Take My Heart

ALSO BY J. J. SOREL

THORNHILL TRILOGY

Entrance
Enlighten
Enfold

THE IMPORTANCE OF BEING WILD

THE IMPORTANCE OF BEING BELLA

https://jjsorel.com/

Take My Heart

J. J. SOREL

Cover Design by Teresa Conner | www.wolfsparrowcovers.com
Edited by Red Adept - Kim Husband

FOR THOSE AGED 18 AND OVER ONLY - Warning steamy sex scenes
All the characters in this contemporary romance are consenting adults. For those readers who like their romance novels peppered with descriptive sex scenes, then this is for you. However, for those disinclined towards steamy boudoir scenes I suggest you either approach this with an open mind, or just pass it on to someone looking for an escape in the arms of a sexy read.

"It's complicated," I said.
"They always are, darling. The exciting ones always are."

CHAPTER ONE

Huffing and puffing, I wondered what had possessed me to walk the entire ten flights. Did those ten years of dance classes account for nothing? Pausing at the landing, I adjusted my ponytail and smoothed back my hair. Why the employment agent had asked for a photo with my hair down was a question that kept revolving around my busy mind. Despite being thin on detail, the employment agent had requested that I be punctual, courteous, and not ask questions. That last clause made my ears prick. Knowing my inquisitive nature, I'd have to watch myself.

The only thing I knew about the position was that I'd be required to keep an elderly person company four hours a day—from four until eight in the evening. For that, I would receive the equivalent of a full-time wage.

"Full-time wage" flashed before me like a lit-up billboard. A flourish of anticipation swept through me, thinking of all the things I could do with my spare time. There'd also be no more running late in the mornings only to be met with a nasty scowl. Or working for a boss who made a sport of inflicting misery. No more forty-hour week morphing into sixty hours. Or the creepy, drunken messages while I slept, reminding me of all the tasks that were humanly impossible to complete in eight hours, let alone two hours.

It had been one month of hell. Therefore, I couldn't believe my luck when I received a call from an agent offering me a position that required someone for conversation and to read stories. I had no idea who I would be working for. Not even the gender—although the "hair down" request did make me wonder if it was a creepy, lecherous man, something Cassie, my best friend suggested to me. But then, she tended toward the melodramatic. Of course, I accepted the role within a breath, because being a recent graduate and in debt to my eyeballs, I needed a job.

Opening the door of the stairwell, I stepped into the hallway and entered into a plush walk down memory lane. Boasting the elegant sophistication of Art Deco, the dimly lit interior exemplified that classic era of Fifth Avenue architecture.

I stood at the door and glanced down at my watch. Noting that I still had a few minutes, I wondered if "punctual" meant exactly on time. Or could one be early? As my knuckles hovered over the door, I lowered my hand and decided to wait. While doing so, I studied the tinted-glass light fittings that jutted out of the wall casting shadowy light over golden frames of women in flowing gowns.

Just as the minute hand hit the hour, I took a deep breath and knocked. After a few moments, I heard slow, shuffling steps, and an older woman opened the door.

"You must be Ava Rose," she said, holding the door open for me to enter.

"I am," I said with an awkward smile, holding out my hand. "Pleased to meet you."

As her frail, wrinkly hand landed on mine, her eyes traveled to my face and remained there as if taking in every detail. I even started to worry that there was a remnant of jam from the donut I'd scarfed down earlier or something up my nose.

"I'm Aggie." She stretched out her arm for me to enter.

"Oh, that's short for Agatha."

"It is," she replied with a hint of a smile. Something told me that Aggie didn't do too much smiling.

All it took was one step into that beguiling, time-trapped room for an eerie sensation to flash through me. It was a feeling similar to déjà vu, or entering a museum filled with the pungency of decay. Not that the room stank; if anything, it smelled like roses.

Slender, with upright posture, Aggie, who I assumed was in her seventies, possessed an elegant bearing matching the opulence of her surroundings.

She pointed to a curvaceous armchair. "Please, sit. Can I offer you a drink?" She raised a brow, which made me wonder if she meant of the alcoholic variety.

"No. I'm good. Thanks."

"I might have one, then," she said, hovering about.

"Please, do. Of course," I replied, unsure if she'd actually asked for my permission or not.

Although slow, her stride was confident and balanced. Wearing pink bell-bottoms and a silky floral shirt, Aggie had a stylish if not unique air about her. With that plait of gray hair twirled into a bun above her head, she reminded me of an ageing ballerina, especially with her long neck and lifted spine. I could see that Aggie had once been beautiful, especially her glistening aquamarine eyes, which, although faded with age, sparkled with a healthy dose of curiosity.

She stood by a silver trolley, picked up a shaker, and poured its contents into a martini glass. After taking a sip, she strolled back and sat opposite me. "A weakness of mine." She held the glass to her painted lips. "Do you know how to mix a martini?"

I sat up. "Um… no. I can't say I do. But I'm a quick learner."

She nodded. "Good. That's part of the job. From four until eight. I like my martinis, and…" She opened a pretty silver box by her side and took out a cigarette. "I smoke." She lit her cigarette with a flick of a lighter. "I promise to leave the terrace doors open." A hint of a smile came and went.

As I watched Aggie puff deeply on her cigarette while clasping the stem of an elegant V-shaped glass, I thought I'd traveled into a scene from a 1950s film.

While the sun filtered through the pink living room, my ordinary life in a tiny bedsit located somewhere in the bowels of the city, where only those scrounging about for their next meal lived, seemed like a distant memory.

Sipping pensively on her martini, Aggie kept switching her attention from me to the expansive view of the Hudson, which was visible through the beveled-glass French doors that opened out to a balcony the size of a small room.

Sneaking a look at Aggie sucking on her cigarette, I thought about the past, when people hadn't heard about cigarettes causing cancer or, if they had, chose to ignore the warnings. That was a far cry from my world, where everyone, including me, stressed about everything.

My guide to happiness read something like this: living a healthy life to at least ninety, which would mean not smoking; shots of tequila only on special occasions, and surrendering them entirely after one had found her dream man; having lots of money;

3

a great husband who supplied one with enough seed for at least two beautiful children whom one could brag about; and multiple orgasms on tap.

"My, you have a busy mind," said Aggie.

My brows drew in sharply. "Excuse me?"

She chuckled. "I can see that pretty head of yours ticking away." Before I could respond, Aggie added, "Now, first things first. I don't like questions. But this being your first day, I'll allow you a few."

All I heard was that it was my first day, which meant the job was mine, even though I had to meet Justin, my boyfriend, at six. But rather than mention that to Aggie, I decided to text him later.

Four hours with an intriguing, albeit an intense woman didn't seem too shabby at all—overlooking the potential of a premature death due to passive smoking. It also meant that my pay would start immediately, thus removing the unpleasant task of asking my mother for a loan. The thought of that had me mentally popping a champagne cork, given that each time my mom handed me cash, it came with a lecture about snaring Justin into marrying me, even if it meant forgetting to take my pill.

At twenty-four, I was hardly ready for motherhood, nor to be the wife of a man who was more interested in his career, buddies, and ball games, interspersed with a quick, hard fuck here and there. When it came to tenderness, Justin, who was probably at the time pumping his fist at the ball game on TV, missed out.

"I have the job?" I asked.

"Don't look so surprised." Aggie butted out her cigarette into a crystal ashtray.

"Do you mind if I ask what you'd like me to do?" A meek smile crossed my lips. "I mean, other than making martinis."

She shrugged. "Just keep me company. I wanted someone young around. That way I can hear about the latest fads. I watch TV, but it bores me. It actually makes me angry at times. All that silly deconstructed, incomprehensible language."

I nodded. "It can be rather shallow and pitched to a lower form of intelligence."

"Yes... So true." She studied me again. "It's as if we've all become dull-witted. Or is it that the dimwits have taken over the controls?"

"Maybe," I replied vaguely. Although politics was not my thing, at forty dollars an hour, I would try and give it my best.

"Ava Rose. That's a pretty name. Has a nice ring about it. That's what attracted me, and the photo, of course."

I sat forward. "I did wonder why you requested an image with my hair down."

"Now you're being plain cheeky." Her eyes had a sting in them. I couldn't tell if she was joking or serious.

"I'm… um… sorry," I stammered.

Her face softened. "The short answer is, I don't like ugly people around me. I couldn't stand the idea of someone with cropped hair painted in a rainbow of colors. Or tattoos…" She studied my blouse. "You don't have tattoos, do you?" Her face expressed concern.

Reminding myself that in Aggie's time, women weren't pierced or tattooed, I answered, "No, I don't."

"Good."

Seeing that her attention remained on my body, I asked, "Is there any specific way I should dress?"

Aggie's head pulled back as if I'd asked a stupid question. "Now you're just poking fun."

"Oh no, I mean. I didn't… I wasn't being facetious."

She laughed. "You're sensitive. I like that. I believe you studied English literature. That appealed to me. I like an intelligent, well-read mind."

"Have you a favorite?" I asked.

"You of all would know how difficult that is to answer. It's like asking what one's favorite color is. It depends on the mood, doesn't it?" Her voice had an edge of authority to it that scraped a little. "*Wuthering Heights*," she said. "I'd like you to read that for me."

That made me sit up. "Oh… that would be a labor of love. It's one of my favorites."

Once again, she studied me for what seemed a long while. "Good. Tomorrow, we'll start with that."

"I'll bring along a copy," I said, pleased that at last, I had something to offer that at least coincided with my degree.

"No need. I have several." Her eyes passed by my face and landed on a dark wooded bookshelf filled with gold-scrolled hardback books.

I went over to take a look.

Aggie pointed. "You'll find them on the top shelf."

Looking up, I discovered hardback copies and a large selection of paperbacks, all of the same title. "You must be a fan."

"I used to collect them." She crooked her finger. "Come and sit. Let me get acquainted with you. But first, how about we start with that martini?"

When she began to rise from her chair, I said, "Oh, there's no need. I can do it."

"I'm not an invalid, dear girl." She rose and gestured for me to follow her. "You'll need some ice."

"This is a large apartment. I notice you have another floor." I looked up at the striking wooden staircase with an exquisite black filigree railing.

"It's a penthouse. Big and lofty. I need plenty of room to fill all of my memories."

"Oh, you have a lot of things?" I asked.

"I have. But that's not what I meant." She looked at me enigmatically, which made me bite my tongue, as a ton of questions banked up.

We walked down a hallway, the walls of which were laden in oil paintings and watercolors. There was certainly plenty to take in, and the first things I noticed once I entered the large kitchen were stained-glassed French doors that opened out to a balcony. My eyes landed on the terrace of the neighboring white-bricked building, where a cat snoozed amongst a clutter of ceramic pots filled with creepers and plants. With golden sunlight filtering in the stainless-steel surfaces sparkled. *"So, this is how the filthy rich live?"* I thought to myself.

Aggie, who must have noticed my wide-eyed appreciation, said, "It's an opulent home. My late husband owned fields of oil. I'm what's known as obscenely wealthy. Not that I'm bragging." A faint smile grew on her face as she pressed a button on the fridge door, and ice spilled into the silver bucket she held.

I went over to help. "I can carry that if you like,"

She handed it over to me. "Good. Now you know where the ice is. There's plenty to eat if you like. I have Louisa, who comes and cooks for me every day. You probably won't see her. She leaves at three o'clock. Apart from Louisa, there's Jennifer, my cleaner, who always leaves by midday. After that, I am here alone." She gestured for me to return to the living room.

Following Aggie's instructions with the greatest of care, I rattled the ice in the cool stainless-steel receptacle and poured it into the stemmed glass. I carried it carefully over to the terrace, where Aggie sat in a white cane peacock chair and set the glass down by her side.

I bit into a nail, watching with a furrowed brow as she lifted the glass to her mouth. "Now, why are you standing there watching me?" she asked.

Taking a step back, I said, "Sorry, I just want to make sure you like it."

She savored the liquid for a moment and then nodded. "Good. Very Good. So much better than all the others."

"*All* the others?" I asked, competing with the rowdy street sounds below.

Aggie pointed to the matching peacock chair next to a large terra cotta pot of creeping roses. "Please. Sit. You make me nervous standing over me like that."

As I went to sit, Aggie said, "Before you do, however, I insist you try one."

I frowned. "A martini, you mean?"

"Yes."

"Oh. I don't normally drink at this hour," I said, feeling stupid for some reason.

"Well, for today, let's break the rules. Live dangerously," she said with a mischievous twinkle in her eyes.

I shrugged. "Okay. A small one, then."

After I poured a half glass from the remnants in the shaker, I took a tiny sip and grimaced. It was sharp, cool, and edgy, a little like Aggie.

She laughed. "Oh, dear girl. The look on your face. I have to admit when I was your age, I didn't have a taste for them either. My late husband's cohort of snobs introduced me to them. Or was it that I introduced myself to them in order to cope with his boring friends?" She said that almost to herself with a chuckle. She switched her focus to the street below. "Oh look, there goes Cecil and his strange little dog. Don't they look like each other?"

My eyes traveled down to busy Fifth Avenue, where I spotted an effeminate man with a pug. "I suppose I can see a resemblance."

She laughed with a rasp. "Cecil's a fag, you know."

I winced. "Gay, you mean?"

"That's right, they call them that now. One has to be respectful. Although I do resent the fact that I can no longer describe myself as gay if I'm having a nice day." She sniffed. "In my day, they were either poofs or fags. I knew a few. They were always fun to have around. I'm sure Ashley was sucked off by one or two."

Having just taken a sip, I reacted to Aggie's crude comment with a coughing fit.

"Are you all right?" Aggie asked.

I patted my chest and waited for it to settle. "I'm sorry, it went down the wrong way."

"I shocked you, didn't I?" Aggie reached into a crystal box on the white filigree table by her side and brought out a cigarette, lighting it with a matching crystal lighter. Exhaling a puff of smoke, she asked, "You don't smoke?"

Shaking my head, I said, "Never have."

"In my day, we did it to stay slim."

"Your doctor hasn't tried to make you quit?" I asked.

She waved her hand as if shooing a fly. "I don't have a doctor. I don't believe in them. They poke around in places. Even when uninvited."

Another loaded comment. I was still gestating the one about her late husband being bisexual and wasn't quite ready to ask if a doctor might have molested her.

"I would have thought it wise to have a doctor to check over you."

"Why, because I'm eighty-two?"

My head pushed back in surprise. "I wouldn't have guessed you to be that."

Aggie studied me for a moment with narrowed eyes. "You're telling the truth."

"I always do," I said.

"That's not always wise." She rose and walked back inside before I could respond and returned shortly, wearing sunglasses. "Mm… I love the sun, don't you?"

"I do."

"Are you a beach girl?"

"I'd like to be," I said, sipping my martini, which grew more appealing with each swallow. At the least, it relaxed me.

"What stops you?" she asked.

"Well, money, I suppose."

"You don't have a boyfriend who spoils you? A beautiful girl like you."

I recalled Justin cowering at the prospect of a shark attack that one time we paddled in the shallows along the bay. "He's not that kind of guy, I suppose."

"Then he doesn't spoil you?"

I shrugged. "Justin's not really into that."

"Get rid of him then," she said, looking out into the distance onto the Hudson River that sat behind the variegated green lushness of the park.

I bit my lip. "He's my boyfriend."

She turned to study me again. "He's well hung?"

I swallowed. "Um... I'm not sure. If he..." I stammered. Was I really about to discuss my boyfriend's penis with an octogenarian?

Aggie grinned at my stunned expression. "Don't fall for that nonsense that size doesn't matter. Monty was hung like a horse. And my, oh my." She fanned her face. Wiggling her little finger, she added, "Ashley, on the other hand, had a tiny little thing, but he had a huge bank account to make up for it, I suppose."

I had no idea how to respond to that. A faint nod was the best I could offer.

For the rest of that afternoon, I watched Aggie drink five martinis, while I barely finished the small glassful I'd poured earlier. Whatever this was— strange, to say the least—I developed a deep fascination for my new employer. And as she saluted me, asking me to find my own way out, I bowed and thanked her profusely.

When I stepped onto the busy avenue, the thought struck me that I hadn't called Justin. Grabbing my phone, I pressed on his number, but it went to voicemail, so I left a message apologizing and headed back to my tiny, messy excuse for a home.

CHAPTER TWO

After what had been an odd, if not eventful week, I kicked back my shoes and slumped back on my sofa. There was a party to go to. And I looked forward to catching up with Cassie, mainly because I wanted to tell her about my new job. I'd already tried telling Justin about it, but his eyes glazed over, as they often did whenever I spoke about myself.

Hating to admit it, but I wasn't sure why we were together. Having never been in love, I had no idea what it felt like. One thing was for sure: whenever I was with Justin, I didn't experience a racing heart or butterflies in the belly. I just assumed that love didn't consume one in real life as it did the characters in books and movies. There was also my mom's take on marriage: that security should come first and that passion was the cherry on the cake.

Justin was hot. Or at least all his female colleagues seemed to think so, going by how they hovered around while hanging on his every word. We didn't really have much conversation. I'd often tried. But Justin wasn't much of a listener. And where sex was concerned, he'd thrust into me a dozen or so times, climax, and then fall onto his back and snore.

All in all, it was ordinary. So why was I with Justin? The short answer was that after being single for a long time, I liked the idea of a boyfriend and had convinced myself that passion would eventually grow.

As I sat there wondering about what to wear to the party, I thought about Aggie and how she'd drifted in and out of sleep while I read to her. Then I'd stop, and she'd wake up. She'd then ask me to continue and make me repeat the scenes where Cathy and Heathcliff ran along the windswept, craggy moors vowing undying love for each other. At times, Aggie waved her hand for me to skip a paragraph or page, as though she wished only to relive the passionate, heart-ripping moments. Her appetite for those passages, like the book itself, began to haunt me.

As all these thoughts percolated away, the sound of the buzzer startled me. I rose with a heavy body to answer it.

"Hey. It's me," Cassie sang.

"Come on up. The elevator's not working," I said.

"Damn. I've got my killer heels on."

"Sling them over your shoulder, then," I said with a chuckle.

I opened the door and listened as her panting echoed up the stairs.

Cassie pushed open the stairwell door and scowled. "You need"—she leaned against the wall to get her breath— "to move somewhere with a working elevator."

"That, and somewhere miles away from the drug dealer downstairs," I said, referring to the comings and goings at all hours of the night, which kept waking me up.

Cassie strolled in, looking gorgeous as always. She had long legs that seemed to go forever, a svelte frame, and high cheekbones framed by bouncy blonde waves. Her big green, friendly eyes, however, were her best feature.

We kissed each other on the cheek and hugged. Friends for ten years, we'd met at a contemporary dance class, after which we became close. We slept over at each other's homes as teenagers and shared growing pains, laughing and crying together, mainly through Cassie's considerable sexual awakening.

Being a slow starter, I had been more into books than boys. Then as I developed some curves that even loose T-shirts couldn't hide, I noticed boys checking me out. Instead of fluttering my eyelashes, I went the color of beetroot. When they handed out the manual for how to be a coquette, I missed out. But thankfully, by the end of my teenage years, I'd lost all shyness around boys. If anything, I probably talked too much.

My mother, who had the same disease, constantly chided me for it. She'd babble on about how men didn't like women who yapped on and on. I would look at her with a furrowed brow. "The apple hasn't fallen far from the tree, Mom. You seem to lecture whoever's within earshot. And you don't discriminate— man, woman, or dog."

I laughed, thinking of how she would chatter away to our dog when no one else was around.

She'd place her hands on her hips and say, "I'm lucky. I landed a man that likes an assertive woman. But that's rare. The movers and the shakers, the rich guys out there, aren't into women who talk too much."

"Oh well, then they won't be leaving their shiny designer shoes under my bed, will they?"

She'd give me one of her glares, while my sweet father, who was always on my side, would giggle. I loved him for that. I could have married a loser, and he still would have supported me. But then, Justin was the catch of the century, according to my mom, so she had little to complain about.

Being the one that always got the guys, Cassie had earned the nickname Male Magnet. The leftovers would flirt with me—the short, slightly chubby, dark-haired girl whose dress sense centered around loose and comfortable rather than sexy and showy.

"Why aren't you dressed?" asked Cassie, her eyes moving up and down my body.

"I just got back," I said, sighing. "And who has a birthday party on a Thursday, anyway?"

She shrugged. "The rich and idle."

I entered my tiny kitchen, which could barely accommodate two people. Opening the fridge, I grabbed a carton of juice and poured out two glasses, passing one to Cassie. "Here, looks like you can use a bit of rehydration."

She took a sip, and then stood up. "Come on, let's see what you're wearing."

My bedroom, the size of a cupboard, was all bed and very little else.

"When are you going to move in with Justin? His apartment's huge compared to this. And at least it's in SoHo. Think of the fun we could have," she said, raising a brow.

Cassie was a party girl through and through. Although she was ready to pounce on marital bliss, I imagined she'd always be that girl who, at the drop of a hat would go out for a drink, shopping, or any outing involving a cocktail, a pretty frock, and plenty of eye candy in the shape of well-built men.

"I'm miles from that, Cas. We've only been dating for three months."

Twirling a blonde lock in her fingers, Cassie said, "That's how long Marcus and I've been together. But you know that. We all met the same night."

I nodded, thinking of that night out. After one of our dance classes, Cassie and I had headed over to a trendy bar in SoHo and met our future boyfriends, who were full of swagger, confidence, and noisy male bravado. Being cousins, Marcus and Justin were similar in many ways, though Justin had the loudest mouth and drank the most.

It was because Justin was a lawyer that my mother obsessed over him becoming her future son-in-law. She'd married my darling father, who made furniture and lacked drive, much to her chagrin. Even though she bossed him around, Dad didn't seem to mind. He always smiled back to me, apologizing for her outbursts. He loved her madly, and although my mom called him a lazy so and so, she was crazy about him too.

Cassie removed three dresses from my wardrobe. "I suppose one of these will do." Her lips turned down. "If only we were the same size. I could have lent you one of mine. It's a fancy affair. You realize the whole family will be there."

I grimaced. "Shit. I'm not sure if I'm in the mood for that. And I look terrible."

Cassie smiled. "You're so pretty with that thick, dark hair of yours. You should wear it out. And I'd kill for your breasts."

"I'd kill for your long legs, big green eyes, and just about everything, Cas."

We stared at each other and giggled.

She took out a green dress. "I like this on you."

"I haven't worn that for a while. I suppose that will do."

"We need to go shopping for some new clothes, Aves. You haven't bought anything new for so long."

"Hello... I've barely been able to pay my rent." I tilted my head.

"That's about to change. And anyway, you're with a seriously rich guy."

"Justin's not that rich. He's doing well, I suppose for a twenty-five-year-old."

"He's an up-and-coming lawyer. Driven and ambitious. And according to Marcus, he inherited some killer stocks from his late father that are kickassing."

"Kickassing?"

Cassie giggled. "Don't go all English lit on me. You know what I mean. Now come on, get dressed. I'm dying for a drink. It's been one of those weeks. My boss and his creepy little fingers."

My brow lowered. "Are you fucking kidding me? You need to punch him out."

"I know. But I need the job. It's a leading PR firm that everyone's dropping their panties to get. I suppose the odd little squashy-feely moment's not going to hurt." Her mouth twitched into a faint smile.

Seriously concerned for my friend, I wasn't buying her stoicism. "Now listen, Cas, you're being sexually harassed. He's so out of line. You should report him. I know you. I can see that he's creeping you out."

She shook her head. "I shouldn't have said anything. And you better not say anything to Marcus or Justin."

"So, what does he do exactly?" I pulled off my T-shirt and lowered my sweats.

"Fuck, Ava. You've lost some weight."

That was music to my ears. "I'm now a size 12. Great, eh? I've been running up flights of stairs and have dropped my daily donut intake to one." I laughed at my one and only bad habit. Sugar. I would have poured it down my throat if I could have. The trouble was my butt always collected every lousy calorie.

I slipped into the green dress with a high neckline and an A-line skirt. Studying myself in the mirror, I could see that it flattered without making me look too top heavy.

"You're looking great, Ava. What are you doing with that hair?"

"I'll put it in a bun, as usual." I twisted my braid to create a bun on top. With my longish face, it suited me to have the height.

"You haven't answered my question," I said.

Cassie sat back on the bed. Her crossover chiffon skirt fell open, revealing stockings. When it came to sexy and stylish, she owned it.

"He touches my arm and often brushes past me. So that I can feel his..."

My face scrunched in disgust. "His dick... Fuck... I'm going to report the jerk if you don't."

Standing by my side at the mirror, Cassie adjusted her floral skirt and then leaned toward the mirror to study her makeup. "Please promise me you won't, Aves. I need this job. I'm only telling you because you're my best friend."

"All right. But promise me you won't go to any of those late-night office parties."

"No fucking way. I'm not that stupid. Anyway, he's fucking Amy."

"Amy? The one that wants your job?"

She nodded grimly. "Yep. A real ladder climber that one. That's the problem. The ones who are willing to fuck their creepy bosses get better roles."

"That's so sad. These ambitious hussies are relegating the sisterhood back to the Dark Ages."

Cassie giggled. "Sweetie, it's always been that way."

"Hm... doesn't mean we should keep putting up with it." I tilted my head.

She just shrugged and continued to fix her hair in the mirror. "Do I need a coat?"

"I didn't bring one," said Cassie, watching me as I took one final look at myself in the mirror. "You need some kohl around your eyes and a bit of lip gloss." Cassie pulled out a kohl stick. "I've got a brown one. It's subtle." She passed it to me.

I stretched the skin of my eye and drew a faint line at the bottom of my lid and under my eye. I turned to face her. "How's that?"

She nodded slowly. "Much better. You look really pretty."

The cab dropped us off at the driveway of one of those large houses that resembled something out of *Dynasty* with its poplar-lined paths and an entrance held up by glistening white columns.

As I gaped at the white-brick McMansion, I whistled. "Holy Moly... I didn't realize Marcus's parents were so rich."

Cassie stood there under the lamplight, her face glowed with expectation. "Isn't it great." She linked her arm into mine. "Now you know why I'm here to stay. Small penis notwithstanding."

I stopped walking, and my head turned so sharply I nearly suffered whiplash. "What?"

A cheeky grin crossed her lips. That was Cassie, always throwing the unexpected at me. We'd never really spoken much about her sex life with Marcus, which was odd, given that sex was one of her favorite subjects. Although Cassie wore her ambition to marry an obscenely rich man, regardless of attraction, on her designer sleeve, I still found myself taken aback.

"It's not the size though that matters. It's what they do with it," I said, wavering slightly. Having never had an orgasm while being penetrated, I wasn't exactly in familiar waters, while Aggie's "size *did* matter" comment entered my thoughts at the same time.

"Just wait till you've had more experience. Although..." She turned to face me. "You're always changing the subject. I bet Justin's hung."

"You're being prurient."

"What does that mean?"

"Vulgar. In any case, I have no idea how big 'hung' is."

Her hands stretched apart. "And so thick." Her fingers circled her wrist.

"He's not like that." My forehead scrunched. "It would hurt, wouldn't it?"

"Oh my God, Ava. You're so inexperienced." She took me by the hand. "Tell me, does he make you come?"

My face heated up.

"He hasn't, has he?" Cassie exclaimed.

I shrugged. "It's not all about that. And he's my first. It all happens pretty quickly, to be honest."

"Shit, Ava. It's meant to be pleasurable. I know I enjoy it."

"But you just admitted to Marcus having a small..."

"Go on, say it. Dick." She giggled. "He's not that small, he's normal sized. I was just exaggerating to get a response. He's a very giving lover, with a nice expressive tongue as well." Her eyebrows bounced up and down.

"Mm... okay." I grabbed her by the hand. "Come on. Enough talk about sex. Let's go in."

CHAPTER THREE

A tall, heavily-built man opened the door and showed us into the predominately white foyer that was so bright I had to squint. Clip-clopping along the marble floor, we headed toward a chorus of voices that increased in volume with each step and entered the large entertainment area, where guests milled about, chatting.

My eyes swept around the room seeking out familiar faces, namely our boyfriends. As it was Cassie's boyfriend's birthday, I'd assumed it would be a younger crowd. Instead, the guests were mixed in age.

"It's a swanky affair, isn't it?" I whispered.

"Yeah. It's lavish. I wouldn't expect anything but." She smiled. "This is the first time I've been here. Shit, I didn't realize Marcus was so loaded." She expressed a quiet chuckle. "I'll have to marry him now."

Knowing what I knew about Cassie's near lack of passion toward her newish boyfriend, I asked, "What about love?" Just as Cassie was about to launch into one of her lectures about marrying for security, almost word perfect to one of my mother's rants, Marcus and Justin headed our way.

Wearing a glazy-eyed expression, my boyfriend looked as though he'd already had his fill of alcohol, which made me cringe. As he swaggered over, I had to admit he cut a fine figure in a tux, reminding me of why I'd been attracted to him in the first place.

He grabbed me by the waist and planted a wet kiss on my lips, after which I pulled away to look at him. "And hello to you, too."

"You look fucking good enough to eat," Justin boomed.

Noticing the guests staring at me, I whispered, "Shh... tell the whole world, why don't you."

Justin drew me in close again. "I will. You…"

I blocked his mouth with my hand. "You've been hard at it already, I see." I looked into his hazel eyes, which were coated in just enough cute mischief for me to forgive him.

He opened his hands in defense. "Hey… Only a few after work. And the bourbon here's pretty nice." He swept his arms about. "Nice house, eh?"

I rocked my head slowly. "Mm… not my kind of thing. It's a bit too eighties glitz and chintz for me."

He pushed back his head. "Come on. It's perfect."

Cassie interrupted. "I agree. It's a gorgeous house." She stroked Marcus's cheek, who responded with one of those sweet, loving smiles. One could almost see the stars in his eyes as he gazed at Cassie. Always polite, Marcus cast his attention to me and held out his hand. "Hey, Ava, thanks for coming." He leaned in close and whispered, "I agree. I hate this house. I preferred our home back in Brooklyn."

Just as I was about to comment, a blonde woman tottered over. Her heels were so high I imagined she wasn't much taller than five feet. I almost experienced vertigo just looking at her shoes. As she flashed a smile that was so bright I needed sunglasses, I trained my focus on her smooth, doll-like face. But then my eyes, with a mind of their own, landed on the mass of pouting flesh pouring out of a low cut, slinky red gown. She was so top heavy with those ballooning bosoms that she needed to hold onto something in order not to topple over. Or so it seemed.

Marcus said, "This is Candy, my dad's new wife." His cool tone betrayed a dislike for his new young stepmom, who was about his age.

I smiled. "Pleased to meet you."

Cassie held out her hand with a matching bright smile. "I'm Cassandra."

"Oh, Marcus's girl." Candy wore such long, thick lashes it looked as though her eyes struggled to remain open. "Pleased to meet you, and welcome to my home."

Candy turned her attention to Justin and flicked a flirtatious smile, which wasn't lost on me, given that I'd already noticed Justin leering at her boobs. Despite them being hard to miss, I still felt my skin crawl at that unsubtle gesture.

"Come and get a drink," she said with a high-pitched, excitable tone. "There's plenty of yummy food. It's catered by Pierre Cheri." Her face brimmed with pride. Not that I'd ever heard of him.

Justin clasped my hand as we followed Candy, whose peachy ass swayed along shamelessly.

"Marcus's stepmom is young," I said.

Justin replied, "Yeah. That's why he hates her."

Cassie, who was on my other side, said, "I'm going for a glass of champagne. Do you want one?"

I nodded. "Yeah. I think I better. The brightness of this room is giving me a headache. Why have four chandeliers when you can have six?"

"I think they suit the room. I love it. It's so *Dynasty*."

Cassie and I may have been seriously close, but our tastes diverged somewhere after the seventies. While I went for natural fabrics and classic lines in art and architecture, Cassie loved big hair, Las Vegas, and polyester.

"Mm… as is Candy," I replied.

Marcus returned with two glasses of champagne. As he passed me the flute, he asked, "What was that about Candy?"

Not wishing to appear judgmental, I said, "She's nice."

"Bullshit. My mother was nice."

Cassie interjected, "Marcus, no one ever likes their stepmom. It's almost cliché, sweetie. I'm sure your dad still holds your late mom close to his heart." She put her arm around his shoulder, and his frown melted away.

Having snuck off to get a drink, Justin returned with a plate of food. "Why's everyone looking so serious? Let's party," he said so loudly that the older guests turned and looked over at us again.

"You should slow down, Justin. It's only nine o'clock," I said.

He ignored me entirely and turned his attention to Marcus. Another kink in his personality, and jarring in many ways, Justin was a man's man.

"So why are you looking so fucking glum, bud? It's your birthday."

"He was talking about his mom," I said.

"Oh? His new hot one, or…"

Marcus scowled. "Listen. Don't you fucking say that ever again."

Justin stepped back and held up his hands in defense. "Hey, dude. It's cool. I was just saying, Candy's kind of out there."

"She's a fucking ex-stripper. What do you expect?" he snapped. "I don't know what happened to my father. He used to be a man of taste. An educated man. Then this…" He swept his hand about the room.

Marcus had been hitting it hard too, it seemed, allowing me to see a new side to him. He'd always come across as the quiet one of the pair. He usually left the spotlight to Justin, who'd been known to jump up on bars and dance or down four shots in succession and sing his favorite team's anthem loudly.

I had to admit, my sympathy for Marcus increased after I caught sight of Candy cuddling up to his dad, who looked more like a biology tutor than a billionaire with a penchant for bimbos.

Justin placed his arm around Marcus's shoulder. "Come on, dude. Forget about it. She's making your dad happy, and that's all that counts."

"Mm… I suppose so." Marcus turned to Cassie and stroked her cheek. "You look gorgeous."

Leaving them to it, I headed to the dining area. Following close behind, Justin pinched me on the butt.

I turned sharply. "Hey, that hurt."

He laughed and drew me in tight against his waist. "I can't help it. You look so sexy all done up. Out of that librarian gear, you scrub up well. And I know what's underneath." His eyebrows lifted.

Mm… Justin was hot to trot. We hadn't seen each other for a week. He'd been busy at being a lawyer, which suited me because I liked my own space. That evening, though, there was something about Justin that irked me. Mainly his heavy drinking and lack of subtlety, which I should have been used to by then.

While I battled with those thoughts, a table of colorful sweets caught my eye, and a little voice within told me to forget about that troublesome boyfriend because life was great again. My stomach cartwheeled with glee at the sight of cupcakes. As my hand hovered over the pretty little thing, I reminded myself that I hadn't eaten since lunch, so sensibly, I headed for the table of savory food instead.

"I'll be back soon," said Justin, touching my ass again.

"Justin, if you do that again, I'll leave. You're embarrassing me."

He laughed. "Oh, come on, Ava. I'm boning up bigtime. Your tits look so big in that dress."

"You're being crass."

He drew me in tight again and planted a sloppy kiss on my lips, leaving behind the sticky flavor of bourbon and Coke. "I'll be back soon. Enjoy, and don't let any of those horny rich dudes feel you up."

I tilted my head. "I'll try to control my urges."

After Justin left me alone, I was faced with the difficult task of deciding on what to eat. Arranged on platters spread over the large oval table, the colorful array of food was indescribable, thus unfamiliar. As I pondered over each carefully decorated selection that resembled more a work of modern art, a yummy aroma drifted up my nose.

A voice traveled over my shoulder. "It's complicated, isn't it?"

I turned and was met by Marcus's dad, who was in his mid-fifties, wearing spectacles and a gentle smile.

"Um… excuse me?"

He held out his hand. "I'm James."

"Oh… Hi. Nice to meet you. I'm Ava."

He studied me for a moment as if trying to get his head around my name. "Ah… Justin's girlfriend?"

"That's me." I smiled.

James pointed to the lavish array of dishes. "I was just saying that it's hard to know what to eat. And I have to admit, I can't figure out what half of it is. I'm told its all the rage. Degustation. Comes from Barcelona. Apparently, they churn the ingredients up and turn it into an artistic statement."

My eyes did a sweep of the food. "That explains it then. Any suggestions?"

"Do you have specific dietary needs?"

I giggled. "Only that I should eat at least one meal a day or else I'll die." A cheeky smile filled my face.

A throaty laugh echoed from his chest. "That's right. Keep it simple. We're so spoiled. These days, before a dinner party, one has to send out a questionnaire. In any case, it's all been catered for tonight." He pointed at the dishes. "There's vegan, peanut, gluten, egg, lactose, and whatever else free and then over there…" He pointed to another table, where I noticed grilled burgers, sausages, and all manner of food that normally appealed to me. "That's where the grownups hang out."

I laughed. "Then, my tummy is demanding a healthy dose of grown-up food. I went vegetarian once and found that at parties there was hardly anything to eat."

We headed over to a table that would have taken an entire cattle farm to fill. "But now you're a born-again carnivore?" he asked, watching me fill my plate with two grilled burgers and a couple of sausages.

Having popped a slice of ham into my mouth, I took my time to respond while chewing away. "Sorry, I'm starving." I smiled. "I was so weak and tired all the time. In any case, I missed burgers."

"I can't blame you." His attention shifted over my shoulder. "Oh my, who's this vision of loveliness?"

I turned and noticed a woman in her forties with a kind smile and a familiar face. "I finally made it," she said with a chuckle.

"Let me guess: the traffic?"

She nodded. Her focus shifted over to me.

James said, "You must know Ava."

Shaking her head, she said, "No, we haven't met..." Her face lit up. "Oh, you must be Justin's girlfriend."

I nodded with a meek smile.

"This is Alice, Justin's mother. And looking lovelier than ever, I might add," he said, returning his attention to her.

I noticed her cheeks coloring in response, which suggested a spark between them. I knew that Justin's father, who was James's brother, had died a year earlier. I could only conjecture that Alice hooking up with her brother-in-law would have seemed wrong, so instead, he had ended up with Candy.

"It's nice to meet you finally," she said. "And where is that troublemaking son of mine?"

"He disappeared a few minutes ago. I'm sure he'll be back. I am meant to be his date." I raised a brow.

"Justin's twenty-five going on fifteen." She tilted her head and smiled warmly. Her hazel eyes, which were the same as Justin's, shone with sincerity.

I liked her instantly.

She looked over my shoulder. "Speak of the devil."

Just as I turned, Justin pounced upon me making me jump. He was so full of energy that I didn't need a crystal ball to figure out what he'd been up to. He claimed me by placing his heavy arm around my shoulders, nearly making me collapse from the weight of it.

"Hey, Mom." He kissed her on the cheek. "When did you arrive?"

"Just now." Her focus shifted from her son to me and then back to James, who stood close by.

An ear-piercing laugh, which was more a squeal, alerted me to Candy, who was close by, flirting with a buff guy. James didn't seem to care, however, given that he appeared more focused on Alice.

"Justin tells me that you're working in a publishing house," said Alice.

"I was doing that. But I've recently switched jobs."

Noticing me shift from one leg to another, Alice said, "It's a high-pressure industry, I imagine."

"Yeah, you could say that. My boss was a bit highly strung. She didn't seem to sleep, because she'd call me at all hours of the night."

Alice grimaced. "Oh… God."

"Blame that on technology," sang James.

"Oh, come on, Uncle, don't go all stone age on us again by blaming everything on technology," blurted Justin.

Ignoring her son's outburst, Alice asked, "Is your current position an improvement?"

"It is. And it gives me free time to pursue other interests."

She nodded thoughtfully. "Then I'm pleased for you. And I must say, Justin never told me you were so beautiful."

I smiled. "Thanks."

Suddenly the guests stopped talking, and their attention was directed at the entrance. Focusing on the same spot, even Candy stopped chatting.

A man appeared. Or I should say a god because his presence was so powerfully alluring that I couldn't take my eyes off him.

He strode in with casual authority, and although for most of the time he stared downward, when he did look forward, his dark gaze was intense and magnetic.

"Oh fuck… What's *he* doing here?" Justin uttered.

CHAPTER FOUR

Alice tapped Justin on the arm. "Don't be like that. Bronson's had a rough time. Be nice to your brother."

"I didn't know you had a brother," I said, stealing another look at the tall, well-built guy, who was so stunningly good-looking that he could have been an actor or a model. But he didn't seem to milk it, given that he wore a serious, downcast expression. To his credit, Bronson lacked that look-at-me vibe that professional hunks with egos as big as their shoulders wore.

"I don't. My late father had this annoying tendency to collect strays."

Alice leaned in and whispered, "Don't be disrespectful to your late father."

Justin grunted something before taking hold of my hand and squeezing it.

"Ouch," I said. My pained frown brought a twitch of a smile to his face. The fact that Justin seemed to extract pleasure from my pain sent a cold shiver through me.

I looked about the room and noticed everyone's attention directed at our corner suddenly. Justin's adopted brother reminded me of a gypsy with those dark features and deep tan. His hair was cut short at the sides, with a thick black mess of locks on top. Shadowed with a thin layer of growth, his chiseled jawline and dimpled chin gave him a ruggedly handsome finish. But it was his dark, penetrating eyes that kept drawing my attention. Although his gaze bore cold disregard, almost taking pride in his own arrogance, something smoldered deeply within. He wore a shirt that molded to his form, revealing a ripple of chest muscles, strong shoulders, and big, curvy biceps. I sensed there would have to be a tattoo in there somewhere because Bronson epitomized the bad-boy in every sense of that term.

As he stood close, a cocktail of earthy male scent and body wash traveled up my nose, landing in my core, while the spark that had ignited after falling into his dark eyes kindled away.

A man had never done *that* to me before.

"Bronson, I'm so glad you came, darling," said his mother, standing on her toes to hug him.

His face softened just a little. But then, within a blink, his brooding expression drew a line on those sculptured full lips, and again he hid behind those dark, almost black eyes.

Holding out his large hand to James, Bronson said, "Nice to see you again. I…. Um…" He combed his hair back with his hands. "I brought a gift for Marcus. It's outside."

Alice was all smiles. It was obvious that she loved her son. Noting a compassionate flicker in her eyes, I got the feeling that Bronson had been through something.

He turned and nodded coldly to Justin, who returned it with an awkward shift of his body. One could almost cut the air with a knife, seeing that the brothers made their mutual antipathy obvious.

Acknowledging me for the first time, Bronson nodded a greeting, but instead of shifting away, his eyes, after a casual sweep of my face, decided to linger. A breath became trapped in my chest, and my face burned. I had to look away first, for it seemed like he'd seen something hidden in me, making me feel naked—not in that sleazy undressing way, but in a way that I couldn't understand, having never experienced that kind of depth before.

I was grateful when Cassie and Marcus joined me.

"Hey, Bron." Marcus hugged his cousin. "I'm so glad you came."

In response, a faint half smile touched Bronson's mouth.

Unable to stay away for long, my eyes returned to his face just as his tongue swept over those cushiony lips in what was the most carnally charged moment I'd ever experienced. Although I wanted to move away in order to stop the wave of heat hijacking my senses, Justin breathed down my neck, holding me close.

Cassie cast me a side glance and with a subtle flick of the head suggested I follow her to the powder room.

When we were out of hearing range, she said, "Holy shit, I didn't realize Marcus's cousin was so damn hot. My panties are well and truly sticky."

I nodded with a giggle.

As we roamed up the long hallway, searching for the powder room, I opened a door and discovered a couple sitting on the edge of a bed, snorting coke. I said "Sorry" and closed the door quickly.

When we finally found the bathroom, we both fell onto fluffy chairs.

Cassie bent down and massaged her ankles. "These shoes are too new."

"They look great. You look great, Cas." Recalling the cocaine-snorting couple, I asked, "Is Marcus into coke, too?"

She shrugged. "I'm not sure. He's never taken it around me. Justin's habit is pretty obvious, though. He's always jumping about, full of energy, whenever we're out."

"God. We've been dating for three months, and I hardly know him. I didn't even know he had a brother."

"Me too. Marcus only just told me." She turned to face me. "Boy, Bronson's fucking hot."

"So you keep saying," I said, heading for the mirror so that I could smooth back my hair.

"He couldn't take his eyes off you, Aves."

My face burned again. I had noticed his gaze returning on more than one occasion, but I put it down to curiosity. "Maybe he wanted to see who his brother was dating."

Cassie leaned in and applied some lipstick. "Mm... I don't know. I think he's attracted. He ignored me."

"You sound disappointed."

"And you seemed pissed off with Justin," she said.

"I didn't think it was that obvious." I took a deep breath. "He never listens whenever I talk. It's all about him. And the way he checked out Candy. I'm sure he's on coke and..." I sighed. "Apart from the lack of spark, he told his mom that I'm still working for Grazilla Ironpants."

Cassie giggled at the ridiculous name I'd given my ex-boss. "He's a bit caught up in himself, I'll grant that. But he's seriously rich. You've heard about the share portfolio he inherited from his dad?"

I nodded with resignation.

"We'll be rich bitches. And then we can have little affairs here and there, just like any self-respecting desperate housewife would."

"Mm… let me guess, buff, barely-out-of-college Latino hunks raking leaves on the massive grounds of our white mansions?" I pulled a face.

Cassie giggled infectiously. "That sounds just right."

"I'm never going to do that." I became serious. "I mean it. It's all good to joke. But when I marry, it will be for love."

"You're such a romantic. What about all the comforts of life?"

"Give me ceiling-banging orgasms over Cartier any day," I said.

"But you haven't had one of those yet, have you?"

"I take it you're referring to the orgasm?"

Cassie nodded with a chuckle.

"Not with a guy. Only my fingers."

"Now I know what to buy you for your birthday," said Cassie.

I shrugged. "A gigolo?"

"No, crazy girl, a vibrator. I love mine. That's how I get my kicks, and Marcus is pretty good like that. He's a giving lover. At least you can train Justin to use his tongue."

"That shouldn't be up to me, surely. In any case, he's a wham-bam-thank-you-ma'am sort of guy."

"Boring," crooned Cassie, opening the door.

Walking down the hallway, I saw Justin brush his nose after closing a door behind him. He noticed our approach and waited. "There you are, sexy girl."

I pushed out of his hold. "You've been doing drugs, Justin."

"It's a party. Now come on, don't go all tight on me. Let's have fun." He winked at Cassie, after which he led me by the hand.

The disco had commenced. Mirror balls spun around while pulsating beams of epilepsy-inducing lights dappled the floor.

Justin grabbed my hand and twirled me around. "Let's dance."

Marcus and Cassie joined us as we shuffled about. Turning it into a workout after the large meal I'd eaten earlier, I revved it up a notch and moved my body about vigorously. Next to us, while owning her exotic-dancer tag with pride, Candy wiggled her butt and shimmied her shoulders. I noticed Justin's eyes settling on her, and after the song ended, I decided on a break.

Recalling the sugary delights, I headed straight over to the table of cakes. My olfactory nerve went into overdrive as I sniffed in the yummy aroma of pure delight. A chocolate mud cake stole my heart and suddenly became my sole ambition in life.

Holding a glass of champagne in one hand and a plate in the other, I found a nice quiet corner outside on the terrace by the pool.

Enjoying the peace, I sank back onto a cushioned, comfy cane chair, and with each mouthful of melty chocolate, I succumbed to shivery pleasure, convincing myself that cake was as good as sex, if not better, given my lack of experience in that area.

From where I sat, I could see Justin dancing so close he nearly rubbed himself against Candy. I looked away and kept indulging in my cake. Strangely, I didn't feel any jealousy. If anything, sympathy for James washed over me, considering his wife wore her flirtatiousness on her plumped lips.

I enjoyed sitting out in the open air surrounded by trees and earthy, floral aromas. It was a clear night with a pearly moon that beamed a ripple onto the swimming pool.

Fanning away smoke that suddenly blew in my direction, I looked up and noticed Bronson, his back to me, puffing on a cigarette. He turned and, noticing me there, distanced himself.

My eyes were drawn to him in a way I wished they weren't. Under the moonlight, he seemed like an almost mystical being bathed in shadow, especially when the smoke formed a halo around him.

He turned again and said, "Is the smoke annoying you?"

I put my fork down and ran my tongue around my lips to wash away the chocolate. "Um… no. It's okay. I'm kind of used to it, anyway."

A slight shift of the brow was his only response, and then he went back to smoking while looking up at the sky.

"I work for a lady who smokes a lot."

He turned and faced me again. I wasn't sure if he wanted to be left alone. He didn't exactly give anything away with that remote stare.

"She makes sure she's on the balcony, though." As I babbled, a little voice within told me to stop, because he wasn't exactly encouraging me with that gaze that bordered on blank, even though I detected a whisper of depth in there somewhere. He just kept sucking on his cigarette as if his life depended on it.

31

Perhaps it was the champagne and the sugar hit because I kept talking anyway. "I read for her, you see. She also makes me mix martinis."

After a moment and one more drag on his cigarette, he said, "With an olive?" A hint of a smirk touched his lips and boy... he wore it well.

I remained transfixed. "Um... no. Hmm... that's funny." I chuckled in a goofy way. "I have to admit I'd never mixed a martini in my life. I hadn't even tried one. Until now, that is. She makes me join her, which means I always leave with a smile."

"She sounds interesting."

"Agatha's a cross between Miss Havisham and Greta Garbo."

"Let me guess," he responded, butting out his cigarette. "A lonely woman with revenge in her heart who slinks about demanding to be left alone."

My eyes brightened. "Justin didn't know what I was talking about when I described her as that earlier. I'm impressed."

He shrugged. "Let's just say I've had plenty of time to read."

"Then you're a rare being because these days not many people read. And to be honest, when I got this job being asked to do just that, reading from a book that I hold so close to my heart, I nearly broke out in a happy rash.... I..." I suddenly lost my chain of thought, mainly because he ran his tongue over his cushiony lips again.

"You were saying?" His voice had a deep, guttural resonance that suited him perfectly.

"Just that I feel blessed. It hasn't been easy lately. I had the worst boss ever, and then I landed this job."

"Do you always break out in a rash when you're happy?" His lips twitched into a hint of a smile.

I giggled. "No. Sorry. I've had a bit of champagne, and I tend to say silly things."

"Silly's entertaining."

His eyes burrowed deep into me again. And the best I could return was a cheesy tight smile. I looked down at my half-eaten cake, and strangely, my appetite had gone. "Do you have a favorite author?"

"Do you?" he asked.

"I think I love Emily Bronte."

"*Wuthering Heights*," he returned. I must have shown my surprise because he added, "Why that look? Am I giving off some kind of illiterate vibe?"

"No. Not at all," I lied, because he was the last person I'd expected to know of *Wuthering Heights*. "I'm sorry. Most younger guys don't really go for books like that."

"I'm not like most younger guys." His eyes darkened again. He'd gotten that right. There weren't too many guys I'd met who read books, let alone looked like him.

He came toward me, and as I sat there staring up at him in suspense, for I wasn't sure what he was about to do, my heart raced.

He leaned in, and placing his finger on my cheek, he wiped it gently.

"You had a brown mark there." His eyes softened slightly. He put his finger in his mouth in a way that made me want to sigh. It was so suggestive. "Mm... chocolate. Nice," he rasped as if he'd dipped his finger somewhere forbidden.

I wanted to speak but lost my voice due to that subtle cologne scent wafting up my nostrils, combined with his melty brown eyes boring into me.

"Um... Yeah, I..." As I stammered, seeking a coherent response, Justin and Marcus came out, holding cigars and laughing loudly.

Bronson turned to face them. The brothers' obvious cold regard for one another made me think of the classic Cain and Abel relationship.

"Hey, Bron, come and have a cigar," said Marcus.

"No. I'm off. I just dropped in to bring a gift. It's at the entrance."

"Hey, you shouldn't have. How are things, anyway? Have you landed on your feet?"

He nodded slowly. "Yeah. Good."

Bronson looked over at me and nodded. "Ava."

A smile trembled on my mouth. The way my name left those lips made me swoon. And then his eyes trapped mine for a final plundering of the senses. I stole a final glance as I watched him swagger off in a way that only he could.

Justin came and stood close to me. "What did he say? Did he try to sleaze onto you? That douche."

"He was nice. In a kind of quiet way. He doesn't say a lot," I said.

"That's Bron. Always been a man of few words. But he's a good guy," said Marcus.

"Bullshit," said Justin with a sulky grimace.

Marcus looked at me and laughed. "Justin's got a bee in his bonnet because Bronson used to get all the babes whenever we went out."

"Don't crap on," Justin snapped before returning his attention to me. "Tell me, was he trying to fuck you? Seriously."

"No," I responded with an agitated tone. Justin's coarseness grated on me. I rose. "I'm really tired. I might go."

His face contorted with disappointment. "But you've only been here for an hour or so. The party's only just warming up."

"I'll call a cab." I kissed Marcus on the cheek. "Happy birthday."

Justin grabbed me. "Hey, can I drop in later?"

I took a deep breath. "I'm really tired. Maybe we can catch up tomorrow night. Is that okay?"

He went dark suddenly. "Whatever." Sulking, he turned his back on me, while Marcus cast me a tight smile as if to apologize for his cousin's petulance.

I went in to grab my things and found Cassie still on the dance floor. Wearing her dance training on that well-toned body, she busted a few familiar moves we'd learned in class. I smiled because that was often me. But for some reason, I was not in the mood that night.

I joined Cassie on the floor, and she spun me around. Leaning close to her ear, I said, "I'm going."

She stopped dancing, and her shoulders slumped. "You can't."

I kissed her on the cheek. "I'll call you."

CHAPTER FIVE

My head throbbed. Could that have been the two glasses of champagne? If so, I'd become a pussy, because I'd drunk far more than that with far less punishment in the past. It was probably more to do with the lack of sleep. Bronson's dark, brooding presence had appeared before me. So lucid was the dream that I felt his finger touch my cheek, just like he'd done at the party. From that point on, I tossed and turned all night, shocked at how a fleeting moment with a stranger could affect me that profoundly.

Too tired to climb the stairs, I decided to ride the elevator. As I stepped into the chamber, I encountered a man in a cute uniform and pillbox hat sitting by the controls. His costume matched the building's vintage. The elevator itself was a work of art, boasting geometric glass-work and a mosaic floor. I almost expected Greta Garbo or Jean Harlow to swan in dressed in slinky pearl-colored gowns. Just like everything about my interesting new job, even the elevator ride propelled me into a twilight zone.

"Good afternoon, Madam. What floor will it be?" the operator asked.

"Ten, thank you," I said.

"Agatha's abode," he replied, dropping his formal tone.

I nodded.

"You must be her new assistant."

"I am. I've been here for a week. I normally climb the stairs." Noticing a slight furrowing of his forehead, I added, "It's my only workout at the moment."

"I see. So how is Mrs. Johnson?"

"Mrs. Johnson?" I asked.

"Agatha, dear," he responded with a kind smile.

"She's good." I had yet to learn so much about my new employer, including her surname. "My name's Ava," I added.

He bowed his head in acknowledgment. "Charlie's my name. Pleased to meet you."

Just as I was about to ask more about my enigmatic boss, the elevator stopped. He pulled open the door, and I stepped out. Adhering to protocol, I placed my hand in my bag and brought out my purse.

He held up his hand and shook his head. "No, dear. You keep it. I only accept tips from the rich." He saluted me. "I'll be seeing you."

As I watched the doors snap shut, I asked myself "Did that just happen?" I stood transfixed for a moment. There were no bright lights, noisy phones, or screechy mega-screens. It was as though I'd climbed a summit somewhere away from humanity.

Finding the door slightly ajar, I knocked and walked sheepishly in. I entered the pretty living room, and as with each time I visited that beguiling space, I landed on something new to feast my eyes upon. This time I noticed white picture rails that accentuated the pink walls, from which hung vibrant and original Impressionist paintings. The wall-to-wall shelves housed a collection of figurines, colored glass vases, and countless fascinating pieces of bric-a-brac.

Looking about for my employer, I spotted Aggie seated on the terrace again, which I'd learned was her favorite spot. She had this uncanny, almost encyclopedic knowledge of the lives of those who passed by regularly. Although they bordered on defamatory at times, I found Aggie's witty comments hilarious.

To avoid startling her, I coughed. Aggie turned, and seeing me, she gestured for me to join her.

"Um... I found the door open," I said, stepping onto the terrace. "I hope you don't mind. I knocked."

She studied me for a moment. "I left it open for you. Just in case I dozed off. The sun's too nice to miss."

"Can I get you something?" I asked.

"The usual. It will be my first. I've decided to cut back." A flicker of a smile came and went.

"Oh... That's good, Aggie."

"Yes, instead of seven or eight, I'll go down to five, I think. I'm starting to find the climb difficult."

I nodded slowly, amazed. Given that one martini had me giggling at strangers whenever I left my daily session, five would have placed me in a coma.

"I can take you upstairs before I leave every day if you wish," I said.

She shook her head vehemently. "Unnecessary."

When I returned, I placed the martini by Aggie's side and asked, "Would you like me to read?"

She shook her head.

Clasping the stem of the glass, Aggie took a sip. "Mm… lovely. You're a natural."

"Thanks," I replied with a genuine smile. Aggie might as well have complimented me for brewing up a cure for cancer because it brightened my spirit learning that I had mastered the art of martinis. Not that it would gain me kudos for future employment.

Aggie pointed to a white peacock chair that resembled a throne by her side. "Sit."

Sinking down onto the floral cushion, I allowed my body to indulge in comfort. I cast my face up to the blue sky as my pores absorbed pleasant warmth from the sun.

"You're not yourself today," said Aggie, reaching over for her cigarettes.

"I'm just a bit tired."

"I appreciate you coming here on a Saturday. Will that work? Seven days. I'll pay double time. I like the company. And I need someone to mix my martinis." A cheeky smirk played on her lips.

"Of course. It's only four hours a day, and you're very generous. I'm grateful to have this job."

"Good. Then tell me why you look like you've been fighting with your boyfriend."

I shifted my position. "I didn't have a fight as such."

Her blue eyes narrowed as she studied me. I'd suddenly developed this irrational belief that Aggie could read my thoughts. Visualizing her white hair loose, I even started to wonder if she was a witch.

"You've fallen in love."

My brow crumpled with disbelief. "What? No… I haven't."

She moved her attention to the street. Aggie's mercurial nature, although jarring at times, was welcome, given that I wasn't in the mood to analyze my love life.

Pointing, she said, "There's Billie. My, he's walking well."

Looking down onto the pavement, I had no idea who she meant, considering the many that marched forward, oblivious to our gawking.

"He's the one with the pale-blue slacks. Ha... he always dresses as if he's on a Contiki tour." She chuckled.

"Contiki?" I asked.

"Organized tours. Mainly for rich geriatrics with no sense of adventure in their decaying bones."

I had to chuckle at Aggie's tone, which was as dry as the martini she sipped. "Okay. I see him now."

"Billie Washington. Related to the famous president, apparently. He has a penchant for leggy blondes. Although in our days he used to chase me around. I let him one night, you know." The shine in her eyes told me there was more to come. When it came to smutty banter, Aggie could hold her own with a bunch of horny frat boys. "Tiny little penis. When he flashed it, I had to try not to giggle. You know how delicate men are about their dicks."

Having only ever seen one in my life, I just stared back blankly.

"You're inexperienced, aren't you?" Aggie sucked on her cigarette, and as she exhaled smoke, she added, "Please don't tell me you're still a virgin."

"No. I've got a boyfriend."

"Oh yes, of course. What does he do?"

"He's a lawyer."

"Oh... one of those. Talks and talks endlessly about himself, I suppose. Can talk underwater with marbles in his mouth?"

Laughing at that ridiculous image, I nodded. "He's chatty."

She turned and faced me. Her eyes narrowed as they did whenever she burrowed into my mind. As though naked, I even unconsciously crossed my arms.

"He doesn't please you. You don't look like a girl in love to me. Although I saw something in you when you arrived. But that's someone else, I think. You've lost your heart to another."

"I haven't," I protested. My eyes traveled to her empty glass. "Shall I get you another?"

"You're being evasive. But yes, please. Have one too. It will relax you. I'm getting your anxiety."

"I'm sorry. I didn't realize I was that transparent."

"There. I knew it."

What was I giving off? I asked myself while standing by the trolley pouring out two martinis.

Careful not to spill anything, I took each step slowly back onto the terrace and set the glass down by Aggie's side.

I settled back into the comfortable Morticia chair and swallowed a little of the firewater, which made my cheeks fire up.

Aggie watched me drink. "There, you look better already. There's nothing that a good martini cannot cure."

"Would you like me to read?" I asked, mostly for my own sanity, because I didn't feel like making my love life the subject of the moment.

"No. Tell me more about whats-his-name."

"Justin."

"Yes. Does he pleasure you in that way?" Her lips twitched into a lopsided grin.

"Well... Yes..."

"He doesn't, I can tell. Does he make you come?"

My face heated up. "Look, Aggie, I have nothing but admiration for your sharp, inquisitive mind, but would you mind if we didn't discuss my sex life?"

Her eyebrows drew in. "But what else is there to talk about if one can't talk about love?"

"I don't mind talking about love. I'm just a private person, that's all."

"I understand. I promise not to mention it. But there is one thing I will throw in. It's vital that a man learns to pleasure a woman. We're subtle creatures. Our anatomy's not as obvious or as big." She looked up at me with one of her cheeky grins. "If you get my meaning."

"Would you like to meet a partner?" I asked, in a bid to shift the focus away from me.

"Oh God, no. I've had one true love. No man will ever compare to Monty. I have memories." She touched her heart. "Lots of them. In any case, I'm dry down there. Closed for business." She raised a brow.

That nearly made me choke, even though I should have been used to Aggie by then.

"Monty was your true love?" I asked.

The way her eyes misted over as she looked into the distance told me that I'd hit a raw nerve. I held back on further questions and sipped my martini instead.

"Look." Aggie pointed. "There's Edith. Oh my, she's using a walker. Poor girl."

Girl? Edith looked close to a hundred years old.

"Would you like to go out sometime? We could go for a walk in the park. I could even read for you there," I asked.

"Oh God no. The only time I'll be leaving here will be on a stretcher." Aggie lit another cigarette. I noticed her hands shaking a little. That earlier comment about Monty had changed her mood.

"You don't like the street?"

"I love the street. I wouldn't live anywhere else. I just don't like people seeing me like this."

"But you look great. You have great style, regal posture, and you're so agile for..."

"For an old girl?" Aggie chuckled. "So I come across as queenly, do I?"

I couldn't tell if she was joking or offended.

She tapped my arm. "It's okay, dear. Just playing with you." She studied me for a moment. "You look better. See, there's not much a martini can't cure."

I smiled. "Is that the only reason why you don't wish to go out?"

"You're asking too many questions, Ava. Remember, no questions."

My mouth turned down. "Sorry."

Her face relaxed a little. "I have this phobia about people. I don't like moving amongst them. Once upon a time, I loved socializing, but now, I'm happy to engage with one other, like yourself or my cook. Apart from that, I have memories to keep me company."

There were so many questions I wanted to ask. Aggie fascinated me. Instead, I bit my tongue.

We spent the rest of the day talking about the people walking by, mainly about their clothes. Aggie had this thing for fashion. And at the end of our session, I was taken aback when she handed me a plastic bag filled with clothes.

"What are these for?" I asked, assuming they were destined for a charity shop.

"They're for you, Ava. Take a look."

I opened the bag and ran my fingers over silky fabrics. Digging in deep, I discovered skirts, pants, and a couple of floral dresses. When I read Christian Dior and Pierre Cardin on the labels, my jaw dropped.

"They should fit. You've got the same figure as I did. Big breasts and ass."

Lost for words, I bit into my cheek.

Aggie added, "I've lost a lot of weight. But when I was your age, I had your figure." She nodded with a slight smile. "The boys liked it. That's for sure."

Being one of those rare women that didn't think much about clothes, I found my breath stuck in my throat as I touched the smooth silk, velvets, and quality cottons. I pulled out an outlandish long-sleeved dress printed in purple flowers and sporting green buttons.

"I wore that with white boots. I loved the buttons. It came with a matching belt. That should be in there somewhere. I bought that in Paris in 1970."

Stunned, I looked at the array of clothes that the city's fashion-conscious would have broken a sprinting record to possess.

"Are you sure you want me to have them?" I asked.

"What? You don't want them?"

"Well, yes. I mean, they're stunning. I've never worn anything like that before."

"I've noticed. You could do with a little more color." Aggie's cool observation reminded me of the tendency I had to dress without much fuss. Unlike Cassie, I didn't think about my wardrobe. Most of the time, I got around in loose jeans and T-shirts. The looser the better. Because, as Aggie had pointed out, I wasn't slim, and therefore clothes didn't hang elegantly on me like they did on Cassie.

I slid the clothes back into the large plastic bag. "They're amazing, Aggie. Thank you. You're really generous. Are you sure you wouldn't prefer to give them to a family member? A granddaughter or something?"

"I don't have any family." Her matter-of-fact tone suggested a lack of concern.

Despite chronic curiosity, I remained respectfully silent.

CHAPTER SIX

BRONSON

I paced about like a tiger in a cage. This time it wasn't bars holding me in but a desperate, almost crippling urge to get back at my asshole brother. Seeing his smug face again had fired me up. I needed to breathe because my revenge had to be subtle but painful nevertheless, because the last thing I wanted was to be locked up in that hellhole again.

It was five in the morning. I hadn't slept. The girl at the party had made a big appearance. And I mean big. Painfully so.

Ava.

The fact I remembered her name surprised me. But then, there was a lot about her that stuck well and truly in my head, and below. Ava's beauty had stolen my breath, though, from the second I fell into those big blue eyes and followed that natural sway of hips. She was a real woman in the true sense of the word, with curves in all the right places, the thought of which flooded my groin with heat. After that little chat we'd had, I'd walked away scratching my head trying to figure out what an intelligent woman like Ava saw in that asshole, Justin.

But I needed to focus. Ava was my weapon. I'd fuck her. That should piss Justin off big time, with that big fucking ego of his.

I'd always gotten the girls. That was why he hated me. Especially after Sandy, the girl he'd spent a whole year chasing, had ended up in my room at one of our parties. And I was the one who ate her cherry. That said, the animosity wasn't just about us as horny teenagers chasing pussy though. It had begun from the moment I walked into that family aged five. Justin, who was my age, did everything he could to terrorize me. Horrible fucking pranks like placing dog shit in my bed, or he'd make a mess and then point the finger at me. But I kept my mouth shut because the thought of returning to that stinking dump that had been my home before Justin's dad adopted me scared the shit out of me.

But now that we were adults, the game had changed. This was serious. Justin had to pay big time for shitting on my reputation. All that bullshit about being innocent. He was the only person who could have stashed the drugs in my backpack because I'd seen him with the bag of white powder earlier that night.

Sleeping with his girl was one thing, but I needed more than that. My ultimate goal was for Justin to go through what I'd been through. Being a pretty boy, he'd have a hell of a time fending off the cocksuckers in jail. Despite possessing a big mouth that fired missiles of hot air, Justin couldn't fight his way out of a paper bag. The hungry fuckers in there would know how to put that big mouth to good use, and it didn't involve sucking lollipops either. My kickboxing youth had come in handy. After I bruised one asshole's cock with my knee, they all kept away. The cash my art and furniture generated also helped, in that the prison officers made sure I was left alone.

I stared out the window, which had become a favorite pastime of mine since being released. The view was not pretty, though, from that fourth-floor shithole I'd recently moved into. My eyes rested on the other equally sad buildings facing a seedy alleyway that probably had enough DNA stuck on its grimy path to fill a prison.

I had to visit Harry, my old boss, later that morning. He'd promised me a job on one of his building sites. Having done time when he was young and foolish, Harry was more of a buddy than anything else.

Moving away from the window, I lowered my body to the ground and pumped out a hundred pushups, followed by stretches that I'd picked up while in prison. Becoming an exercise junkie had been the only good thing about being in prison for a year. I liked how it made me feel. And along with drawing and woodwork, it was the only thing that kept me sane.

I wiped my face with a towel, after which I decided to go for a run.

When I got to the ground floor, I exited the cracked glass doors and, as always, stepped over spilled garbage. The alley smelled of shit, as it always did. Watching my step, I noticed soiled, torn panties, which only added to the alley's grunginess.

As with every morning, the park, which was close to my place, wasn't exactly a picture of beauty either. Empty bottles and cartons lay strewn all over the grass, suggesting a big night for those sleeping rough.

I clutched my arms. The air was sharp. Just as I was about to start jogging, I stopped when I discovered there were bodies scattered about, in what was a sad sight. As a cold hand gripped at my soul, I raked through my hair, wondering if that could have been me had I not been saved by Elliot Lockhart, my late adoptive father.

How my life had changed. Two years earlier, on my way to carving out a better life, I'd started an architecture degree at Columbia. And then that fucking party, from where I left handcuffed while being pushed and shoved by cops as I pleaded innocence until my throat became raw.

A dog scrounging for food looked up at me with big, sad eyes. I opened my arms. "I haven't got anything, buddy."

I headed for the pavement and ran my heart out. That was my way of dealing with shit. Exercise. It had started with playing football. I became addicted to the high it delivered, which was better than any drug I'd ever taken. Not that I'd taken many; only weed on occasion. And then there I was in jail, doing time for an apparent coke habit. Even fellow inmates couldn't figure me out, especially when I passed on deals that were taking place right in front of me.

The shabby looking office suited the paunchy, middle-aged P.I., who didn't exactly strike me as someone ready to pounce on facts. If anything, he looked like he'd slept less than me. And that was saying something, since thanks to acquiring insomnia in jail, I hadn't had a good fucking night's sleep in ages.

"Okay, take me through it," he said, slouching back in his chair.

"It's not a long story. While my parents were away, my brother threw a party. By midnight, after the neighbors complained, the cops came around. They scrounged about and found a bag of coke in my backpack."

"So let me guess, one of the guests planted it there?"

I nodded. "I know who it is, too. It's just that I can't pin it on him."

"Then what do you want from me?"

"Follow him. He doesn't hide his coke habit."

"That's easy enough to do. But then how's that going to connect him to the crime?"

"Good question. Just get me some photos for now, and I'll fill in the blanks as I go."

He pushed a clipboard with a form on it toward me. "Here. Give me as much detail as you've got. The more the better. Then leave it to me. I charge double on weekends."

"Whatever it takes."

"Good. I'll need a deposit before I start. You're good for that, I suppose?"

"Yeah. Why wouldn't I be?" I bristled at his implication that because I'd been locked up, I wasn't to be trusted.

Frustration bit into me—was that how I would be defined from there on? Ex-convict scum, and not that guy with a promising future in architecture.

"Just asking. How long were you in?"

"One year."

He let out a long breath. "That's tough. At least you're a strong-looking guy. I'm sure that helped."

My lips twitched into a mock smile, recalling the showers and the hungry looks coming from some of the inmates who'd been locked up for ages, men who hadn't even known they liked dick until they were caged. The worst were the weedy ones, in there for white-collar crime. They'd seemed the hungriest.

"I punched my way out of trouble. Years of martial arts helped," I answered.

He scrutinized me for a moment. "All right. Stay in touch."

That night, I went back to my family home. It was my mother's birthday. In spite of my reluctance, given that I'd only rubbed shoulders with the clan earlier that week, I attended out of respect for her. Carrying a small coffee table, a gift for my mother, I took a cab back to my old life in Brooklyn.

As I peered at familiar landmarks that I'd walked past for nearly twenty years, I relaxed. Things weren't too bad, in that at least I'd landed a job starting straight away. Having a ton of projects on the go, Harry needed someone with my carpentry experience, and he was so desperate I could virtually name my price. I'd never had a problem finding money. And I liked to work hard. One thing was for sure, I needed to clear out of that apartment as soon as possible. The late-night antics from the floor above were keeping me up—loud orgasms or someone being battered about, the thought of which stressed me out. I'd even contemplated investigating but had to stop myself, given that it was the type of place where people played with guns for fun.

The cab dropped me off at the brownstone, two-story home, which had been my home from the age of five. Before that, it had been one institution after another, each just as creepy as the prison I'd just left. In fact, they were so frighteningly similar that the first week of being locked up, I couldn't stop throwing up.

I placed the small table on the street when a couple of girls walked by and whistled at me. I returned a smirk. Why not play up to it, I thought. I hadn't been with a woman for over a year and craved the taste of some pussy.

"Cute table," one said.

I grinned back.

After climbing the stairs, I pressed the bell despite owning a key.

My mom opened the door and stepped out of the way for me to enter.

She hugged me. "Darling, I'm so glad you came."

"I made you this," I said, setting the coffee table down in the hallway.

"Oh, it's lovely. You made that?" Her eyes shone with admiration at the oval-shaped mahogany table. It was one of the many pieces I'd made in prison. Even though the officers had taken almost everything I made, I'd managed to keep the best one for my mother.

I nodded.

"You're such a clever boy, my darling. Come on. Let's get you a nice cold beer."

"Who's here?" I asked, hearing voices and giggles.

"Just the family."

Family, I could just do. And as that thought turned over, Justin stood before me. "Twice in one week. It's almost like the bad old days," he said with that smug grin that made my fists clench.

"Be nice," said my mother, looking at Justin.

When I entered the dining area, even though a collection of familiar faces turned toward me, my eyes zeroed in on Ava.

She'd raised the bar pretty high where women were concerned, which wasn't the only thing she'd helped raise. Considering my plan for revenge, I hated how Ava did things to me that I'd never experienced before. I even tried to convince myself that was due to the lack of female contact for more than a year.

Dressed in purple, she was hard to miss. But as my eyes traveled back to those eyes, which had already cast their spell on me, I struggled to turn away. One couldn't help being drawn into those deep blue eyes that echoed a hint of purple from her dress. And that mouth-watering body, the promise of those full breasts rubbing against me, had already launched a few explosions thanks to my dirty mind. The green buttons on her dress seemed to pop right out. A fantasy for later would go something like this: One by one, I'd undo them to find a silky piece of lace holding in a nice pair of tits waiting for my hungry mouth.

I just had to accept that she'd mess with my hormones all night. But the question remained: Was I ready to mess with Ava by seducing her for ulterior motives?

Floating back to reality, I greeted my Uncle James, his new bubbly and literally bouncy young wife, Candy, Marcus, his girl, and my old neighbors.

"Bronson, how good to see you again," said Dora, who must have been at least eighty. She stamped a lipstick stain on my cheek, while her husband, Phil, shook my hand.

I had a soft spot for Dora. She'd cared for me when I was young while my mom worked part-time. Being one of those gentle types, Dora had a ton of patience. I did wonder, though, if they'd called the cops the night of *that* party. Maybe that was something I'd never know. And I couldn't blame them, considering how the noisy party had spilled onto their normally quiet street.

My mom fussed about. She was never good at standing still for long. I also sensed a spark between her and Uncle James. I always had. Although I was certain that they'd never had an affair. She'd loved my late dad too much for that. In any case, it would have broken my heart to know otherwise. For non-biological parents, they were wonderful, affectionate people that I wouldn't've hesitated to give a kidney to for rescuing me from that hovel. Experts say that most people don't recall life before the age of three, but I did. Every cruel minute of it— from the cold eyes, stench of piss and vomit, to the gut-wrenching cries. It was woven deeply into every cell of my body.

"Bronson, darling, go and get that lovely little table you made me," said my mother.

I bit into my cheek. I wasn't exactly the type who liked to parade his creations before people but fueled by my mother's encouragement and her insistence, I brought in the table and placed it beside the recliner she favored.

"Oh… that's so interesting. It's beautifully finished," said Phil, who had lent me his tools after I'd developed an interest in woodwork as a teenager. While Justin had been out and about getting drunk and picking up chicks, I spent time in the shed, sanding pieces of timber I'd collected at scrapyards.

"Bronson's always been creative," said my mom, running her hand over the polished table.

"I love the legs. It's so original," said the angel.

I looked over at her, and when she smiled back shyly, our eyes locked. I soaked her in as someone starved of beauty would.

Noticing how drawn I was to his girl, Justin came over and claimed Ava by taking her hand.

James tapped the chair next to him. "Why don't you take a seat, Bronson."

I sat next to him, from where I had a perfect view of Ava.

"Would you like a beer?" he asked.

I ran my hands through my hair. "Yeah, sure." I stood up again and said, "Stay. I'll get one." I checked his bottle. "Can I get you another?"

"Why not. I'm not driving." He chuckled.

I looked over at the guests' drinks. "Can I get anyone anything?" Of course, my eyes settled on Ava again.

"Yeah. Another beer here," said Justin with that loudmouth of his.

I headed into the kitchen, where I opened the fridge door and grabbed three Coronas.

In the background, my mom moved about, preparing plates. "Mm… that smells good. Do you need a hand?" I asked.

"Maybe you can carve the meat if you don't mind." She smiled sweetly.

"Yeah, sure. I'll be back. I'll just deliver the drinks."

CHAPTER SEVEN

"So, how's that architecture degree going?" asked Phil.

For some reason, everyone stopped talking and centered their focus on me, making me cringe.

"I've had to put that on hold," I said.

Unsure of whether my old neighbors knew anything about my imprisonment, I kept it brief.

My eyes settled on Ava again, who'd spent most of the time chatting and joking with Marcus's girlfriend between stealing little glances here and there. I even noticed a streak of pink on her cheeks whenever our stares collided.

"Bron's been away for a while," said Justin with a smirk that registered straight down to my fists as always.

"You've been on a holiday?" Dora asked me.

I shrugged. "Yeah, something like that."

By the way, Phil gently tapped her hand under the table, I sensed he knew something.

Marcus looked over at me. "You're looking really fit, Bron."

"Yeah, I try."

"So, are you working?"

I nodded. "I've just scored a job on a site starting Monday. Building pre-fab homes."

"That's interesting. I remember you were into designing them. Are they using your ideas?"

"Not as such, but Harry's expressed interest in checking them out sometime."

I noticed Ava following our conversation which pleased me. Not so much because I wanted to get into her panties, but because I wanted Ava to know that I wasn't just some dirtbag felon.

"I liked the sketches you showed me a while back," said my uncle. "I'm looking for something to do. I could be interested in backing a project."

I nodded, casting a sideways glance at Ava, who remained fixed on our conversation.

"The shares are performing brilliantly. I imagine you're happy about that," said James.

My eyebrows drew in sharply. I had no idea what he meant. Just as I was about to comment, Justin blustered into the room with Candy by his side. By the cheesy grins on their faces, it was pretty fucking obvious that the pair had been doing sniff. That pissed me off big time, given that I could have snapped a shot of Justin snorting, saving some cash in the process.

Candy stood by James, giggling loudly. He turned away from me and whispered something to her, and after he returned his attention to me, I asked, "What shares?"

Justin jumped in and said, "Let's not talk shop. Let's party. It's Mom's fiftieth." He stood beside Ava and wrapped his arm around her shoulder.

Going by the nervous look on Justin's face, combined with my uncle's perplexed expression, I sensed something wasn't right.

"What shares?" I persisted.

"I just cashed in the same shares that your father bought, which have reached stratospheric heights."

He cast his attention to Justin, whose back was turned away, but from where I sat, I could see that he'd gone slightly pale.

"This is the first time I've heard about that," I said, thinking about the shiny red BMW convertible that Justin had posted a photo of on Facebook.

Justin pounced in. "Did you see the ball game last night? I mean, that fumble cost us the game." Falling for the subterfuge, my uncle, who'd always been a football fanatic, nodded. Justin then continued rambling on about the game, and that was that.

Something suddenly didn't smell right. As always, it had my shady brother's dirty fingers all over it. I recalled how, as a child, Justin had always stolen my Christmas presents or swapped them for the ones he didn't like. He'd always been on the take.

Tired of listening to Justin blabbering overlaid with Candy's piercing giggles at his every utterance, I decided to head out to the garden.

Standing on the porch, I lit up a cigarette, a bad habit I'd taken up in prison, which I'd planned to kick as soon as things settled.

The sky was clear. Taking my interest was a bright star that I speculated was Jupiter because of the flickering colors. That was something else I'd learned from my late father, who, being a keen amateur astronomer, had instilled in me a similar fascination with the galaxy.

"It's a lovely night," said a sweet-sounding voice from behind me.

I turned, and there before me stood the angel. "Hey."

"Sorry. I hope I didn't startle you," she said with a gentle smile.

"No. I'm just indulging in my one and only bad habit," I said.

"Only one?" She raised a brow.

I'd always been a sucker for blue eyes, and Ava well and truly won the prize for owning the prettiest set I'd ever seen. As I gazed at her, I tried to push aside the steam of attraction that threatened to overthrow my scheme.

Tearing my eyes away, I told myself to stay on the page, that seduction was close within my grasp. My chance to set up the payback.

"Mm… I guess," I finally answered.

"Are you on a health kick?" she asked.

I blew smoke in the opposite direction. "Not with this dirty habit, I'm not." I grinned. "But sure, I'm trying."

She studied me. "I love that coffee table you made. Are you into working with your hands?"

I nodded slowly. "I like carpentry."

It was like a drug, those sweet eyes flickering with possibility, and just as I toyed with the idea of finding another way to get back at Justin, he stepped outside. Spotting us, he strutted over to claim his girl. While noticing's Ava's forehead crease, I didn't get the vibe of a woman happy to see her man.

"Can I ask you something personal?" I asked.

"It depends on what it is."

"What's a woman like you doing with that dick?" I lifted my chin toward Justin, who'd arrived within earshot.

She shrugged while shifting her weight. I'd obviously challenged her.

"That's not much of an answer," I challenged.

With the moonlight on her face and wearing a tight smile, she looked up at me, and once again, our eyes locked before she turned away and regarded Justin, who'd stepped into our space.

"Are you hitting on my girl?" He wrapped his arm around Ava.

Just to piss Justin off, I didn't answer him and instead saluted Ava. "Nice talking to you."

Leaving them to sort out their shit, I headed over to the shed. I stepped into the workshop, where my dad used to tinker about and where my interest in carpentry had begun. That familiar scent of freshly cut wood flushed me with nostalgia. Everything was where it had always been, as though nothing had changed. When I was a boy, that shed quickly became my little refuge. It was where I'd bonded with my dad, a relationship that made Justin seethe with jealousy. He'd even tried to join us but was so useless and lazy he lasted one hour. A welling of emotion gathered around in my chest as I recalled my father. The fact that he'd died while I rotted in prison had broken me because I hadn't even been able to say goodbye. In many ways, that had been what hurt the most about being locked up.

The old transistor radio that my dad would have blaring while we worked stood on the ledge, where it had always been. He'd sometimes sneak the odd cigarette against a background of sixties and seventies tunes, which I quickly developed a taste for. I slumped into a chair and wondered what unlucky star had touched me. Because one year earlier, I'd been in a great place. Then that party. Bang. It all changed, and suddenly, thrown in with a bunch of scumbags from the dark fringes of society, it seemed as though I'd done a full circle. That I was back where I'd begun. On bad days, I'd even convinced myself that I belonged there.

Reaching into my pocket for my cigarettes, I'd just stretched out my legs when a scream made me sit up.

Ava yelled, "Don't!"

At first, I thought Justin was just clowning around. I knew it well. That ugly snigger and then protesting his innocence by insisting his nasty prank was only a joke.

After I heard Ava crying out, "Justin!" I ran out to investigate, and hiding behind the thick bushes, I saw Ava struggling in Justin's arms.

"Don't, Justin," Ava said.

"Oh, come on. Don't go frigid on me."

"Don't!"

"Rough is fun." He chuckled.

"Justin!"

By that stage, Justin had Ava up against the wall. "You're a cockteaser, Ava. I need a fuck."

"Not here. You're hurting me."

That was no play, I thought. Witnessing Ava's face scrunching in terror, I was convinced that was not the face of a woman who wanted her boyfriend to play dirty.

CHAPTER EIGHT

AVA

There was no doubt that the little stirring of desire I'd felt for Justin had dried up. I put it down to his drinking, which only seemed to strengthen his fierce determination to take what he wanted. We'd slept together about six times over the three months we'd dated, which seemed ridiculous as far as relationships went. But the heavy drinking and the smell of his cigar-infused breath nauseated me.

I kept seeing that dark, almost dangerous look in Bronson's eyes after Justin had tried to force me. Instead of fear, he made me feel safe. And something more.

Adamant and persistent, Justin had pulled a playful grin. His disregard of the pain he'd caused still iced my veins. Had Bronson not stepped in, Justin would have gone through with it, given that his fingers were hooked inside my panties.

My mouth remained agape as I leaned against the wall and watched in horror as the brothers pointed into each other's face, spitting vitriol.

It was Bronson that my eyes sought. The fire in his black gaze made my heart skip a beat and my knees go weak. There was something magnetic and primal about him.

I couldn't take my eyes away from him, even though it was wrong.

Really wrong.

The brothers hated each other. That was patently clear.

Bronson clenched his fist, while his eyes fired up with fierce determination to protect me. That really freaked me out, given we barely knew each other.

"Let her go, Justin," he growled.

Justin turned sharply. "Keep the fuck out of it. This is between me and my girl."

Bron looked at me as though seeking some kind of affirmation, but I remained wide-eyed and speechless. "Then why was she screaming?"

"None of your fucking business. You're nothing but a fucking disgrace to the family. Why don't you crawl back to that prison cell where you belong?"

The words "prison cell" deafened me. But when I refocused, I noticed Bronson pushing Justin against the wall. The sinews in his large arms bulged as his fist headed for my soon to be ex-boyfriend's jaw.

My screams alerted Marcus and his father. They came running out just in time to stop Bronson from throwing a punch that would have knocked Justin out. He had, however, managed to shake Justin around as if he were a ragdoll.

After pushing Justin away—who, as a consequence stumbled back and fell on his butt—Bronson ran his fingers through his hair. His handsome chiseled features bore a film of sweat. His eyes were cast down to his feet. I sensed frustration or something more complex going on there. When his eyes returned to mine, I saw struggle and a deep longing that both frightened and touched me at the same time.

I wanted to thank him. To tell him it was okay. But my throat remained tense. And by the time I'd found my voice, Bronson left without uttering another word.

Lowering myself to a bench, I wasn't ready to see people, while at the same time, James led Justin away. And although they couldn't see me, I could hear them.

"What the hell was that about?" James asked.

"Stay out of it, Uncle."

"I won't stay out of it. Your heavy drinking is worrying your mother. I've seen you twice this week. And the other night at my house, I found some streaks of white powder on my Eagles album cover. Candy admitted to me she'd shared a line with you."

"Your trophy wife, you mean. The one that offered to go down on me."

It wasn't so much what he said, although that did sicken me, but the manner of his smarmy retort that I found truly disgusting.

"What happened with those shares? Elliot told me while he was in the hospital that he planned to carve them up in three equal portions: for Alice, yourself, and Bronson."

"Dad changed his mind after Bron was convicted. As anyone would. He probably would have blown it on drugs, anyway. He's the jailbird in the family, after all. Even though you all treat him as if he were some kind of fucking hero."

"We don't. He had a tough start to life. He's worked hard and shows talent. In my book, that kind of person deserves respect."

"I'm sick of talking about that douche, who's not even my real fucking brother."

"This isn't the last of it, Justin. If I find that you haven't done the right thing, I'll step in."

Justin mumbled a response, after which I heard their treads fade away.

Lost in thought, I jumped when the buzzer sounded.

Discovering that it was Cassie, I waited for the sound of the elevator before opening the door for her. She entered wearing a sunny smile and clutching a parcel that radiated that unmistakable delicious aroma of donuts.

Falling onto the sofa, Cassie plopped the sweets on the table. "Here, I thought you could use something nice after last night's shenanigans."

I grinned and nodded. "Yeah. I'm single again."

Cassie studied me for a moment. "I hope you know what you're doing."

"Coffee or wine?"

"Wine," she said.

It was early afternoon, and because I had Aggie in a few hours, I settled for a coffee.

After I'd polished off two donuts with Cassie watching, I asked, "Aren't you going to have one?"

"Maybe just one. You're so lucky, Aves. When you put on weight it goes to all the right places. With me, it just settles here." She pinched her belly.

"There's nothing there. You're really skinny, Cas. To be honest, I worry about you."

"Hey. I'm no longer sticking my hand down my throat after meals. I've put that behind me."

A slow breath left me as I studied my friend, who'd been body obsessed since her teens. If anything, Cassie's unhealthy fixation with body image had made me rebel, in that I'd decided to enjoy eating. Especially sweets. Even if my jeans had tightened around my growing ass.

"That's good to know." I stroked her arm and gave her an encouraging smile.

"So what happened? God, Marcus's dad and Justin were giving each other the evil eye after you left."

"I don't know. There's something not right there. Justin's fucked up. I can't be with him. He nearly raped me outside, you know. If Bronson hadn't stepped in..."

"But boyfriends don't rape. They play a bit rough at times. A bit of dirty play is kind of exciting."

"There's a big difference between playing dirty and nonconsensual sex."

Her plucked eyebrows lifted. "He was that rough? Tell me what happened."

"Just that he groped me, pushed me against the wall, and was ripping my panties."

"But that's hot." I could see envy in her eyes.

"I get that point. And that's probably right. That's why I know that Justin's not for me. You realize we've only slept with each a few times. I've tried. I know he's really good-looking, but when Justin kisses me, nothing happens."

"Has a kiss ever turned you on?" Cassie asked.

A frustrated sigh sounded in my chest. "That's the thing. It hasn't. I mean, I've kissed a few guys and whatnot. You know all about that. We've shared on all our kissing experiences." I tilted my head. "I've never felt that fire that's meant to take over. Or is that just Hollywood and Harlequin filling us with unrealistic expectations?"

"No way." Cassie shook her head. "I've been there. With Gino. Remember that sexy Italian?"

"Yeah. The impoverished one that worked at the local café. The one that you shunned because he offered no future prospects."

Her mouth turned down. "I know. But it's hard out there. And look at my mom and dad. My mom married for love, and they've been struggling ever since. The net result being me having to work two jobs since I was fifteen. I'm fucking exhausted, and I'm only twenty-four." She brushed back her blonde fringe. "At least Marcus has money. Life's suddenly gotten easier for me. He pays for everything. He even paid my rent last month. And he bought me these." She pulled at her stretchy designer jeans.

"But I bet you wouldn't have minded Gino ripping your panties off," I countered.

A slow smile grew, and her face reddened. "Mm… who's says he didn't?"

I giggled. "You're a minx. So, do you still see Gino at the café?"

"Yeah. He's married." She sounded disappointed.

"But that's the point, isn't it?"

"What is?"

"That fuzzy, heart-leaping feeling. Life's too short to rob ourselves of that."

With a wistful sigh, Cassie said, "Yeah, I suppose." Taking a sip of wine, she added, "Justin's gutted, Marcus tells me."

"I don't care. He's a brute. And if Bronson hadn't intervened…"

Cassie interjected. "There it is."

I shook my head. "What?"

"That look in your eyes. I've known you forever, and I haven't seen that before. You like him. And he likes you. And boy, he's fucking hot, and a little dangerous, I think, with that big body, tattoos, and intensity of his."

Churning up like a stormy ocean, my emotions became a tangled mess again. The warm shower that cascaded over me from hearing that Bronson liked me went cold as I reflected on his shady past.

"He's been in jail," I said.

"I know. So bad-boy. He's fucking sexy. I bet you wouldn't mind him ripping your panties off."

Even though I painted on a shocked frown of disbelief, there was no denying the little swelling ache taking place below. "Unlike you, I'm not into the bad-boy type."

"Did you see those arms? God, he's big in all the right places. I bet."

"Yeah. So you keep saying, Cas."

I rose from the couch and strolled over to the tiny little balcony, where again, my eyes lamented the chunk of decaying wall blocking the sky.

"I'll admit, Bronson's seriously good-looking, and he does make my heart pump faster than I'm used to."

"Ah… there." Cassie pointed at me. "You do like him."

"Hello… He's been in jail."

Recollecting Bronson's wild-eyed fury as he went to hit Justin, I said, "Maybe he killed someone. We don't even know what he's been in for."

"For cocaine. Marcus told me Bronson was locked up for a year. They found it on him at a party at their family home."

"You know my feelings about drugs. That's another reason why I had to dump Justin. He snorts coke. And when he's on it, he becomes horribly rowdy and aggressive."

"But he's really rich, Ava. And good-looking."

"You sound like my mom. She'll be seriously pissed off when I tell her. But I'm only twenty-four, for God's sake. I've got time to get it right. And Justin's creeping me out. Rich or not." I looked at the clock. "Hey. I've got to get ready for work."

"Who works on a Sunday?"

"I do."

Cassie followed me into my bedroom. On the bed lay the purple floral dress that Aggie had given me.

"That's such a loud dress. It is so unlike you. Miss Jeans-and-T-shirt Girl."

"I know."

"But it suits you." Cassie stared at the label. "Shit, Dior."

I nodded. "Uh-huh… You should see what else Aggie gave me."

"Let me see. Please." That shouldn't have surprised me. Cassie loved clothes.

I placed the contents of the bag, which I hadn't had a chance to hang, on the bed. It had been a spur-of-the-moment decision to wear the purple floral dress, especially after I'd tried it on and discovered the fit was perfect. It also went with my eyes and hair. I couldn't resist. As it turned out, Bronson had been the only one that commented on how unique and attractive the dress was.

Cassie lunged for a pair of pink and green striped bell-bottoms. "Oh my God. Vivienne Westwood. They're outrageously divine. And bell-bottoms are in at the moment." She held them up against her.

"You can have them," I said.

Her blue eyes shone with wonder. As she held them against herself and looked in the mirror, she said, "They're too big. They'll fit you, though. God, you're the same size. What a coincidence."

I nodded. It had struck me as oddly coincidental for some reason.

She picked up a Pierre Cardin shirt with a tie around the neck. "This is pure silk and so classy. You've hit the jackpot. You could sell these on eBay."

"I won't be doing that. I'll wear them."

"Even the striped bell-bottoms?"

I rocked my head. "Well, maybe not those. Why don't you take them and have them adjusted? Here." I handed them to Cassie. "And take this as well." I handed her a yellow silk gypsy blouse.

"Givenchy! Freaking hell, Aves, are you sure?"

"Of course, I'm sure. And anyhow, yellow's more your color."

She leaned in and kissed me. "You're the best."

On that note, I reached into the pile and picked up the purple dress again, for some reason. Perhaps I wanted to show Aggie my appreciation of her generosity. I'd also grown seriously fond of it.

CHAPTER NINE

Aggie stood at the door, and for a moment, I thought I could see something in her eyes that spelled deep, heartfelt emotion.

"That dress. Oh my... And your hair is loose. I've never seen it like that. It's so long and lustrous."

I remained at the entrance, biting my lip. She had a dazed look on her face, leading me to think that maybe she'd had one martini too many already.

Aggie stepped out of the way, and I entered.

"You don't mind me wearing it?"

She replied, "Oh no. Please come like that. I prefer color. And you're a beautiful girl, Ava. You need to take advantage of that wonderful hair. Don't ever cut it."

I smiled, thinking of my mom, who kept saying I looked too old-fashioned with it long.

"Come, come. It's a lovely sunny day again. Let's sit outside," said Aggie. Following along, I ambled behind her, and noticed that she was dressed in her regular pink slacks with a pink-and-white polka-dot shirt.

"I must say, Aggie, that shirt's really nice. It suits you."

She touched the shirt. "This old thing. I picked it up at Harrods in London in the sixties. A cheapie. But nice. They used good fabrics back then." She lowered herself onto her favorite chair, which looked more like a cane throne.

"Can I get you a drink?" I asked.

"Of course. It's that hour. I've been a good girl today. I only had a glass of wine with my lunch."

"That's great, Aggie. You're looking really well."

"I slept well last night. I had a long beautiful dream. An old love of mine came to visit." She raised a brow, making it seem as though it had actually happened.

When I returned with her martini, Aggie looked disappointed. "You're not having one?"

"I might abstain for now. Maybe later," I responded.

"What's happened to you? There's been a change. It's for the better. I can see that."

"Are you aware that you're clairvoyant, Aggie?" I said, surprising myself, for my tone was forthright and not the usual wavering one I used around her.

"I'm not normally. But for some reason, you're very familiar to me. You're easy to read, Ava."

My eyebrows contracted. "How so?"

She ignored my question. "Okay, so there's a change. Tell me, have you left that joyless boyfriend of yours?"

Aggie's sardonic tone made me grin.

"I have."

"Good. There's another, though. Because I see color in those cheeks of yours. That doesn't happen after a break-up."

For some reason, I ended up telling Aggie everything that had happened. She even grimaced when I described how Justin had pushed me against the wall.

"So, this tall, dark and handsome man saved you. How gallant. Very romantic." She lit a cigarette and looked out into the distance.

"I suppose. Only, he's just gotten out of prison."

Her head turned sharply to study me again. "It wasn't murder, though."

The conviction in her tone made my spine stiffen. "No. How did you guess?"

"By the way... you described him." That falter in her voice struck me as odd. "He reminds me of Monty."

"He does?" My brow lowered.

"Tell me then. Continue. What was he in for?"

I took a deep breath. "Drugs, I'm told. Cocaine."

"Oh, is that all. Mm..." She sat back and sipped her martini. "I used to have the odd sniff at parties. Around here, it was all the rage. That and marijuana. I enjoyed cocaine. It made the blood boil. Great for sex. But I knew a few that fell into the grip of it. It's a demon drug, that's for sure. It didn't do that to me, though. Cigarettes and martinis are my only weaknesses."

As usual with Aggie's raves, my jaw dropped. Possessing the type of genes that addicts would have given a kidney to possess, Aggie wore her hedonism with pride.

"Why are you looking at me like that," she asked.

"I guess I'm awestruck by your…"

"My wild ways?" She raised her eyebrows. "Darling, life is to be had. None of that herbal-tea-and-yoga nonsense for me. I got my exercise from sex and shopping. My nourishment came from eating out at some of Manhattan's finest restaurants, and of course, I kept myself happy by not worrying about my bad habits." She laughed.

"These are such different times, I suppose. We're all reminded to care for ourselves. That our bodies are temples."

"I'm an atheist, darling." Her low drawl made me giggle. "Okay, so this sexy man was in prison, and that has put you off him. Am I right?"

I nodded. "I hate to admit it. But yeah. I suppose. His eyes…" I drifted off as I saw them in front of me again.

"Describe them for me."

"They're dark brown, sometimes even black. There's something deep that wants to erupt… a kind of hidden fury. He often reverts to a remote stare when no one's watching. But then when he looks at me, his eyes soften just a little, even though there's an element of mistrust or even shame in there. He does seem a little messed up, I suppose," I said, looking at Aggie with a tight smile.

"My, you do like him." A dreamy expression coated her stare. "Monty had dark eyes that turned black. He rarely smiled. The brooding type, you know? He loved and hated with equal intensity. In many ways, Monty's passion frightened me. But oh, how I couldn't do without him either. Time stood still whenever we were together."

"Did Monty visit you last night?" I asked.

She nodded slowly with a little smile. She looked younger suddenly.

"How did you meet?" I asked sheepishly, thinking of Aggie's rule for no questions. But she didn't seem her normal inscrutable self that day.

"My father adopted Monty when he was five and brought him home one day."

"Oh… so he was your brother." My eyebrows met.

"Not by blood." Aggie turned to look at me.

"Of course, I mean. I didn't…" I stammered.

"My mother didn't want him at first. And my brother Clarke hated him. They would fight." She chuckled. "Of course, Clarke would end up on the ground. Monty was fierce. Well-built and strong. Even as a boy. He became a builder. Even though his money…"

"His money?"

"My father, who adored Monty, left him the lion's share of his assets. As a result, Monty became fabulously rich."

"What happened to your brother?"

"Clarke died young. From alcohol abuse. He never recovered after his wife died."

"That's sad."

"Mm… I suppose. But Clarke was horrible to Monty. As a young boy, he would lock him up in cupboards and put spiders in his bed. But I protected Monty. We were thick. By the time we were teenagers, we'd escape to Central Park. It became our wonderland. There's even a tree there with our names carved in it. Aggie and Monty forever." She chuckled. "Childish. But sweet. A love heart, you know." She looked up, and her blue eyes seemed larger, almost youthful.

"So did you become sweethearts young?"

"Oh yes. I gave every part of myself to Monty."

I didn't have the courage to ask how young.

As though reading my thoughts, Aggie said, "In my days, a woman was mature at thirteen. At least, I was. I had a very shapely body, and my desires were well and truly developed by then."

I flinched at the thought of sex at thirteen and wondered if it had been illegal in Aggie's days.

"Our passion was too powerful. It had a force of its own. Almost in a supernatural way. We were meant to be together. Then all that changed." She sighed. "I went to visit the Johnsons at the Hamptons. It was summer. Monty refused to go. He hated Ashley, who was close to Clarke." Her eyes had that remote looking-back-in-time glaze, as though she was watching it taking place. "Ashley was tall, blond, blue-eyed and super-confident. He was that charmer who'd enter a room and sweep a girl off her feet by blending a little cheeky comment with a compliment. And they were recklessly wealthy."

"The Johnson family?"

"Yes. Parties, and so much revelry. I was eighteen, and well, I succumbed to his advances. I remained there for the whole summer, and by the end of it, we were married."

"And Monty?"

"I broke his heart." She held her arms and rocked. A tear touched her cheek.

Seeing that Aggie's glass was empty, I rose. "Can I get you another?"

Clearly distracted, Aggie nodded.

I grabbed a tissue from my bag. "Here."

Aggie took it and blew her nose.

After I returned and placed her drink by her side, I asked, "Did you see Monty after that?"

"It took two years to see him again. He went away to Chicago. I'd moved in here with Ashley. At first, it was a happy marriage, even though that spark soon died between us. But then Ashley started to drink heavily, and we grew apart. But the worst was yet to come. That happened when Monty returned with a wife. God, how I hated her." Her edgy rasp prickled the hairs on my arms. "Penelope. Penelope Black."

"Oh… was that Monty's surname?"

"Yes. It's my maiden name. Montgomery Black. It suited him. Tall, strong, dark, and handsome. Women melted around him. He didn't see it though. He was too intense and internal for that. I don't know what he saw in Penny. She talked endlessly about nothing with that high-pitched vaporous voice of hers that used to grate on me. I could barely stay in the same room with her. Corrosive jealousy ate at me. I know I had no right to be. And Monty too..." She took a deep breath and grabbed a cigarette.

After a long pause, I asked, "You were saying about Monty?"

"We were equally jealous. You see, Monty was a part of me and I a part of him. We should have been together. The family wouldn't allow it. Society at the time would have ostracized us. Monty didn't care. But I did. That was my vital flaw—giving a shit about what the Joneses thought."

"Did you continue to see Monty after he married?"

Aggie peered over the balcony. "Oh look, there's Edith."

Frustratingly, I'd lost her. I was desperate to know more.

"Why don't you read a little for me," said Aggie. Her eyes were heavy, and I sensed she'd doze, as she always did whenever I read to her.

"But I always put you to sleep."

"That's why I like it. You have a lovely, soothing voice and I have nice dreams and Monty…"

"Monty?"

She fluttered her hand. "Just read."

CHAPTER TEN

BRONSON

"Here," he said, handing me the USB stick. "They should all be there."

I studied the unshaven investigator for a moment. "That was quicker than I expected."

"I've got my sources. And your guy gets around. As it was, he got the shots from a restroom in a bar frequented by lawyers. It was a Friday night, an after-work shindig." He sat back in his chair. "You know how some lawyers like to powder their noses."

Nodding slowly, I pulled out my wallet.

"Just give me another five hundred. That should do it. It was pretty easy. Only took one outing."

Having expected to pay at least double, I was pleased with that.

When I got home, I jumped into the shower. It had been a long day, and my hands ached. Now that I'd been working ten-hour days, six days a week, my bank balance had bounced back to life, despite my body feeling it.

The hot shower worked miracles in soothing my overworked muscles, and after grabbing a beer from the fridge, I settled in front of my laptop, where I brought up the images the P.I. had taken. There before me, nice and clear, was my scumbag brother bent over, doing a line. As I studied the image, I did wonder what good it would do, considering that Justin didn't hide his habit. But the courts didn't know.

And if it took me a lifetime, I was determined to clear my name.

I kept scrolling down to look at all the photos. One made me pause. I enlarged the image and spotted a familiar face at the bar by his side. It wasn't a surprise—if anything, rather predictable—but it still hit me hard. The blonde in the photo, rubbing shoulders with Justin, was Candy. I looked for Uncle James, but only noticed those two, looking at each other in that unmistakable way, for I could tell they weren't just talking about the price of bananas, more the size, I imagined.

My uncle was a good guy. He'd always supported me over the years. He resembled my late dad, which wasn't unusual, given that they were brothers. Both good, salt-of-the-earth men. It pissed me off that Candy was cheating on him, even though it didn't come as a shock.

I thought about Ava again, which had become a favorite pastime of mine since I'd seen her at my mom's. My skin crawled as I thought about that bewildered reaction on her face following Justin's outburst about me being me a jailbird. A beautiful, refined girl like Ava would never look at me the same way again, let alone allow me to seduce her.

One thing was for sure, my need to have her had grown. The trouble was, I couldn't work out if that was still about revenge or whether my desire for her was something deeper and therefore harder to define.

Whichever it was, I had to see her again.

I asked the cab to drop me off at the end of the avenue. In need of some air, I soaked in the damp earthiness of the established gardens, which was one of the pleasures of being in the suburbs. I had a thing for old architecture, with a preference for gables rather than the flat asymmetrical shapes of modern design—which was often described as bold and intelligent by that well-spoken English dude on cable.

Marcus had called to invite me to his engagement party, which came as a surprise. Knowing how thick he was with Justin, I assumed that I'd been banned from future family occasions following that confrontation at my mom's fiftieth.

Although I was still in touch with my mom, a month had passed since that spat with Justin. I did wonder if Ava was still in the picture. She struck me as too sensitive and intelligent to stay with that shallow, abusive asshole, especially after what had happened.

I stopped before the lantern-lit driveway to my uncle's piece of millionaire fantasy. Enjoying the smell of freshly mown grass, I fed my lungs something wholesome after the noxious fumes of city living.

While locked up in prison, I'd had plenty of spare time to dream, culminating in a plan. I was determined to create a wealthy, successful future. Not because I wanted to ponce around and live in a house that looked like it had been flown in from Disneyland but because I was determined to have a life that was creative and clean—well, maybe a little dirty in the bedroom—and breed children that I could love and cherish and encourage to make the world a better place.

First, however, I needed to rub my brother's face in shit and, even more importantly, find out why my biological mother had dumped me outside that hospital twenty-five years ago. Something that had shadowed my life, and I couldn't hold my head up high while weighed down by that question.

The door was open, so I strode in.

Laughter and people's voices filled the air as I stood in the white marble entrance that was so bright I needed sunglasses.

"Whatever happened to moody lighting?" I asked myself.

I remained there for a moment, psyching myself into facing a crowd of cheery faces. Turning around, I decided to go back out and have a cigarette first, but my mother caught sight of me.

"Bronson, darling." She came toward me with a big smile and opened her arms.

I kissed her cheek. "Hey, Mom. Sorry, I haven't been around much lately."

"I understand. You sound busy. I hope you're not overworking." She stepped away to look at me. "You're looking handsome in that tux."

I tugged on my shirt cuff. "I rented it. It's a bit tight, I think."

"Nonsense. It fits you like a glove. You're looking healthy. You've got more color on your face."

"I've been working outside in the sun."

Taking my hand, she said, "I'm proud of you."

That touched me in a spot buried so deep I had a hard time navigating it. Instead, I reverted to my uniform half grin.

"Come inside, sweetheart. Let's get you a beer. The food's delicious."

As I entered the large ballroom, people stopped and stared. One thing I'd learned in my short life was that someone different or who'd fallen on difficult times seemed to cut a figure of fascination amongst those with ordinary lives.

Ignoring the attention, I looked around the room and settled on an aura of pink in the corner. From that moment, as though I'd been drugged, I fell into a pleasant haze of arousal.

Dressed in a pink gown that revealed a curvy, mouthwatering figure, Ava looked like she'd stepped out of one of those sixties James Bond movies. She epitomized sheer class— sexy and feminine without having it all on show.

Wearing that same fear and bewilderment as they had when we'd last parted, her eyes met mine. I wasn't ready to make my desire for her obvious, so I looked away.

A battle raged between my dick, my heart, and my head as a cold, sinking feeling crept in. Ava was an intrinsic part of my plan. I needed to remain focused. Revenge required a strategic plan adhered to step by step.

I snuck another glance. It was impossible not to. The pink folds of fabric from her beautiful dress cascaded to the floor, clinging lightly over her shapely ass. Just to add to her beauty, Ava had tied a ribbon around her swanlike neck accentuating its slenderness.

I channeled the asshole within, a character I'd perfected after a year of soaking in bitter fury. No matter how beautiful Ava was, the game was seduction. To rub it right in Justin's face. Not to have and to hold.

As Justin hovered around Ava, her rigid spine and tight expression told me they were no longer an item. Now that warmed my veins. I could read Justin like a book, not because I'd grown up with him but because when God handed out subtlety, Justin had been out pissing on a freshly painted wall in the middle of the day.

Oh, how sweet it was watching the asshole sweating it out.

Still, I couldn't blame him. If that were me, I would have bashed down a fortress that even challenged superheroes on steroids in order to win Ava back.

CHAPTER ELEVEN

AVA

I excused myself and headed for the restroom, which seemed aptly titled given that I needed a rest from all the attention.

Justin had been skulking around me all night with those puppy-dog eyes and exaggerated down-turned lips, pathetically trying to win me over. I should have been used to his fawning, considering that we'd already broken up once before but a week after that, I had capitulated and accepted a date with him. My mom's relentless begging to give Justin another chance had something to do with that decision.

The following day, after he'd tried to take me by force at Marcus's party, Justin had called and promised to stay off cocaine and abstain from heavy drinking. He said he'd do anything to make it up with me. A few days after that, he turned up with flowers, his handsome face filled with remorse, which then morphed into a big smile. I ended up accepting a dinner date with him, after which I went home with him.

The same thing happened. No fire. No foreplay. Just six or seven pumps in and out and it was over. He ended on his back, panting, and within a few minutes, he snored. As I stared up at the ceiling, I thought about Aggie's gut-churning regret for having married the wrong man.

A few days later, we were back to being that same couple. Justin's eyes would glaze over whenever I talked about my day. We'd watch dull reruns or any kind of sport known to mankind—even a quoit tournament of all things.

Nothing had changed, so I ended it.

But I could hardly skip my best friend's engagement party— precipitous as it was, considering Cassie had been with Marcus only four months—so there I was.

Rather stupidly, I'd told my mom about Cassie's engagement. Her finger shot into the air like a missile. "See, she has the good sense to marry a wealthy man."

And once again, she reminded me that Justin was just as rich and promised a comfortable future…yada…yada.

"A boring future with no passion," I'd muttered to myself. Talking to a parent about sex had never sat well. I wished I could have told my mom that as a twenty-four-year-old, I owed it to myself to experience sheet-gripping, heart-pumping lovemaking at least a few times before settling for its bland opposite.

Standing before the mirror, I wiped off a lipstick stain on my cheek, and for the umpteenth time, I stroked the silky chiffon cascading from my hips, which floated into a full circle when I twirled.

After I'd mentioned that I had an engagement party to go to and that I needed to buy a dress, Aggie had tapped my arm and asked me to wait. Ten minutes later, she'd descended the stairs slowly, carrying an exquisite pink Dior gown that would have taken my annual salary to buy.

"Here. This should fit," she said, holding it before me.

"Are you kidding me? But this is too precious," I protested— meekly since I wanted that dress.

She waved her hand dismissively. "Ah… I've got tons of them. And it looks like a perfect fit. All I ask is one thing."

Stroking the fabric as one would a pet, I looked up at her.

"That you wear your hair down. It will look nice that way. You have such a lovely long neck. Wear a little ribbon around it. You know, as they did in the Victorian Era. That always drives men wild."

My brow squeezed in tight. "I don't know if I want to drive men wild, Aggie."

"Whether you want to or not, you just will," she said with a confident nod.

As I hugged the layers of silk that emanated an intoxicating floral perfume, a strange feeling wafted over that Aggie wished to relive her past through me.

Removing a tissue from my bag, I wiped my armpits before applying some fragrance. My night had been hijacked by tension, which had little to do with Justin circling around me.

It had started the moment Bronson entered. Even from a distance, he robbed me of air. The way he filled that tux as if it was stitched onto his strong body made me sigh. With that undressing gaze boring straight into me, I had to prop myself against a wall. His dark hair sat up in a perfect tangle, I couldn't ignore those full lips that opened slightly as if about to ravish something.

But he was a criminal.

He'd been to prison.

He was wrong, wrong, wrong.

In every way.

But how could a man look like that and not make a woman dissolve into a puddle of desire?

Every time his eyes fell into mine, I felt so exposed. I even started to believe that actual steam rose out of my skin.

I did wonder if Bronson looked at every woman like that, as though he were fucking them with his eyes. I hadn't noticed his attention shift from me. And when he did look away, he focused down at his feet.

Even though I kept reminding myself he was potentially dangerous, my hormones raged on nevertheless, inflaming me with desire.

I flicked a strand of hair back over my shoulder and made my way back to the party. On the way, I caught Cassie coming toward me. She looked beautiful in a blue gown that hugged her lissome tall frame like magic.

"You look like you've stepped out of a fairy tale in that pink dress," she said, taking me by the arm.

I swished the silk skirt. "I feel like I'm in *Swan Lake*. If I have enough champagne, I may even jeté across the room." I laughed.

"I'd join you, but this little frock's a bit tight," she said with a giggle. "Hey, have you seen Mr. Dark and Dangerous in that tux?"

"Mm… yeah, he's pretty hard to miss." I looked around, but I couldn't see him.

"He's got Candy going all gaga, that's for sure. Here he comes. Or I should say, swaggers. Ah… he's heading over to us."

"Don't make it obvious, Cas. I'm going to get a drink."

She chuckled. "I knew it. He's got you all hot and bothered. And he keeps looking at you again, like at Marcus's party."

I rolled my eyes in response, which was a ruse because I liked knowing that.

After filling my glass with bubbly from the champagne fountain, I headed out for a little air. On my way out, a lovely little cupcake caught my eye, so I grabbed one.

It was a balmy, perfect night. There was no wind. Warm air caressed my flesh as I rested on a white iron bench.

Biting into the fluffy, sugary treat, I sighed as it melted in my mouth.

"That good?" A husky voice resonated nearby.

I turned and saw Bronson with an unlit cigarette hanging from his lips. My eyes landed on them, lingering for what seemed an inappropriate length of time.

"Um…" While I searched for a response, a little bit of saliva mixed with cake escaped my lips and slid down my chin, making me want to crawl under a hole and die.

While wiping it off with a napkin, I noticed Bronson's attention on my lips while I licked them clean. I said, "The cakes are delicious." I spoke in a hurried tone, which emulated my racing heart. "I have no control when it comes to sweet things."

His lips twitched into a half smile and then straightened quickly. Something told me Bronson didn't smile much.

"Is that the only thing you have no control over?" he asked. Lighting his cigarette, he moved away so that the smoke wouldn't annoy me.

"I suppose it is. Sugar's always been a weakness of mine. I'm pretty boring in many ways. I don't have any bad habits other than that."

He studied me as he sucked on his cigarette. Even the act of smoking seemed carnal on those lips.

"It depends on how one defines bad." His eyes remained on my face.

"All the unhealthy things, I suppose. But then, Aggie, that's the woman…"

"You work for," he interjected.

"Oh, you remember?"

"I remember everything."

"That's useful if one's studying for exams, I suppose," I said, setting my plate down on a ledge by my side.

I waited for a response, but he remained quietly absorbed in my face. His eyes scorched my flesh again. "I was saying that Aggie wears her bad habits like a badge of honor. But then, she is 82. I suppose she can get away with her at-times-inappropriate take on life."

His black, perfectly arched eyebrows contracted slightly. "Inappropriate?"

"Well, let's put it this way. She has a salacious tongue and a dark wit about her."

"Salacious tongue?" He tilted his head with a glimmer of a smile.

"That means… dirty-mouthed…"

"I know what it means," he said, standing closer and making me gulp down my champagne. "I am educated."

"I'm sure you are."

He raked his fingers through his hair, making it sit perfectly as if placed there with product. His unshifting gaze unnerved me. I had to look away even though I wanted to keep staring.

"So, Aggie has a dirty tongue, then," he continued with a hint of a smile.

Noticing his emphasis on the word "tongue" I felt I had to clarify my comment. "I meant when she speaks."

"I'm playing with you, Ava."

"Oh… you've remembered my name," I said, sounding more ridiculous by the minute.

His playful grin faded. "I remember everything about you."

As he stepped closer, Bronson ran his tongue over his full lips.

I parted my mouth and lowered my eyes.

When a voice from behind said, "There you are," I jumped.

I turned, and Justin stood before me. Bronson looked away. The tension between them was as palpable as always.

My heart still raced, though. My body wanted that kiss badly, despite my head telling me I'd dodged a bullet.

"Why are you talking to him?" Justin asked.

"I can talk to whoever I like," I answered.

"He's no good," he whispered.

I looked over his shoulder and noticed Bronson step behind him.

"You heard her. Ava's a grown-up. Now fuck off," said Bronson.

Justin sniggered at him and then looked at me. "Can I have a quiet word?"

I shook my head. "No, Justin, you can't."

Boy, did I want to do a retake of what might have happened before we were rudely interrupted. One little taste of those full, sexy lips would have sufficed—dangerous or not.

CHAPTER TWELVE

BRONSON

My mom mentioned that it was off between them, which is why I'd decided to pounce. And we'd come so close. The seduction wasn't going to be as easy as I would have liked, which shouldn't have surprised me. Ava was a classy girl. An intelligent, sensitive woman who, I was certain, didn't fuck around.

I liked that about her. I liked a lot, probably too many things about her.

But I needed to stick to my plan. That asshole brother, who had an ego the size of Niagara Falls had to suffer. Not that taking Ava from him could ever compare to being locked up for one year, even if my body disagreed because the pleasure of spending a whole night caressing Ava's curves while being deep inside her would come pretty fucking close.

I watched Ava sway off, her gown swishing side to side. While drawing back her lingering scent, I cursed Justin for interrupting us.

"Bronson."

I turned and saw my uncle. "Hey, James."

"How's the designing going?"

"Yeah. Good. I've been up pretty late getting some sketches down. I showed Harry. He likes them, but he's up to his neck in an apartment contract, which is where I'm working at the moment."

"You're a hard worker, Bronson. I like that about you. You always were. And talented."

I smiled tightly. I'd never been good at receiving compliments, despite loving them. But they were so rare that I never knew how to respond.

"Why don't we get together for dinner soon. You can show me what you've got. I'm itching for a project," he said.

"I'd like that." I studied him for a moment. "I would have thought you'd have plenty to do. This is a big property."

"All I do is write endless checks for Candy and her daily shopping sprees. Her shoes take up an entire room." He shook his head.

That image of Candy and Justin looking lovey-dovey pricked my conscience. I knew I had to tell him somehow. But I didn't wish to cause a stir at his son's engagement party. My uncle had always been respectful and supportive. After I'd been released from prison, both he and my mother had supported me emotionally, which meant the world to me.

I looked at James for a moment. "You know I'm innocent. I've never been into coke. I'm certain Justin put that coke in my backpack."

He took a while to respond. "Your mother mentioned that to me. It puts us in a precarious position. Everyone's aware of Justin's habit, but Bronson, without proof..." He opened out his hands.

"I know that. I just want you to know that I'm no drug addict or dealer or anything like that. I might have had one fight too many, and I don't smile that often, but I'm not some waste-of-space drug addict."

He touched my arm. "We never believed you were, Bronson."

The grip in my muscles unwound. "That means everything."

An off-center smile settled on his face. He touched my arm. "Next week, then. We'll set up a meeting and get this project happening."

I nodded. "My sketches should be ready by then."

As I followed James back into the party, I went to look for Ava. Taking a deep breath, I psyched myself into asking her out on a date.

Standing in the corner while chatting with Marcus's fiancée, Ava looked up, and her eyes settled on my face. At first, there was that uncertain expression that involved her eyebrows indenting slightly and the biting of her bottom lip— her usual response to my attention. Normally, I would have looked away to give her some space, but this time I held on and was rewarded with a sweet smile.

Ava's friend turned to see who'd taken her attention.

Although it wasn't my style to break in on anybody's conversation, I needed this to happen, then and there, because despite having only arrived a short while earlier, I didn't want to hang around for much longer, or else my knuckles would end up sinking into Justin's smug face. After all, I had only really come to the party to see Ava and to congratulate Marcus.

On my approach, Ava stopped giggling and stared wide-eyed at me, as if I were a ghost. Despite that discouraging reception, I continued anyway.

I preferred outside alone under the moonlight, and definitely not at a party filled with people who stopped talking every time I entered the room. Frozen in silence, the guests seemed to watch my every move as if I were some common criminal.

Ava touched Cassie's arm, who, much to my relief, walked away.

"I need to ask you something," I said, looking around me.

Justin had just entered the room, and although I enjoyed watching him suffer as I twisted a knife into his jealous gut, the last thing I wanted was a shouting match.

"Not here, though. Do you mind if we step outside for a moment?"

I felt her tension while she held my stare. "I'll meet you there in a minute."

It shouldn't have been that difficult. I'd never found it hard to attract a girl before. Normally I let them pounce on me. But this was different.

Ava was different.

Staring up at the starlit sky, I sensed Ava's presence and turned.

"Hey." She stood before me.

I fell into those big blue eyes and lost myself again. Ava was so deep, I could imagine drowning in her. A voice from within told me to stop this game. After all, I could get at Justin in other ways. But as I soaked in her beauty, I remained rooted on the spot.

Her rosy-cheeked face seemed to glow under the moonlight.

"You look very beautiful," I said.

"Is that why you wanted to see me, to tell me that?"

I nodded. "Yeah… pretty much. And to also ask…" I combed back my hair. "Um… would you… I mean, be interested in…" My stammering did me no favors. I sounded like a fool.

"Interested in what?" She tilted her head.

"Going out to dinner with me."

Her mouth had just opened to answer when my fucking brother came stumbling out.

"Here comes fucking trouble again," I uttered under my breath.

With a cigar in his mouth, Justin blew the smoke in our direction.

Waving it away, Ava said, "Justin, can you smoke that somewhere else?"

I decided to kick the boot in further by taking Ava's hand and staring into her eyes.

"She's too good for you," Justin snapped.

I turned to face him. "She's too good for you. You're nothing but a drug addict."

He came and stood close, pointing at me. "And you're nothing but a dirty criminal." He looked at Ava. "You know he's a drug dealer, don't you?"

Ava's face crumpled in dismay. "I can't do this."

My shoulders slumped in frustration as I watched her run back inside.

I grabbed Justin by the neck. "Listen, you fucking prick, you know those drugs weren't mine, because they were yours." I pointed my finger inches from his face. "I'll get you."

I kicked him in the shin, leaving him to cry out in pain.

Smoothing down my jacket, I brushed back my hair and went back inside.

Ava was nowhere to be seen.

Assuming she'd gone to the powder room, I headed in that direction and found her leaning against a wall.

Enough was enough. No more pussyfooting around.

Sensing my presence, she turned, and I spotted tears in her eyes. I brushed her cheek, and a deep need to hold her swept through me. I took her into my arms, and Ava melted into my body.

The fit was perfect, as if she was meant to be there.

Her body's warmth fused with mine while I took a deep whiff of her fresh, fragrant hair. I kissed her cheek and then my lips landed on hers. They trembled at first as I caressed them with mine, slowly and tenderly, savoring every little moment, because that was the sweetest tasting kiss I'd ever experienced.

As I drifted off into a sensual world of voluptuous softness, something darker and needier took over. I pressed against her curvy body, while my hands landed on her tiny waist and drew her in so close, I could feel her heart beating.

Impatient and hungry, my tongue entered deeply, possessing her silky tongue in a delicious tangle.

While still locked in her arms, I managed to open a door and, not caring whose bedroom it was, waltzed Ava into the darkened space.

We fell onto the bed, and before I knew what was happening, my hands were sliding up her smooth thighs.

Frightened it would end any minute, I was driven by a force so intense and desperate that I knew I had to taste her. To smell her.

Blood raged to my groin at the thought of entering her. My cock pushed against my pants. There was nowhere to hide. I was so turned on that I could no longer think about anything else.

We remained in a crush as my mouth devoured her swollen, moist lips. I cupped her head in my hand, tipping it back so that my tongue could plunge in deep.

A loud breath deflated my chest as I felt the fullness of her breasts.

Traveling up her thigh, my hand landed on her silky panties. They were drenched, which sent my pulsating cock into a frenzy.

Salivating at the thought of tasting her, I had to control the urge to rip her panties off and to tear every shred of fabric from her so that I could savor every inch of her flesh. But the fear of being discovered excited me, making me desperate to at least take away something of hers.

Unlike my normal approach to sex, which was to fuck hard and fast, I wanted to take her slowly.

Ava whimpered as my fingers landed on the flooding heat of her pussy. As I entered between her folds, my finger needed to know what it would feel like to be inside her. My chest collapsed with impatience as the tightly muscled walls crushed my finger. She was so small and tight. My cock ached.

I sucked on my drenched finger and buried my head between her legs.

She opened wide.

Ava wanted this.

Good.

Because I was famished. Famished for her sensual beauty, a sort I'd never experienced before.

All that mattered suddenly was being inside of her.

When my tongue settled on her clit, she winced.

Ava tried to move away, but I clasped onto her curvy firm butt and kept her still.

"I haven't…" She murmured.

"You're like a flower," I whispered, and she instantly relaxed.

I placed my tongue on her inflamed and sticky bud. Ava's gentle moan inspired me to continue. I was determined to have her trembling in my hands before long.

I licked from back to front slowly, rotating my tongue around her clit, fluttering and sucking her erect, responsive bud gently. Determined to make her come, I ate away at her as if she was a delicious piece of candy. Her addictive flavor was like none I'd ever tasted.

I entered her deeply with my tongue and released a flood from her. Ava cried out as she shuddered through a long release. She ejaculated musky cream onto my tongue and I sucked it back like one thirsting after days in a desert.

"I need to be inside of you," I said.

Panting, Ava fell into my arms.

My lips crushed her mouth.

CHAPTER THIRTEEN

AVA

His moist lips tasted of me. Instead of feeling repulsion, I burned with a need so deep, especially with that hard cock pushing against my thigh, that if he didn't enter me, I would scream.

I wanted every bit of him. Badly.

Danger or not. Criminal or not. I didn't care.

I just wanted him to take me. Do something to me that was wrong, but yet profoundly fulfilling.

Having never had a tongue on my clit before, I'd recoiled at the thought of it, even after Cassie had spoken glowingly about it. But as soon as his tongue started stroking my bud, I couldn't have opened wide enough. I even recalled gripping his head as I exploded through an orgasm. That was how it felt, so much more intense than I could have ever imagined.

His earthy scent, a blend of maleness and bath soap, did things to me that no drug or drink could ever achieve. I thought I would lose my mind as I drew from his neck a brew of virility that only added to the burn going on in my core.

The room was dark. Driven by lust, I surrendered into his strong arms.

He undid his zipper and lowered his pants. A huge bulge pushed impatiently against his briefs.

My hands traveled under his shirt and indulged in the hard ripple of stomach muscles. I traced the curves up to his equally firm pectorals that had a smattering of hair between the rigid, smooth mounds of muscle.

He lowered his briefs, and my breath hitched. Justin was tiny in comparison. I opened my legs wide as Bronson held his cock, the thickness of which resembled my wrist. It was so long I had no idea how it would fit, but my mouth watered at the thought of it anyhow.

Unable to stay out of each other's arms for long, we held each other again, his mouth on mine.

Bronson whispered, "I haven't got a condom."

Sharing his frustration, I said, "I'm on the pill."

"You would trust me?" he asked.

His surprised tone reminded me how irresponsible I was about to be. But rationality no longer mattered. Driven by that pulsating burn between my legs, I allowed lust to take possession of me.

Our arms unlocked, and he looked at me with a serious flicker in his eyes. "I haven't been with a woman for a long time, and my last blood test was clean. But you don't know that."

As he stood up, the lights came on.

It was an image that would remain etched in my memory forever.

Bronson's hair was messy in the sexiest way possible. His shirt was half undone, and that large erect cock rested in his hand.

Justin's eyes went from me to Bronson, and when they landed on his cock, they widened in shock. He went pale.

Knowing how men were about their penises, I didn't doubt that envy would eat away at Justin, given his insecurity when it came to his meager member. The bewilderment on Justin's face almost made me laugh. I didn't, because I quickly scrambled to cover my thighs and cross my arms, unable to recall how Bronson had managed to undress me.

"What the fuck?" yelled Justin.

Bronson was the coolest of all three of us. A smirk filled his beautiful face, suggesting that he actually enjoyed infuriating Justin. He faced his brother, not even attempting to cover himself up as if to say, "Now who's the real man here?"

My jaw opened to speak, but I couldn't because I was still dazed and flushed from a cocktail of hormones after an orgasm to beat all orgasms.

"Get out, Justin," I said.

He headed for the door and, just before exiting, blurted, "This isn't the last of it."

Bronson regarded me with a shrug. "Did you ever see that scene in *The Holy Grail*? Where that torso of a sliced-up knight bounced up and down on the ground screaming at his attacker to come back and fight?"

The cheeky smirk on Bronson's face made me giggle. "Yes. I have." I put on a silly English accent. "I'm not dead yet."

"That's the one."

"And your point?" I asked.

"Justin's a sucker for punishment, that's all. He's sunk. Or at least, I hope he is." He tilted his head.

"We're no longer together if that's what you're asking." I rose. "I wouldn't have let you touch me otherwise." Lifting the zipper to my dress, I smoothed my mane, which was a tangled mess.

Bronson did up his trousers and tucked his shirt in. He combed down his hair with his hands.

He stood before me. His gaze burned into me again.

Taking me into his arms, Bronson kissed me deeply and tenderly. I melted again. He robbed me of my senses as his hand snuck up to my butt and squeezed it.

After we separated, Bronson smoothed out my dress.

We walked to the door. As he reached for the doorknob, Bronson stopped. "Will you go out with me? Dinner or a movie, or both?"

He looked like a boy almost. A different Bronson. Not as intense, but sweet and hesitant.

My senses had finally returned, reminding me that Bronson was a criminal. I chewed into a nail.

His brow creased. "Look, Ava. I'm not sure what you think of me. But one thing's for certain, I'm not into drugs. Justin planted those drugs on me. If you won't go out with me, then let me at least prove I'm innocent."

"I didn't say that… I wouldn't…" I stammered. "It's just that this tense relationship you have with Justin stresses me out."

Bronson stared at me for what seemed a lifetime. He exhaled a deep breath. "I only came here tonight to see you."

"But you're family. Marcus is your cousin," I said, challenging that unexpected confession.

He continued to gaze deeply into my eyes as if trying to read every thought my busy brain produced.

"I came to see you," he repeated, pulling out his phone. "Can I have your number? I promise to call at a respectable hour." His lips twitched into a smile, which softened his face and made him look sweet, almost vulnerable.

My hearted melted. I was putty around him.

I took his phone and tapped in my number.

As Bronson took it from me, our hands touched, and he tranced me out again.

If only he wasn't so damn hot, I thought. "You know you'd make a great hypnotist," I said.

"I'll bear that in mind. Maybe in my next life. This one's already taken."

I giggled. "Now you've got me intrigued. I look forward to hearing all about it."

"That's a yes then?" he asked, cocking his head.

I nodded slowly.

He tapped something on his phone, and mine pinged.

"I wonder who that's from." I grinned.

A knock came at the door. Seeing Candy standing there snapped me out of my mesmerized state. "Now, what have you two been up to?" Her high-pitched voice made me wince. A stunned look was the best I could offer, which, I imagined, confirmed her suspicions. Reverting to being Mr. Cool and Inscrutable, Bronson left the room without uttering a word.

After mumbling something, I left her and headed for the powder room, where I slumped onto the fluffy chair and let my racing mind spill its contents in the comfort of privacy.

My little moment of reflection, however, was interrupted when the door swung open. Therefore, I sighed with relief upon discovering that it was Cassie.

"Hey, there you are," she said with a puzzled frown. "Shit, Ava, you've got mascara down your cheek, and your hair's a mess. Have you been getting hot and steamy?" Her wicked smile made me chuckle.

Making my way to the mirror, I gasped at the wreckage before me. Bronson had forgotten to mention that I looked like I'd been swept away in a tornado.

"Shit. I look terrible." I took my brush from my bag and sat down again. My thick, long hair demanded patience.

"You've been with Bronson," Cassie said at last. "That's why Justin was acting like such a dick."

An image of my ex's deranged expression flashed before me. "Oh fuck, what have I done?" I buried my head in my hands.

"You did what any self-respecting, hot-blooded woman would have done." She giggled. Her infectious lightness worked wonders, making me laugh too, despite my giggles largely driven by nerves.

"What was it like? Did you go all the way?"

"By all the way, you mean did he fuck me?" I asked, continuing to rip into my hair. It was hard to remain patient and calm when talking about Bronson.

"Tell me, is he as sexy underneath those clothes as he is dressed?"

A slow, cheeky smile formed on my lips as I relived Justin's shock when he'd seen how well-endowed Bronson was. "Better, I think."

"It was yummy, then?"

"We didn't get that far. No condom."

"Oh… damn. So, you ended up hot and bothered."

"Not me so much." A slow smile grew.

"Did he go down on you?"

I nodded slowly.

"Nice."

"Better than nice," I said.

She let out a little scream and jumped up and down. "At my engagement party. How sexy is that? I love it!"

"It's so damn complicated, though," I argued. "Bronson insists that Justin planted drugs on him that sent him to prison. Do you think that's true?"

"Justin uses cocaine, Ava. Does Bronson?"

"No. Or at least, I don't think so."

"But then, Bronson's got that bad-boy vibe, whereas Justin's more the boy-next-door type," said Cassie.

"Justin's not, though." I sighed deeply. "Shit. Shit. Shit."

"Hey, babe, don't worry. Just hang out with Bronson for a while. Have some seriously hot, dirty sex, and then find a nice boy and marry him."

I laughed at her matter-of-fact commentary.

"Come on, let's get drunk," she said.

"I'll be there in a minute," I said, recalling the message on my phone.

After Cassie left, I pulled out my cell and read Bronson's text. "You tasted exquisite. I look forward to the main course."

As a sharp, hot ache pulsated deep in my core, I closed my eyes, and a large smile claimed my face.

CHAPTER FOURTEEN

BRONSON

One useful habit I had picked up in prison was to keep a journal. If anything, it helped me get my head together. Flicking through pages that contained drawings and scribblings, I landed on my "mission" page.

It read: 1. Find dirt on Justin. 2. Seduce his girlfriend. 3. Fuck her. 4. Receive an exoneration from my sentence. 5. Sue the pants off Justin. 6. Set up my own building firm. 7. Find my real parents.

So far, I'd only managed to fulfill points 1 and 2.

And that was where my scheme had hit a slight snag.

Aside from the satisfaction of seeing Justin fume after catching me with my dick out, my spirit sat somewhere between deflation and elation. In other words, I was conflicted.

I'd fucked girls that Justin had dated before, but Ava was something else.

She was in a league of her own.

I could understand why Justin was doing everything to win her back. He definitely didn't deserve her, though. She was way too good for him.

In the spate of twenty-four hours, Ava had become more than a prize. She'd become something almost unattainable, only because I, too, didn't deserve her. At least, that was what my jaded spirit told me.

My mission had become infected by emotion, in that I couldn't get Ava out of my head or body.

My fingers tingled at the thought of those curves.

I still salivated at how she'd tasted, and I'd been walking around with a hard-on all week just thinking of her.

No woman had ever possessed me that way before.

It wasn't just her considerable physical beauty but everything about her that I craved.

Each time I looked at her, I lost myself in her beauty. My eyes were addicted. And whenever she spoke, I could have kept listening all night. Not only did I like the things that exited that smart mouth but also the caressing tone of her voice.

I decided not to call Ava.

It wasn't from a lack of desire, because I'd begun to tap on her number many times. Then the thought of using Ava for my own twisted ends stopped me from calling her. But over and above everything, it was that Ava thought I was a criminal.

I had to clear my name first.

Ava had to see me for who I really was and not some convicted drug dealer.

I walked into a bar close to my childhood home, where my uncle waited for me, sitting at the bar.

"Hey, James. Sorry I'm late," I said, pulling up a stool.

"Beer?" he asked.

"Yeah. Sure."

Picking up the bottle the barman had set down, I took a thirsty gulp. Wiping my lips, I said, "That feels better. Okay, then, let's get down to business."

"Before that"—he squared his shoulders—"I need to tell you something."

Taking a sip of beer, I looked up at him.

"Something happened after you left the party the other night. I'm still trying to get over it." He gulped down his bourbon. "It's really rocked me. Although it shouldn't have come as a surprise."

"What's that?"

"I found Justin all over Candy."

I stared down at my hands for a moment. "Have you spoken to Candy about it?"

"She insists Justin came on to her."

"That's plausible. It wouldn't be the first time that Justin's forced himself on a woman."

"Are you serious?" My uncle studied me for a moment. "I know that you've got issues with him."

"I'm serious, all right." I pulled a mock smile. "As you already know, I'm convinced Justin stashed the coke in my backpack. I had him followed and obtained some snaps of him powdering his nose while cozying up with Candy. She looked pretty happy."

My uncle stared blankly at me.

"Look, um, I'm sorry. I should've said something."

He patted my arm. "Don't worry about it. I'm the stupid one. I should have known marrying an ex-stripper wouldn't turn out nice."

The question on my lips never made it out, even though I was dying to ask it.

James smiled grimly. "Why did I? I hear you ask."

I nodded slowly.

"I suppose, like most middle-aged men frightened of that downward slope, I needed something to make me feel young. But to be honest" —he sipped his beer solemnly— "It was one big fucking mistake. And now it will cost me for sure."

"You're divorcing her?"

"You bet. I don't know where's she's been. I've even asked her to get a blood test."

"Ah… That's not good. That's one thing a marriage should offer, loyalty and condom-free sex."

He sniffed. "That's right. Anyway, I wanted to share that with you, because I know about your struggles with Justin. And to be honest, I'm pretty fucking pissed off with him."

"That's understandable," I replied.

"He's the dirty one in this game. Candy was always going to slink off with someone younger. That was predictable. But Justin's part in this just makes me sick. I've told your mom that I don't want anything to do with him. Marcus has gone off him, too. And they were pretty thick, as you know."

I nodded sympathetically. At least I had my uncle on my side.

He gulped down his drink and beckoned to the bartender for another. "All right, to business. Show me what you've got."

I took a folder from my backpack and placed it on the bar. "That's a quick drawing of the village. And over the page, you'll see the individual designs. I've created seven prototypes."

James spent a few moments flipping from one page to another. I sat nervously by. I'd never been confident about my sketching skills. My mom was the only one who had seen a few drawings here and there, not just images of houses and designs, but portraits of women and landscapes. If anything, sketching had kept me sane in prison.

He looked up at me, shaking his head. "Bronson, these are incredible drawings. By hand too."

"Yeah, well. I prefer the old-fashioned approach to drafting. Harry, my boss, thinks I should go digital. And I probably will for some of his jobs. Big boxy apartments, that type of thing." I scratched my neck.

"They're brilliantly rendered. I'm taken aback. I didn't realize. I mean Alice mentioned you were creative, but wow. I hope you get back to that degree you started."

"I'm working seven days a week at the moment. I don't really have a lot of time. But with this project, who knows. That's if you're interested."

"I am. I love the village idea. It almost looks like an old English setting."

"That's where I got my ideas from. A German village, actually. I studied it online. Hopefully one day I can visit it."

"You will, I'm sure. Bronson, I get this feeling you're going to amount to something. These are great designs."

"That makes me feel positive. I wasn't sure what you'd think. You're the first person to see them."

"These are truly inspiring. Have you got any idea on where?"

"I have. There are three places just outside the city. Old industrial wastelands that are being offered for a song."

"What about chemical waste?" he asked.

"There are these revitalization grants, where they cover the cleanup costs in return for a project like this one."

"Great. I'm excited. Something for me to do. And it looks like a money spinner."

I raised a brow. "That's the plan, Uncle."

CHAPTER FIFTEEN

AVA

Turning the key tentatively, I unlocked the door. When Aggie placed a key in my hand to her apartment, I was naturally taken aback, considering how private she was. I still hadn't made it up those stairs to the private rooms, though. Not for lack of curiosity. Each time I asked about the rooms above, she either changed the subject or responded vaguely.

Predictably, I found her sitting on the balcony. I coughed on my approach to avoid startling her. Aggie turned and nodded. Her hair was in a meticulous bun, as always, and she wore a floral shirt over her regular pink bell-bottoms.

She studied me closely. And summoning up weak acting skills, I painted on a bright smile, which was a battle, given that my emotions were anything but sunny.

"What's happened to that man who made your cheeks all rosy?"

Was I that transparent? I wondered.

Aggie hadn't heard of my encounter with Bronson at Cassie's engagement party, although it was not for lack of trying. She'd even intuited I'd gone somewhere forbidden from the vibe I apparently gave out.

I couldn't bring myself to tell her, though. How could one tell an old woman, albeit a sexually liberated one, that a virtual stranger nearly made me swallow my tongue from ecstasy after devouring me within an inch of sanity?

A week had passed since that steamy encounter. And the fact that I hadn't heard from Bronson had made for a restless and difficult time.

"Um… there's no man, Aggie."

"Bullshit. There's always a man." Mischief leapt from her eyes. Her voice softened. "You're not yourself, Ava. And you would have looked so beautiful in that dress. I knew you'd snare him."

"Snare who, Aggie?"

"I'll ask the questions, Ava. That's why I pay you."

Her snappy tone made me flinch. "A martini?"

She nodded and pointed. "I insist you have one. You need it. I can see that."

I couldn't argue with her on that front. In any case, I'd grown fond of my newly acquired one-martini-a-day habit. Aggie had even tried to ply me with more, but given the tipsy state I left in each day, I wished to avoid stumbling home.

As I thought about drunkenness, I summoned up unpleasant memories of Justin after he'd turned up late at my place the previous night, clutching a bunch of flowers. He'd made such a noisy fuss on the street below, I'd had no other choice but to let him in. With the benefit of hindsight, I should have left him there to blend in with the other raucous misfits doing drug deals. If there was one little street where one could yell their lungs off without causing a stir, it was my street.

From the moment he'd stumbled in, I regretted opening the door. Slurring his words, Justin kept going on about how small his penis was. It was pathetic in many ways, especially after I had to repeatedly insist that I hadn't broken off our relationship due to the size of his penis. There was more to life than a man's penis, I thought. Apart from breeding, of course, in which case size played no part. And the fact that Justin kept at me about it confirmed my views of him being a shallow, self-centered boor.

He fell onto the couch. Then, holding his head, Justin went on and on about how evil Bronson was.

I said, "Look, Justin, I need to sleep. You have to leave now." I pointed to the door.

Downcast he rose and lumbered to the door. He turned and stared at me. "There's no hope for us?"

I shook my head.

"He's no good for you."

"I'll be the judge of that," I said.

As I watched him disappear down the stairs, I shook my head in disbelief over how stupid we both were— me for letting him in and Justin thinking the size of his dick had caused our breakup.

I placed Aggie's martini by her side, after which I sat down and took a sip of the fiery liquid, hoping it would ease the agitation caused by a restless night.

"You haven't slept well. And it's not due to pleasure, either."

"No." I sighed.

"He's kissed you, hasn't he?"

I nodded slowly. My mouth turned down. I had to gulp back a lump. Bronson had gotten so deep under my skin that it seemed as though he'd taken total possession of me.

Aggie scrutinized me for a moment. "I can see he's affected you, dear girl."

I sipped my martini a little faster than usual. "He was supposed to ask me out on a date but hasn't called."

"How long's it been?"

"A week," I replied.

"And tell me, did you both...?" She tapped her fingers together to signify copulation.

I studied her for signs of amusement. Instead, I was met with the type of sympathy a mother might radiate.

"Kind of," I said, shifting in my seat.

"By kind of, you mean he didn't go all the way. But he touched you?"

I nodded.

"Cunnilingus?"

My mouth turned up in an embarrassed half grin. I nodded.

"Then you want to keep him. Those type of men are rare. Ashley never went anywhere near there. He was too nice and clean for that kind of sauciness."

"It's complicated," I said.

"They always are, darling. The exciting ones always are."

"Bronson's just gotten out of prison."

"A strong name. I bet he's a strong man."

"He is. But he was locked up in prison, Aggie."

"But he didn't murder anyone. It was not for violence," she argued.

I'd discussed him with her before, and knowing her view on drugs, I didn't feel like opening up that discourse. "He insists he's innocent."

"Do you believe him?"

I nodded slowly. "I do. Only, he promised to call, and he hasn't."

"Then go and claim him. Who says that it's the man's job to get down on his knees? Isn't that why women burned their bras in the sixties?"

"I wouldn't have taken you for a feminist, Aggie." I smiled.

"I'm no such thing," she snapped. "Men are physically stronger, and women are mentally stronger. It's not a battle of the sexes. It's simple. We're both equally capable and incapable." She snorted. "All that breast-beating, nothing but nonsense."

"But equal pay, the vote…" I argued.

She sighed. "I liked being a kept woman. I didn't do one day of work in my life. So what does that make me?"

"You came from another time. These days, women's voices need to be heard. We are part of the workforce. And at least we're finally being listened to in matters of abuse."

Her brows drew in slightly. "I'll own my wealthy, idle lifestyle guilt-free, thank you. That's why I married Ashley and gave up the only man I'd ever loved." A cigarette trembled in her hand.

"You wished you hadn't married Ashley?" I asked, dying to know what had happened to Monty.

Aggie looked at me, and said, "Ava." I braced myself, expecting an admonishment for asking a question. "You're very beautiful. You could and should be able to dictate your own terms, dear girl. Don't let all that feminist nonsense about being independent and doing your own heavy lifting force you into a lonely, loveless existence."

"But you didn't go down that independent path, and I sense your loneliness," I argued.

"That's because I chose the wrong man. The one I should have chosen, had I been less impulsive, would have given me everything: wealth, love, passion, and probably children." Her voice quivered.

I turned sharply to study her.

She was wearing shades, so I couldn't see her eyes.

"I'm sorry to hear that. I take it you didn't give birth."

She puffed out some smoke. "Ashley was firing blanks, as they say."

"I'm sorry."

"Enough of that. I'm good. Life's good. I have all the martinis I want. I have some superb memories. And Monty visits me all the time."

"In your dreams?" I asked.

"Oh, everywhere. He's everywhere." She pointed. "Oh look, there's Melissa Bloom swanning about with that young, dark and handsome guitarist. He's young enough to be her son."

"Do you have photos?" I asked.

"I have plenty of photos."

"I'd love to see them," I said.

"Let's leave the past alone. And you, Ava"—she pointed at me— "must promise me to go and get this Bronson fellow and give him what he wants and more. If we use our feminine charm and wiles to our best, men eat out of our hands. That gives us control. It always has." She followed that with a throaty laugh. "And he's already been somewhere private and intimate. He's yours now. Call him. Live dangerously."

She sat down again. "Now read to me. The part where Heathcliff visits Catherine for the first time in her marital home, just before she's about to die."

I'd lost count of how many times I'd read those passages of Heathcliff declaring his undying love by pledging to meet Cathy beyond the grave.

As I read on, Aggie's body surrendered into the chair, as though those words had been intended for her and not the dying heroine.

I left Aggie at eight, asleep on the sofa. As usual, I offered to walk her up the stairs to her bedroom, but she'd murmured for me to leave her alone. She had, however, encouraged me to call Bronson. Not that it took much convincing, and the martini helped.

I ran down the stairs, and after my breath settled, I leaned against a wall in the quiet lobby and pressed Bronson's number.

My sticky palm gripped the cell tightly as I waited for an answer.

"Ava." His sexy rasp helped settle my pounding heart. The fact he'd picked up straight away helped too.

"I just rang to say hello..." I said.

"I'm glad you did. It's nice to hear your voice," he said.

Even on the phone, that low, husky voice of his caused a swelling ache in my groin.

"I was wondering if you wanted to catch up for a drink or something..." I stammered again. What had happened to me? I'd always been comfortable talking to anyone.

"Where are you now?"

"I'm on Fifth Avenue."

"It's a nice evening. How about we meet in Central Park? Have you eaten?" he asked.

"No."

"Let's meet there. I can be there in thirty minutes," he said.

"Okay. How about at the angel fountain?"

"Sure. The perfect place to meet an angel."

I chuckled nervously. "Okay, then..." I lingered for some reason.

"I'm glad you called, Ava."

Not knowing what to say, I uttered, "Bye."

Suddenly it hit me. I looked horrible. I had no makeup on and was dressed in jeans and a loose blouse. As usual, I hadn't really thought about my clothes that day.

Passing a shop window, I looked at myself in the reflection. A big smile had supplanted the long face I'd been carrying around all week, and my cheeks had a healthy streak of pink. *That would just have to do*, I thought.

CHAPTER SIXTEEN

BRONSON

When I heard Ava's breathy voice, my earlier resolve to put off seeing her until I cleared my name vanished there and then. She'd been on my mind all week. All I could think of was how Ava felt. The promise of finishing what we'd started dominated every cell in my body.

Although I had to put the finishing touches to my designs, given that a meeting with the council had been set for the next day, I dropped everything. Luckily, I'd just showered after another long day working at a dusty building site. I changed into a fresh shirt, and then instead of driving my new car, I grabbed a cab to avoid the nightmare of parking.

Even standing among a crowd by the fountain, Ava stood out. Dressed in jeans that hugged her curves nicely, she had that natural appearance I preferred in women.

Noticing me heading toward her, she smiled shyly. The closer I got, the brighter her smile grew, which helped me loosen up a bit.

As I bent down to kiss her cheek, a scent of jasmine flooded me with memories of how she'd felt the night of the engagement party.

"Hey," I said. "Sorry. The traffic was crazy."

"Hey, that's cool. I only called an hour ago." That same unsure expression touched her face again.

Without makeup, Ava was even more beautiful. Noticing my blatant ogling, she said, "I'm sorry about my casual look. I've just finished work. It was a spontaneous decision to call you."

I took her hand. "Hey, I'm glad you did."

Her eyebrows shifted slightly, and then, pulling her gaze away from mine, she said, "This is such a beautiful fountain."

I nodded. "I've always been fond of it myself. I used to come here as a child and pray."

"Are you religious?"

"Maybe. I'm not sure yet. I'm looking for something."

"Tell me when you've found it. I stopped looking a while back," she said with a dry tone.

"But you're still young, Ava. Miracles happen. Or at least, I hope they do. So far, only one's happened for me."

Her head tilted. "Only one?"

"That's enough, isn't it?" I asked, taking her by the hand. "Come, let's walk."

Ava studied me. I could see her mind ticking over. "I guess," she replied, as we sauntered down to the tree-lined avenue.

She stopped walking. "Am I allowed to know what that miracle was?"

"Are you hungry?" I asked, being deliberately evasive.

"I am." Ava stopped walking and faced me. "You changed the subject."

"I'm too hungry to go into anything deep, Ava." I paused, stealing another look of her pretty face. "What do you feel like eating?"

"I'm not exactly dressed for eating out. I didn't call you for a dinner date or anything."

"Why did you call?" I stopped walking and faced her.

A glimmer of a smile touched the side of her mouth. "You tell me your miracle first."

I was quickly learning that beneath that shy smile existed a feisty woman. Having always been a sucker for a woman who stood her ground, I liked that.

Returning Ava's challenge with a half grin, I replied, "Let's eat, first. And by the way, you look great, especially in those jeans. They were made for you."

"I've been on the cakes again. I'm a bit chubby." Her mouth turned down.

I couldn't help but check out her ass, which was the sexiest, curviest butt I'd ever seen. "As wicked as you make it sound, I like the result." As she stared at me, trying to see if I was for real, my grin faded. "You're perfect, Ava." I stood close and stroked her arm.

She pulled her arm away, and although she did it gently, it still felt abrupt.

"Is there something the matter?" I asked.

"Why didn't you call me?"

I took a deep breath. "It's a long story, Ava. Let's grab something to eat. Then we can talk."

That little touch of her arm still tingled on my fingers as we walked side by side. With each step, I was pulled in closer, as if drawn to her by a magnet. I even felt a spark when her shoulder touched my arm.

We headed toward the lake and noticed a café.

"That looks inviting," I said, turning to Ava.

"Yeah. Why not." She smiled shyly again as if we'd only just met.

The balmy, still evening was perfect for dining outside.

After the waiter directed us to a table with a fantastic view of the lake, I asked, "What would you like to drink?"

"A chardonnay," Ava said, looking up at the waiter.

When the waiter returned his focus to me, I said, "I'll have a Corona, and the menu, please." He nodded and set down two menus. "Have whatever you want, Ava. My life's about to change."

"Oh?" Her forehead creased.

"It's a long story."

"Another one." She cocked her head slightly. "I'm a good listener, you know."

A wisp of hair had fallen over her high cheekbone, which I gently brushed aside. "You looked beautiful the other night, Ava. I wish I had a photograph."

Her eyebrows gathered tightly. "You haven't called me, but yet you want a photo?"

I sighed. "Okay, look…" The waiter turned up and delivered our drinks just in the nick of time. I needed something badly to help ease this rise of emotion between us.

Lowering our drinks onto the table, he asked, "Are you ready to order?"

I nodded and looked over at Ava.

"You go first," she replied.

"I'll have the grilled steak, medium, fries, and salad," I said.

The waiter scribbled that down and then looked over at Ava who replied, "I'll have the same, thanks."

After he left, Ava looked up at me. "You were saying?"

Taking a deep breath, I said, "You know about my recent…"

"Stint in prison," she said.

I knitted my fingers. "I'm innocent. I've already told you that. But I need you to believe that. I need to prove it to you. So that you don't keep staring at me the way you do."

Her head pushed back. "What do you mean?"

Staring down at my fingers, I sought the right words. "I guess it's like you're trying to figure out if I'm bad or some kind of loser not to be trusted."

Her brow crumpled in disbelief. "That's not what I see when I look at you. That's your own insecurity talking, Bronson."

"Then why do you always have that puzzled, almost suspicious frown whenever I say something? Like now, for instance."

"I'm sorry, I had no idea that's how I was coming across. It's just that you're a pretty intense guy… I feel like there's so much going on inside of you, that any minute something might erupt. It's not because I think you're a criminal. I find you fascinating. And to be honest, I believe you."

It took me a moment to still my frazzled emotions before her last comment finally hit me. I looked up sharply. "What did you say?"

"I believe you," she said with a reassuring smile.

Whatever had kept me bound for weeks, especially since meeting Ava, released its hold on me. I could breathe at last.

Placing my hand in hers, I said, "Thank you. I can't tell you what hearing those words means to me."

A compassionate smile radiated from her. "That's understandable. What happened to you is so reprehensible, it infuriates me, to be honest." She nodded decisively. "The more I've come to know Justin, particularly this last month, the more I've noticed something rotten in there. Whereas"—she paused while I caressed her hand—"I believe you're genuine." While Ava took a sip of wine, I searched for something to say. But then, she added, "Justin's got a drug habit. And I've seen how much he's challenged by you. He's jealous. He admitted that much the other night when he came to my place. Uninvited, I might add."

My brow gathered tightly. "Uninvited? Did he try to hurt you? Or force himself on you again? Tell me."

Ava flinched at my aggressive tone. "Not really... Although it was stupid of me to let him in. But I managed to kick him out."

The pounding in my chest settled a little. I placed my hand on top of hers. "Promise me that if he ever comes near you, you'll call me straight away."

She nodded.

As our hands remained in a tight clutch, it felt as though I'd known Ava all my life and that I'd arrived somewhere comfortable and familiar at last.

"You really believe me, then?" A faint, hopeful light brightened my spirit.

She nodded slowly. "I do. You've got this depth about you that I've never experienced in anyone before. You strike me as being honest."

I took her hand and kissed it. "I'm so glad you called me, Ava." Now it was my turn to be inquisitive. "Why did you call me?"

Her cheeks reddened slightly. "Aggie suggested it."

"The woman you read to?"

"Uh-huh." She toyed with her glass before lifting her eyes up to meet mine.

I wanted to devour that shy smile. Ava unconsciously teased me when her sweet tongue swept over her rosy sensual lips. "If you keep doing that, Ava, I'm going to have to take you here in the gardens and finish off what we started."

She laughed. "That could get us arrested."

"So Aggie suggested you call me, ah? Did you tell her about us?"

"Us?" she asked.

"For me, there's an us." A half smile grew at the side of my mouth. "You didn't answer my question."

"Yes, I told her about you. She'd already guessed, anyhow. Aggie's clairvoyant. I'm certain. She freaks me out, to be honest." She paused for a response. I wasn't sure what to say to that, so I just nodded. "Anyway, she noticed something in my mood and asked if I'd met someone. That was the day after *that* night…"

"Hm… I've been hard all week because of *that* night." Noticing her eyes switch from my face to her fingers, I asked, "Sorry, am I being too crass?"

She shook her head. "No… I like knowing that you desire me."

"It's deeper than that, Ava." My smile disappeared.

CHAPTER SEVENTEEN

AVA

Bronson had this mystifying way of throwing loaded comments at me. I was about to respond when our steaks arrived. The sizzling aroma headed straight for my gut, and despite a sudden profound need to delve into the sexiest man I'd ever set eyes on, I said, "Just hold onto that for a moment, I need to eat."

"Me too," he said, carving into his steak.

We ate away in silence. It was a comfortable silence, though, and nothing like that not-knowing-what-to-say awkwardness that I'd experienced on dates before.

Bronson wiped his lips. "That's one good steak." He gazed up at me. "I'm glad you like eating."

I laughed. "You've met women who don't?"

"Yeah. The skinny ones. They have a weird relationship with food. I love food, and I love sharing it."

"Me too. Cassie's got that problem. I don't think I'll ever be skinny." I turned my mouth down slightly. I'd always seen myself as fat. Especially in junior high where I became the butt of everyone's joke, literally, given my big ass.

"Ava. You're a woman. In every sense of the word. Believe me."

I took a deep breath as his heavy-lidded gaze added sexy promise to the type of compliment I'd never tire of hearing.

Bronson's apartment was clean and ordered, which pleased me for some strange reason. Maybe because, being naturally untidy, I presumed that it fitted neatly with that cliché of opposites attracting. Not that I needed any further justification for being drawn to Bronson.

Breathing in the cool night air, I stood on the balcony and studied the view of the bay. Twinkling with a blur of color reflecting from surrounding city lights, the bay resembled a modern art painting. As I feasted on the sky, I caught sight of a shooting star and gasped in wonder. It was like a celestial orgasm: short, sharp, and exciting. Analogies aside, the cosmic omen showered me with hope and magic.

One thing was for certain, Bronson's apartment was a far cry from my little shoebox excuse for an apartment, which I was planning to move from soon. The money Aggie deposited weekly into my account had me saving madly for a new apartment in which I didn't trip over the toilet to shower.

I remained on the balcony to give Bronson privacy as he took a call. Explaining that he had a meeting in the morning, he apologized for having to take it. Not that I minded. I'd crashed his evening, after all. Still, I was glad I'd listened to Aggie and called him.

My heart raced with every stolen glance. I couldn't get enough of him. Each time I looked, I saw something different in that handsome face. Bronson could have starred in Hollywood as an action man with that body or as a brooding, mysterious lover with those dark, swarthy features.

After dinner, we'd taken a walk through the park.

I couldn't say what startled me more, the Swiss army knife Bronson pulled out, or the fact that he went over to a tree and carved a heart with our initials into it.

We belonged together, he told me, causing my breath to hitch.

The impetuosity of that action, considering we'd only just met, shocked me. However, my heart saw it differently, for I was so hopelessly attracted to Bronson that I fell into his arms and surrendered my mouth to his.

The hasty nature of our connection had my sensible side in a spin, but I'd never experienced anything like it before. Even though we hadn't even slept together, it felt like I'd known Bronson forever.

There was this inexplicable familiarity about him, the way his eyes shone with belief and sincerity, along with that faint uncertain half smile that he reverted to naturally.

Bronson held me, and as I leaned against the tree, a tear touched my cheek. That simple act of carving our initials seemed so innocent and pure, but yet as I drank in his hooded gaze and felt Bronson's hard arousal against me, it was anything but innocent. His moistened lips took to mine with a ferocity of need as his tongue penetrated deeply into my mouth. It was hot, dangerous, and if we didn't go somewhere private soon, potentially obscene.

He pulled away. "As much as I want you here and now, there are too many people about. Will you come back with me?"

I nodded as if in a trance. A tingle of anticipation settled into my core, while my feet barely touched the ground as we moved along. Driven by an intense desire of the like I'd never experienced before, I would have followed Bronson into a pit of burning embers. Even hell.

After he ended his call, Bronson asked, "Can I get you something? I haven't got wine. It's only beer and bourbon." He tilted his head in an adorable boyish way.

"You look different when you smile," I said.

His eyes wandered over me. "That's because it doesn't come naturally to me. Around you, though, I feel light."

"You haven't had an easy life?" I asked.

Placing his arm around my waist, he drew me close, which made my pulse race again. "No. But you're here now. So, can I get you anything?"

I shook my head. All I wanted was him.

My eyes landed on the coffee table and noticed some sketches. "Did you do these?"

He bent down and gathered the sheets of paper. "Yeah, just a few drawings for tomorrow's meeting."

As I focused on the well-crafted drawings, my jaw dropped. "They're excellent. You're a very capable artist."

"Why the surprise? Just because I'm a bit edgy doesn't make me a loser."

Bronson's defensive response made me wince. "I'm sorry. I didn't mean it that way. It's just that you haven't really spoken much about what you do."

His face relaxed, which in turn eased the tension in my legs. Pointing to a drawing depicting a village scene, Bronson said, "This is my vision: to build affordable housing developments on vacant industrial sites. But not like your typical tenements. Cottages." Bronson searched through his pile of drawings. "More like these."

I stared down with wonder at the charming gabled homes. "They remind me of houses in fairy tales."

"I like classic lines."

"These are fantastic."

"I'd like to make them affordable. And even have some set aside for the homeless if I have my way. The plan is to create both. Bring activity to the area and then design a village-like atmosphere that motivates businesses to move in. Very European."

"It is." I looked up at him. "These are genius."

His brow contracted. "I don't think they're that. But they've kept me focused for a year. That's what I did in prison."

"I'm seriously impressed."

He sat down next to me and drew me in close again. "And I'm seriously turned on."

Although Bronson was so alluring it almost didn't matter what he did, his considerable talent had just made my attraction rise to stratospheric heights.

Lifting me up effortlessly, he carried me to his bedroom, where he placed me on his bed and stood before me for a moment, running his hands through his hair as if uncertain.

His hesitation made me sit up. "Is there something the matter?"

Shaking his head, Bronson undid his shirt buttons. I'd felt his torso and chest and strong arms, but I'd never seen him in the flesh.

As he dropped his shirt to the ground, my breath hitched.

Bronson embodied male perfection. His scrolled tattoos emphasized just how big his biceps were.

"Are you going to just sit and stare?" he asked, cocking his handsome head.

"Oh... sorry, am I?"

He leaned in and kissed me. "You are. Now it's my turn to stare. You're wearing too many clothes."

I pulled my blouse over my head and realized I'd worn comfortable but boring underwear. Crossing my arms over my breasts, I smiled awkwardly.

"Uncross those arms, Ava."

"If I knew we were…" I stammered. "I would have worn nicer underwear. I shudder to think of my bottoms." I giggled.

He smiled. "They're not going to remain on you long enough for me to notice. Now uncross those arms."

I did, and his eyes darkened. "You're beautiful."

He lowered his jeans, and his large bulge stretched the cotton of his briefs as if pleading to be unleashed.

My heart pumped so hard it landed in my dry throat.

He lowered his briefs and came toward me. Having forgotten how big he was, I gulped.

Bronson fumbled around with the clasp of my bra, and my breasts tumbled out. He trailed his soft lips over my puckering flesh and then sucked on my nipples, while caressing my breasts, causing an aching swell between my legs.

CHAPTER EIGHTEEN

BRONSON

When it came to my perfect woman, she had nice firm tits that spilled out of my hands and an ass to match. I liked my woman to be on the voluptuous side. And boy, Ava had the type of curves to keep me up all night in the true sense of that word.

I ripped off her panties, which wasn't hard to do given that they were already torn.

"I'm sorry, I should have worn..." Ava murmured.

I kissed her swollen, moist lips and then pulled away to gaze at her again as my fingers caressed her warm softness.

She parted her moist lips and let me slide in. I tasted her silky tongue and went into overdrive from the promise of what was to come.

My tongue trailed down her puckering flesh. She tasted like an exotic fruit. Her nipples spiked onto my tongue as blood charged through me.

Walking down her silky thighs, my finger entered between her heated folds and was drenched by her tight muscles.

"You've fucked before, haven't you?" I asked, finding it difficult to speak due to a flood of blood hijacking my senses.

She answered with a breathy "Yes."

"Wait a minute," I said, unraveling from her hold.

I opened the drawer by the bed and pulled out a sheet of paper.

This was no longer a game. After tasting her at the party, my cravings for Ava had intensified. I wanted our first time together to be magic. And for that to happen, it had to be skin on skin.

In any case, catching Ava and me naked together would have Justin pissing blood. Not that I blamed him. Losing a woman like Ava could break even the strongest of men.

She lifted herself up. "What's that?"

I handed it to her. "A blood test I've just had."

Ava's chestnut hair cascaded over her breasts in what was a drawing crying for my sketch pad.

"You had this done two days ago?" Her lips parted.

"I just needed you to know that I'm clean. I need to feel you"—I caressed her smooth, milky skin—"properly."

Without even looking at it, she passed the document back to me. "But you didn't call me."

I scratched my prickly chin, which was in desperate need of a shave. "Hey, I was always going to call you, angel." Sitting on the edge, I stroked her cheek. "Thank you."

"For what?" she asked, looking up at me with those big glistening eyes.

"For believing me."

She buried her face in my neck.

Enough talking. It was time to ravish her, and my cock, which was twitching like mad against my belly, agreed.

Landing on her swollen clit, my finger glided over her bud. Her sighs told me I'd found the right light touch.

My tongue watered for a taste. As I moved down her body, she stroked my penis gently. Not having been with a woman in over a year, I was really close to that edge of no return.

"Ava," I said, struggling to talk. "I'm going to come pretty quickly. I'd prefer to be inside of you."

She removed her hand. "Sorry, it's just that you're nice to touch. Do you want me to put it in my mouth?"

"No, darling. Not now. Maybe later."

My tongue landed on her clit. Her moans grew as she writhed in my clasp. I fluttered over it and licked slowly.

I needed Ava lubricated. She was too tight, and I didn't want to hurt her. As my licking increased, I felt her ass clench in my hands, telling me that she was close, so I entered her first with my tongue and then my finger. Just as I did, she spasmed around my finger, squeezing it tight as she groaned through a creamy release.

I wiped my lips on the sheet. That was for later so that I could smell her. Gross, maybe, but a serious turn-on.

She opened her supple thighs wide. Her pink, creamy cunt made my cock go blue.

She took my dick in her little hand.

"Guide it in," I said.

"You're so big."

"Do you want me to stop?" I asked in a strangled voice.

Ava continued to push gently toward me. Her tight pussy squeezed the senses out of me.

"No." Her plead inspired me to enter deeply.

As I tentatively slid into the farthest point, a groan left my mouth. The fit was exquisite. I was so stimulated by the sensation of her heat I stayed there for a moment to soak in her juices.

I pulled out and slowly entered again, only to find the same breathtaking resistance.

My thrusts increased.

The friction was so intense that it challenged my staying power.

I gripped her ass as Ava moved her sensual hips fluidly.

She felt really good. Almost too good.

As I rested weight on my arms, Ava dug her nails into my biceps as my thrusts became more urgent. My balls tightened as my cock plowed through her tight pussy.

"I'm going to come," Ava moaned.

Her convulsing muscles gripped and released, soaking my cock, just as I groaned through what was the longest stretch of euphoria I'd ever experienced.

My head fell back, and a loud rumble erupted from my chest. It felt as if I'd ejaculated a whole year's worth.

Holding her in my arms, I uttered "Ava" with the last bit of breath I had.

When we tumbled back to reality, holding each other close, Ava laughed.

Pushing back my head to look at her, I laughed too.

A weird response, but nice anyhow.

I'd never been much into laughing, but since meeting Ava, I'd probably laughed the most I'd ever done in my life.

It was hard to know whether I slept or not because it was as if I floated in and out of consciousness. Melding into Ava's curves, my body rested properly for the first time in ages, while my heart felt light and full. It was a perfect fit in every sense of the word, both inside and out.

When she wriggled into my groin, I rubbed my hard cock against her, craving another feast.

I looked at my watch, something I never removed because I hated running late. It was seven in the morning. I didn't want to wake her, so I continued to spoon her while drawing in her scent.

I felt Ava move, and then she turned to look at me. The morning light touched her face, and her dreamy eyes smiled back.

I couldn't believe we'd fucked every which way earlier, for she seemed so young. Her body wasn't, though. I'd discovered, much to my cock's delight, that Ava enjoyed hard, dirty sex.

She smiled. "Good morning."

"Good morning, angel." I kissed her.

"I must taste horrible," she said.

"You taste like us."

"Us? But I haven't…" she licked her lips.

Mm… that really made my cock go hard. "Shower?"

She looked disappointed.

"I need to be at a meeting at nine, Ava. But you can sleep in if you like."

"No." She caressed my arm and smile sweetly. "I'd like that shower. With you." She rose from the bed. "I must look a sight."

"Your hair is wild and sexy, and it's making me hard as hell." I stood up and stretched.

"I can see that." She ran her tongue over her lips, and I leaned in and kissed her. Then, taking Ava by the hand, I led her to the shower.

Satisfied that it was the right temperature, I stood away and let Ava step in. She crossed her arms over her breasts.

"What's the matter, Ava?" I asked, pinching her butt, which made her giggle.

"I'm a bit shy about my body. I feel fat."

My addicted hands slid along the contour of her waist and hips, with a little squeeze of her ass along the way, as the warm water cascaded over us.

"You're not fat, angel. You're perfect. Really perfect." I pointed down at my hard cock. "He's pretty hot for you."

She stroked it. "Mm… I've noticed." Getting down to her knees, she took my dick and placed it between her spongey lips. She sucked on it gently and then continued to move up and down while holding onto the base of the shaft.

A deep sigh of indescribable pleasure sucked air out of my lungs as I leaned against the tiled wall.

Her mouth moved up and down while her tongue licked the head. As I watched her luscious mouth cling my dick, her pretty eyes looked up at me, and that really brought blood charging wildly down to my balls.

"Mm… Ava… I'm going to shoot if you keep that up."

She continued anyway.

I closed my eyes and fell into a spell of pure lust. "You can pull out now because I'm about to…"

Ava held on, determined to swallow me whole. Surrendering, I released deeply down her throat.

After returning to the land of the living, I took Ava into my arms and held her tight.

"That was amazing. Where did you learn to do that?"

"Um… with a banana." Her voice sounded so dreamy that at first, it didn't register, mainly because blood flow hadn't quite made it back to my head.

I looked to see if she was joking. "What?"

Grabbing the sponge, I squirted on body wash and proceeded to rub it over her breasts. "So, you practiced on a banana?"

Ava giggled. "I went to a class."

I stopped sponging her. "You're fucking kidding me?"

She shook her head. "Nope. It was at a bachelorette party. It was so ridiculous that I ended up eating the banana."

I pulled a face. "You're a good learner. Only, my neck's good for a little bite here and there, but"—I cocked my head downwards—"Not him, I'm afraid."

121

Ava laughed. "Don't worry. I know the difference between a dick and a banana."

"Good, I'm glad we've established that." I smirked.

Unfortunately, time moved along quickly, and because it was such an important meeting, I had to arrive on time. Unaccustomed to an audience when dressing, I buttoned up my shirt with Ava sitting back watching me. I liked it, though, and looked forward to ogling her in return.

"I have to run," I said, brushing her cheek. "Just take your time. There's coffee and cereal. Help yourself to anything."

She looked at me with that big smile of hers. I shook my head. "What?"

"Nothing, I'm just enjoying the show."

"The show?" I grinned.

"Yeah." Ava, who was dressed in my shirt, stood up.

"And seeing you in that shirt is making me lose my mind. Promise me you'll be here when I get back, in that shirt."

Her brow drew in sharply. "You'd like to catch up later?"

I nodded. "You bet." Reading a flicker of uncertainty in her eyes, I asked,

"Am I coming on too strong?"

She shook her head and fell into my arms. Her fragrant hair brushed my nose.

"You can come back here after Aggie's. If you like. I'll give you a key."

Drawing away from me, she studied my face. "Are you serious?"

"I've never been more serious."

"But we've only just met," she said.

"So?"

CHAPTER NINETEEN

AVA

I naturally assumed Bronson was playing with me. With that occasional dark humor of his, he was, at times, hard to read. But Bronson was dead serious, which was where he generally parked his emotions.

He rummaged in a drawer and brought out an entrance card.

After he placed it on my damp palm, I said, "Um… okay." Left speechless, I actually had a head full of questions.

He combed back his hair, making it sit up perfectly. His freshly shaved skin rubbed smoothly against my cheek. As I sank into its heat, a sniff of herbal cologne made me melt.

Dressed in taupe chinos, which fitted his thighs and butt snugly, and a crisp white shirt highlighting his tanned features, Bronson looked smoking hot. I could have imagined him on the cover of *Alpha Male Monthly*.

"You look really handsome."

A glimmer of a smile touched his lips, making his cheeks dimple and adding to his beauty, if that were at all possible.

Bronson leaned in and kissed me again while running his hands over breasts and squeezing my butt along the way. He pulled away and stared into my eyes. "I wish I didn't have to race off, Ava."

Gathering the designs spread out on the table, Bronson placed them in a black folio case. Popping it under his arm, he looked as though he was about to conquer the world.

He stood at the door and said, "I'll call you after the meeting."

"I'd like that." I smiled. "Go kill them. You're going to do good. I'm sure."

A tender, off-center smile grew on his face. He lingered a moment longer before closing the door behind him.

Taking it slow and easy, I made myself a coffee. That was another advantage of working for Aggie: there was no need to rush about in the mornings. I appreciated having the time to gather my thoughts and make plans.

That morning was like no other I'd ever experienced, however.

A long, sated sigh left me as I plonked down on the sofa, indulging myself in reruns of our lovemaking. My pussy ached in a pleasant way, a bit like that first workout after a long period of idleness. Only this was a million times more satisfying.

I kept staring at the key on the table.

Were we about to jump straight into a relationship?

I recalled him carving our initials on the tree. Even that almost sealed the deal for something lasting.

Nothing like that had ever happened to me before.

Although an adolescent act, that heart with our initials carved inside was so profoundly romantic that it spoke to my soul. And then there was his intense belief in *us*. Startling as that was, it sparked possibilities and adventure rather than niggling doubt. And so there I was, sighing with satisfaction while sinking into the spongey cushion and succumbing to the delicious promise of Bronson.

As I bounded along Fifth Avenue with a big sunny smile, I noticed people staring at me suspiciously. At first, I assumed my loud purple dress was the reason. But then something told me it was more to do with that punch-the-air vibe pushing me along, given that women wore all kinds of weird and wonderful designer outfits along there. A vintage seventies frock was hardly going to raise an eyebrow.

Walking under the red canopied entrance, I pushed the glass doors and stepped onto the mosaic floor. Lights encased in frosted glass created a shadowy foyer, almost making me forget that it was daylight.

I headed straight for the elevator, which as usual seemed to be there waiting for me.

I climbed in and greeted Charlie.

"How's our lovely Aggie?" he asked, cheerful as always.

"She's good. I've offered to take her over to the park, but she refuses to leave her apartment."

"I haven't seen Agatha for at least ten years," he said.

"Really? You've obviously known her for a while, then."

"Oh, sure. I've been here for over fifty years. I knew Ashley well." He placed a hand to the side of his mouth as though about to reveal something confidential. "He liked his boys."

"Huh?" Despite recalling Aggie's admission about her husband and men, I was still shocked.

"Mm… Well, they all had to hide back in those days, I'm afraid." His sad tone inferred that he too had a thing for men.

A flood of questions banked up suddenly. But then we arrived at the tenth floor, and a silent, frustrated sigh deflated my lungs as I stepped out, and waved goodbye to Charlie.

Rummaging in my bag for my keys, I grabbed hold of the keychain that had just become a little heavier. *That* key had so much significance attached to it that my heart hadn't quite settled since Bronson had handed it to me.

I opened the door and stepped in and, as always, went straight to the balcony, only to find that Aggie wasn't there.

She wasn't in the kitchen or in the bathroom, so I fell onto the floral armchair in the bright living room, grateful for the rest. There I fell asleep and lost all sense of time.

When I slumped forward, I woke and jumped up. Shaking away my tiredness, I lifted my weary frame from the comfortable chair. I wasn't sure how long I'd been out. Curiously, there were no clocks around. Aggie had everything else in that room, which made sense in many strange ways because time seemed frozen there. Time didn't even count. Not only in that penthouse but the whole building in general. Even Aggie had alluded to that in one of her many mysterious little rants.

I grabbed my cell and realized I'd been out for a whole hour. There was still no Aggie.

I looked up at the forbidden stairs, and taking a deep breath, I crept along to the base of the attractive, dark-wooded staircase. My first thought was to call out, but I desisted since I didn't wish to wake Aggie. That was, if she slept because my heart thumped away at the thought that she might not even be alive.

With all that playing out in my head, I broke the rules, and up I went.

When I hit the landing, I paused before two large portraits. One depicted a young woman with long dark hair and big blue eyes. I presumed the portrait to be Aggie when she was a young woman. It was weird, because she looked like me, only prettier. My attention then moved to the frame next to it, a portrait of a male with a long face and a high forehead. The wave of hair sitting on top elongated his features further, and like the picture of Aggie, he too wore a serious, almost dramatic expression.

By that stage, I naturally accepted that I was looking at a young Agatha and her husband Ashley.

As I continued to study the images, I heard chatter in the distance. I decided to move toward it down the hallway. The closer I got, the more it sounded like someone in despair.

Pausing at a door, I didn't quite know what to do. But then, recognizing that it was Aggie's voice, I relaxed a little knowing that she still breathed, so I decided to leave and go back downstairs. Just as I turned to leave, I heard what started as a moan turn into a cry.

The door was unlatched, so I pushed it open.

I found Aggie in bed crying out, "Don't! Monty!" as she thrashed about.

Riddled by indecision, I didn't know what to do. Then just as I was about to leave her alone, she murmured, "Who's there?"

"It's Ava. I…"

She motioned to me with her hand, so I went to her bedside.

"Are you okay, Aggie? I heard cries."

When she tried to sit up, I placed a pillow against her back. Her arms were cold, trembling, and fragile as I helped prop her up. I hadn't noticed how skinny they were until then. In fact, Aggie was skin and bone, which only added to my concern for her well-being.

"Can I get you something?"

Her heavy lids opened slightly.

"You seem unwell, Aggie."

"I'm not unwell, child. He's marrying that witch."

"Monty?" I asked.

"Yes. That gigolo. He couldn't wait."

"Wait for what?" I asked tentatively.

"For me. I had a plan."

Aggie looked beyond me as if hallucinating.

"What plan?" I asked.

"Poisoning Ashley. It's all the rage." She turned to face me. Her pupils were dilated. I couldn't tell if Aggie was drugged. She was certainly delirious. "That's how to get rid of a tiresome husband." She laughed in a raspy, frightening manner, sending shivers through me.

"Did you poison Ashley?" I asked quietly.

She shook her head. "No. He died of a heart attack. Just after Monty married." Her eyes filled with tears. "Why did he have to marry that witch? I broke his heart. He was my first. We made love all the way to the end."

"Up to when you married Ashley?"

"Oh, God, no. We made love all the time. He was married to that frigid, flat-chested Penny, and I was married to a fop. I needed a real man. And Monty was that, and more. His big dark eyes would eat me alive. And he was so well endowed he made me see stars. I devoured him, as he did me. We were insatiable. He was my first and my last. As I was his first and his last."

I winced. My heart started to pound. For some reason, Bronson flashed before me just as Aggie described her dark affair.

"Why didn't he leave her?"

"Ha… The bitch was pregnant. Unwavering loyalty made and broke the man. Monty had trapped my heart and wound it tightly around his own. But with that child on the way, something changed in him. Duty got in the way of us. We were meant to be together forever. And now we will be. Soon."

"Soon?"

She sank back under the covers. "Leave me. I need to sleep. Tomorrow. I'll see you tomorrow."

"Are you going to be okay. Should I call a doctor?"

"No doctor. Please go."

I left with a heavy tread. My head was pounding with so many questions: Had Aggie poisoned her husband? And if so, was that what had caused the heart attack? And her affair with Monty seemed damaging but yet profoundly romantic and extreme at the same time.

After I left Aggie's, unable to think straight, I crossed the road and headed for the gardens. With each step I took, the haywire of thoughts concerning all kinds of conspiracies slowly started to ease. Taking a deep breath, I found a measure of sanity again and lowered myself onto a bench.

I liked Aggie. She was generous and deeply fascinating, but that glint in her eyes as if she were possessed by some other force, not to mention her psychic abilities, made my veins chill.

Then I recalled the paintings upstairs. The eyes in that portrait were like mine. How could that be? What had brought me to this woman who had looked like me when she was young? Coincidence or some supernatural force?

Manhattan was hardly the setting for that. Maybe a gothic estate in countryside England, a far cry from Fifth Avenue. But then, the building did seem rather empty. It was as if time had been trapped in there, given how out of place the sophisticated eleven-story structure seemed alongside its monolithic neighbors.

Taking another deep breath, I felt like screaming from the sheer weight of endless questions.

While musing over the fine line that existed between coincidence and the supernatural, I jumped when my cell pinged. It was from Bronson, and almost miraculously, that dark veil of mystery lifted.

The message read: "The meeting went well. I'm with Harry on the site. Will catch you soon, wearing little, I hope."

I giggled loudly and wrote back. "Only your shirt."

Within a moment, my cell pinged again. "Lucky I'm wearing loose pants. I'll see you in an hour?"

I tapped back, "Yes."

When it came to sexy banter, I was out of my depth. Even so, the thought of his bulge made my panties that little bit stickier.

As I made my way back to Bronson's apartment, I thought about Aggie and her belief that Monty would soon be in her arms forever.

Considering her daily intake of martinis, enough to challenge even the most seasoned drinker, I thought that maybe all that booze had finally made her crazy.

I exhaled a long, slow breath.

For now, passion, and maybe—even if somewhat impulsive to think of it that way—*love* called.

Aggie's eccentric little world would just have to wait.

CHAPTER TWENTY

BRONSON

After the receptive committee studied my designs, an in-depth discussion followed. And judging by their nods of satisfaction, when answering their questions, I felt that I'd captured their interest. A blonde woman kept giving me the eye. I got the vibe that she would have given me more if I'd taken her up on that drink, she'd subtly invited me to. Although she was sexy in that unbuttoned-shirt, heavy-cleavage kind of way, no woman could even touch Ava in the perfect-body stakes.

Although it wasn't just Ava's curves. I loved being around her. I could be myself, something I'd never had with anyone before. Not that I was into the New Age or anything like that. Even that one yoga class in prison had made me pine for a punching bag. But I'd read somewhere about how everyone has a twin flame. I recalled thinking at the time that that was bullshit, mainly because I couldn't imagine anyone fitting comfortably with me.

There was no doubt that Ava was *my* twin flame.

Once the meeting was over, James invited me for a beer. Although I couldn't wait to get back home to see Ava, we did need to discuss the project. As it turned out, there were more pressing issues to discuss.

After grabbing a couple of beers, we settled down in a quiet corner of the bar.

"That went better than I expected, Bron. Wendy was pretty hot to trot. You had her undivided attention." He laughed.

"I'm more interested in getting their undivided attention where the project's concerned," I said.

"I think they were really impressed. They should be. Your plans are well thought out, achievable, and visionary."

My lips twitched into a half smile. "Thanks."

"You know I'm divorcing Candy, don't you?"

I nodded.

"There's something else I need to tell you. There are two things, actually."

I sat forward. "Is it about Justin and Candy?"

He nodded. "Yep. They've hooked up. And to be honest, I get the feeling that Justin's wearing his lawyer's screw-him-for-everything-he's-got hat to get at my cash."

"You've only been married for a year or so. You didn't do a prenup?"

He took a deep breath. And looking grim, he shook his head. "Stupid, eh? Anyway, I've got a good lawyer." He sipped his beer. "There's something else I'd like to talk about. Two more things."

"What's that?"

"When your father was in the hospital, he asked me about the stocks that we'd both invested in. When I told him that they'd skyrocketed, his face lit up. He then told me that everything he possessed would go to your mother. But he did state in his will to split his portfolio three ways: between your mother, Justin, and yourself."

I sat up. This had already been alluded to at my mom's fiftieth, and despite not giving it much thought, given my focus on Ava and a busy schedule, being cut out of my late father's will had hit me hard. It wasn't so much about money, though. It was the assumption that my late father had written me off due to my conviction. That he'd died thinking of me as a felon. Now that really fucking hurt.

"I didn't get anything," I said coolly.

He studied me for a moment. I thought he could read my pain even though I remained stone-faced.

"That's out of character for Elliot." He paused. "I asked Alice, and she said that when he tried to discuss the will, she'd been too upset to listen. Having expected Elliot to have included you all, your mom was speechless when she discovered that you'd been overlooked. Alice even mentioned that she'd offered you half of her portion but that you'd refused."

I looked down at my fingers. "I wanted her to keep it. She's off on that European trip she's always dreamed of. I want her to be comfortable."

"We're talking about at least one billion dollars, Bron. She'll be more than comfortable."

"I know… So that asshole, Justin, who's now a billionaire, is urging Candy to fleece you." A ton of dirty words sat in my mouth unspoken. "I hope I don't see that prick again."

He shook his head in disgust. "Justin's turned out rotten, all right." He pointed. "You, however, have made the most of what was given to you. Your father would have been proud of these designs, I'm sure."

I responded with a sad smile. "Mm… me, the orphan that Justin used to beat the shit out of."

He winced at my grim tone. "Alice mentioned that Justin had a hard time accepting you." He paused. "I'm going to look into that will. If need be, we'll contest it."

"But how? It's finished business, isn't it?"

"We're within our legal rights. I'll do some digging. When it comes to sleuthing, I think I missed my calling." He nodded with a grin.

I checked my watch. "I've got to go. I'm meeting Ava."

"Ava? Isn't that Justin's ex?"

I nodded. "At least I got the girl."

He studied me closely. "You're not with her to get back at Justin, I hope. Ava's a lovely girl."

"She is, and more." I looked James directly in the face. "At first, I flirted with that idea, because I was so fucking angry at that dirtbag. But as I got to know Ava, I fell hard." I took a sip of beer. "Anyway, we're together. It's real. For me, at least."

Although I noticed his brows lift, given how rash that admission seemed, I could see James was happy for me.

"Hey, what else were you going to tell me?" I asked.

He fidgeted with the coaster for a moment. "It's about your mom." He looked me squarely in the eyes. "We're together."

Now it was my turn to show surprise. "Really? When did that happen?"

"Last week. I've always loved Alice. Even from the beginning, before Elliot proposed to her. He just got there first." He shrugged. "But with respect for Elliot, I kept my distance."

An image of the last party entered my thoughts. I recalled how happy they had seemed together. "That's really great news. I could see it all along."

His brow creased. "Do you think your father noticed?"

I shook my head. "No. And in any case, theirs was a great marriage. They were really close and affectionate. I'm blessed for having been brought up around so much love. I just could have done without Justin's ball-breaking antics."

He patted my hand. "You brought a lot of joy to your parents. Elliot often spoke with great pride of how intelligent and creative you were."

"That means a lot to me." I hated how my voice trembled. Rubbing my neck to release the tension, I asked, "Did he ever tell you if he met my real parents?"

Having taken a sip, James coughed. A serious glint coated his blue eyes. The same eyes he shared with my late father.

"Bronson, no one knew anything. Not for lack of trying. I know that Alice went back over everything. All they had was that token you were found with. And as you already know, there wasn't a note."

I played with my fingers. "I thought Dad might have said something."

"There are no secrets, Bron."

I patted him on the arm. "Hey, I'm glad to hear about you and Mom."

"And I'm happy to hear about Ava. She's a beautiful girl."

"That she is. I hope she's not too good for me," I said, surprising myself since I normally hid my insecurities.

"You're handsome, talented, and about to become wealthy. Bronson, you're a catch, so to speak."

A glimmer of a smile claimed my mouth. A couple of months ago, after being released from that stinking prison, I would never have seen myself as anyone's catch.

Maybe my luck has finally changed, I thought.

An impetus to succeed, the like of which I hadn't experienced before, pumped through my veins.

I climbed off the barstool and stood tall.

CHAPTER TWENTY-ONE

AVA

I picked up some nibbles, wine, and a few other groceries on my way to Bronson's place. Hugging a large shopping bag of goodies, I'd gone all domestic. I hoped Bronson wouldn't mind. Considering we'd only been together for so little time, the connection between us seemed natural.

He was on the fifth floor, so I rode the elevator. As I leaned up against the wall, my heart raced at the thought of seeing him. I hoped he hadn't returned. That way I could change into his shirt as promised.

Deciding to knock first, I waited for a response. Hearing none, I used my new key.

Strange how a key could mean so much.

I entered and placed the groceries on the table so that I could sit for a moment. It had been an eventful twenty-four hours, and my breathing had yet to settle back to a relaxed rhythm, it seemed.

Looking around the room, I noticed there were no photos or any of the normal bric-a-brac usually found in a person's home, which was unlike my place that bordered on a hoarder's den. Sentimentalist to a fault, I'd kept everything, even my toys and first scribblings as a toddler.

Enjoying the peace after traversing the crowded city, I stretched my legs out on the sofa. In so doing, I accidentally knocked over a notebook, which fell open on the ground. Bending over to pick it up, I noticed the bold handwritten title: *Things I Must Do.*

Although I shouldn't have, I did the unthinkable and read on. My eyes landed on the first line: Find dirt on Justin. Seduce his girlfriend. And fuck her.

Pausing there, I read it again and again before dropping the book as if it was poison.

Nausea churned away, and my veins iced.

In a daze, I lifted my frozen form and walked out.

Two hours later, I turned my phone on, only to discover countless messages from Bronson. Peering down at the screen, my eyes burned from an endless deluge of tears.

Why carve our names on the tree? Why the key?

Questions kept running through my frantic thoughts.

My phone rang, and I jumped. This time I picked up. I wanted an explanation. Taking a deep breath, I waited for my chest to relax so that I could speak. "Hello."

"It's me, Cas," she said.

"Hey."

"You sound surprised," she said.

"I was expecting someone else," I said.

"You don't read your screen?"

"Normally I do. But I'm having a bad time." My voice cracked up. Tears banked up again. Where had they all come from? It was as though I'd cut the carotid artery equivalent to despair.

"Bronson called Marc," she said.

"Oh?" I sat up. "That's normal, isn't it? They are cousins."

"The call was about you. Bronson's worried. You were meant to meet, apparently, and you weren't picking up the phone. That's why he asked Marcus to ask me to call you."

I almost laughed. That was so unlike Bronson, Mr. Private. It must have taken a lot for him to do that.

I sighed deeply. "We actually made out." I cringed. That sounded weak and childish. Our lovemaking meant more to me than some loose sexual encounter.

"You did?"

The surprise in her voice made me wince.

"Bronson carved our initials into a tree and he gave me a key..." I cracked up again. Sniffling, I grabbed a tissue and blew my nose.

"That soon? I mean you seemed chatty with one another. Shit. Ava. He's kind of bad, isn't he?"

"No. I mean, maybe… Oh fuck… What have I done?"

"You're not pregnant?"

I laughed through my tears. "That's ludicrous. We only got together last night for the first time."

"And he's given you a key and carved your initials into a tree?"

Her incredulous tone made me want to laugh, scream, and cry all at the same time. "I know it seems a bit rushed. But he was hard to resist."

"I get it, Aves, Bronson's seriously hot. Was he worth it?"

"Ha?" My head was somewhere else. All I could think of was that notebook.

"He must be crazy about you because he made Marcus promise he'd get me to call you. According to Marc, Bronson was really freaking out, which apparently is not like him because Bronson rarely expresses his feelings."

I exhaled a deep breath and told Cassie about point two on the list: fucking me to get back at Justin.

"Ouch. Right. But he seems crazy about you. He's obviously had a change of heart. Because from where I'm sitting it sounds like Bronson's fallen hard."

"Like me. I've fallen hard, too, Cassie."

"Sweetheart, call him and talk about it. He's been through a lot. Maybe that was the deranged version of him. I can't imagine what it would be like locked up in prison. And Marc's convinced Bronson was innocent."

She spoke so much sense that a weight lifted off my shoulders. "Cassie, thanks for calling. I need to go. I'll call you soon."

"Are you going to call him?"

"Probably."

I closed the call, and stretched out on my sofa, resting the back of my hand on my forehead.

My cell rang again, making me jump.

That thumping intro to "Smoke on the Water" had to go. It was Justin's doing. He'd mucked around with my ringtone as a joke one night.

This time I checked the screen. Seeing that it was Bronson, I took the call. "Bronson." I kept my tone cool and formal.

"Ava. Why?"

"Why?" I asked.

"I can see you've been here by the groceries on the bench. But why run off and then not take my calls?"

"Was there a camera hidden somewhere in your bedroom?" I asked.

"What?" His surprised tone reminded me how crazy my question must have sounded.

"How else were you going to prove to Justin that we'd fucked?"

CHAPTER TWENTY-TWO

BRONSON

My eyebrows couldn't squeeze tight enough. I had no idea what had come over Ava. "What do you mean?"

"Didn't you seduce me to get back at Justin? And fucking me was the prize."

Who'd gotten into her head? I wondered. "Have you been speaking to Justin?"

"No, Bronson. But I saw it written there in your diary."

"You read my diary?" I asked.

"I didn't mean to. It fell on the ground, and when I picked it up, that passage to get back at Justin by fucking his girlfriend jumped out at me…" She paused to clear her throat. "It was impossible not to notice. I didn't read anything else. That's not my style. I'm not the snooping type."

I wanted to hit my head against a wall in frustration. "Shit" was the best I could offer.

What could I say? That *had* been my aim.

But *not* anymore.

"Are you there?" I asked.

"Yes. But only just."

"Ava, don't hang up. I want to see you. To explain. I'm not good over the phone. Words don't come naturally to me. I wrote that before I met you. But when I got to know you the game changed."

"So, it is a game?"

"Hell, no. That's a figure of speech. Ava… please don't do this. I need to see you. To explain. I just wanted to get back at fucking Justin for taking a year of my life away. I didn't realize I'd fall so hard…."

"So hard?"

A jagged breath left my lips. "Say you'll see me."

There was a pause again. My heart had sunk so low I could barely breathe.

"We can meet. Tomorrow. At the same place by the tree."

"The tree?" I asked.

"You've forgotten already?"

"No. Of course, not. I'm just not thinking straight. I'll be there. What time?"

"It has to be after I finish work. After eight."

"That's too long to wait. But I'll be there, Ava."

"Okay then," she said.

I could hear her breathing, which reminded me of her sweet breath on my ear as I held her close.

"I meant everything that I said last night. Everything. It's not just that tree that you're carved into but also deeply in me."

There was a pause at the other end but I could hear her breathing. "I'm deeply affected too, Bronson. It feels like a lifetime of emotion rolled into twenty-four hours."

"Tomorrow, my angel."

"Okay. Bye."

Setting down my cell, I headed straight for the bottle of bourbon.

The light was so bright that I squinted as I sat outside an office. Nightmares had made for a bad night's sleep. And I felt jumpy after four cups of strong coffee.

Ava was everywhere.

When I fell into bed, her scent assaulted me, which brought our lovemaking back vividly. Fragrances were like that. My body still tingled with her memory. But after I fell asleep, the nightmares came in relentless waves. One ugly image after another. Distorted faces and voices. The sounds were the scariest. Voices in the distance like ghosts calling out my name. I woke at four with a jolt and never made it back to sleep.

The secretary showed me into an office. Being called in had come as a surprise, given that we'd only had a meeting yesterday.

Amber Moore had called later that same afternoon, explaining that she wished to discuss my designs.

I couldn't tell her age only because of all the work she'd had done on her face. One thing I could tell, though, by the way her eyes wandered from my eyes all the way down to my crotch, that she was hungry for some cock.

Standing up, she came toward me. I looked up at her, and my brow flinched.

"So, Bronson Lockhart, I hear you've only just got out of prison."

My jaw tightened. "And?"

A slow smile formed on her plumped lips. "Your designs are impressive."

"Okay. Thanks. Look, Miss Moore…"

"Call me Amber," she interjected with a breathy voice.

"You said that you needed to see me urgently before the submission could be processed. James Lockhart's running the company, as no doubt you're aware. Shouldn't he be the person you need to speak to?"

She went over to a cabinet and lifted a bottle of bourbon. "Can I offer you something to drink?"

"No. I'm good."

"I just wanted to meet you—the man of the moment. You've made a lot of people excited… me included."

"Okay. Good. I worked hard for a year on those designs."

"In prison?"

I sat forward. "Miss Moore. Amber, I mean. What's this really about?"

Her eyes once again roamed over my body. This time they remained. "I've always had a thing for bad boys."

I crossed my arms, and her eyes settled on my shoulders before traveling down again. My legs were slightly apart, my natural seated position. One didn't need to be clairvoyant to sense that Amber was hitting on me big time.

"I just wanted to meet to tell you how impressed we were. And that after James delivers a workable budget, we'll probably sign off on it. I wanted to give you the news personally."

The "personally" sounded like a purr.

I nodded. "That's good news." I tried to keep it brief and professional because I got the vibe I might need to fuck for my supper. Which was not going to happen.

Not with Ava's scent on my skin.

She rolled her tongue over her lips. Walking past me, she dropped her pen—deliberately I was sure, since she bent down, giving me an eyeful of tits as she remained longer than necessary.

"Amber... I'm seeing someone."

She rose and adjusted her tight skirt. "So?"

I stood up. "That's great news about the project. Thank you. Is there anything else?"

She studied me for a moment, sucking on her pen as if it were a dick. "I wouldn't mind seeing you without your clothes on, prison boy."

My forehead lowered sharply. "What? Is the grant contingent on me showing you my dick?"

She shrugged with a slight cock of her head. "Maybe."

"You're fucking kidding me."

"You're seriously hot, Bronson. And I'm horny as hell."

"I'm in love with another woman. If that's the only reason why you're backing our project, then all I can say is..." My throat was tight from agitation. "Thanks, but no thanks."

I softened my response at the last minute because I really wanted to tell her to go fuck herself.

Rushing out before it turned nasty, I headed straight out of the building with black glass for walls.

When I got to the street, my eyes settled on a bar. A stiff bourbon suddenly had my name on it.

After two shots, my nerves settled.

Replaying what had just taken place, I felt profound sympathy for the many women who were hit on inappropriately every day in workplaces. Amber had just demonstrated what fucking for one's supper felt like. And as much as I probably would have fucked her if Ava hadn't stolen my heart, the merits of my project suddenly lost out.

I called James.

"Bronson."

"Hey… Um… something just happened."

"Tell me."

I exhaled a deep breath. "I was called in for a meeting with Amber Moore. And she basically tried to seduce me."

"She made no secret of her attraction yesterday. I'm not surprised. I take it you didn't return the favor?"

"No fucking way." I took a deep breath. "Anyway, we may have lost out because of it."

"You can't be serious."

"I'm not sure. But I got a bit pissed off."

"Right. Well… that's understandable."

"It means we may have lost the funding. Without that, it's not going to be possible, is it?"

"Leave it with me. I'll do some digging. I might even call this Amber myself. The buck doesn't stop with her anyway. Remember, she's one of a committee of twelve. If anything, this could get her into trouble."

"I don't want to take it further, James. My life's complicated enough as it is." I let out a frustrated sigh.

"Leave it with me. We'll talk."

"Thanks," I said, gulping down my shot.

After I left the bar, I passed a tattoo parlor and paused for a moment before walking in.

A heavily tattooed man looked up from his newspaper. "Hey, man, what can I do for you?"

"Something tasteful, not too big. How long will it take?" I looked down at my watch and saw that it was five o'clock. I had three hours before meeting with Ava.

I'd already been counting the minutes away.

"Depends on the colors, the detail. What are you after?"

Undoing my shirt, I touched my chest. "Here in the heart area."

He pointed for me to sit on the chair.

Holding a book with designs, he asked, "Let me guess, a girl's name?"

I nodded. "Have you got a rose in a heart?"

"Sure have. That's a classic. What's the name?"

"Ava."

"That shouldn't take long. Short and sweet." He opened up his designs and showed me a red rose embedded in a heart. "How about that?"

I nodded. "Yeah. Nice. And her last name happens to be Rose."

"Good." He studied me for a moment as if sizing me up. Even though I'd had that all my life I'd never gotten used to it.

"Is there an issue?" I asked.

"None, man… Only, it's going to hurt."

"Anything to do with the heart generally does," I said, tilting my head. "I'm a grown man. I'm no pussy when it comes to pain."

"I'm sure you're not," he said with a throaty laugh. "Are you sure she's the one? I mean, this is indelible."

"I've never been more certain. Even if she walks. I'll still hold her here." I touched the spot to be inked.

He nodded. "We're passionate about our women, us men. They think it's only them. But when we love, we go all the fucking way." His dark eyes had that worn, trusty glow about them.

My lips curled up at one end.

CHAPTER TWENTY-THREE

AVA

Charlie greeted me with his customary cheerful smile as I stepped into the dimly lit cubicle. "What floor, ma'am?"

Maybe he was going senile after all, I thought. The fact I'd only ridden the elevator the day before took me aback. "Ten, please, Charlie." I emphasized his name.

He nodded. "Agatha's it is."

"We spoke yesterday, and you mentioned Ashley, Aggie's late husband." I jumped straight in. Knowing that we had precious seconds, I needed all the information I could get.

"A good, upstanding man. Great tipper. Aggie wasn't so good. Depended on the day. And how much she'd had to drink." He chuckled.

"Was Aggie a big drinker back then?"

"No more than any of us. We all like a bit of fun, don't we? And banning booze had made it so difficult. Hanging out with mobsters to get a fill."

"Ha?" I replied, just as the elevator arrived.

I remained on the spot. "You were around during the Prohibition?"

"I've been here from the beginning." A smile crossed his face again. "Have a good day, ma'am."

I stepped out of the lift. Aggie owned the entire floor and above. But what about below? I wondered. And why was the elevator always on the ground floor whenever I arrived?

I'd never seen anyone in the lobby. It felt as if I were in an episode of *The Twilight Zone*, a show my dad had introduced me to and one that I'd grown very fond of due to its themes of parallel worlds and time distortions.

When I arrived at the door, I knocked before turning the key.

I crossed the large, sunny living room, and looking through the French doors onto the terrace, I discovered Aggie on her cane throne.

Despite the relief at finding her well again, I felt a tinge of disappointment too. Curiosity had gotten the better of me. Upstairs had become that place of mystery that I found myself thinking about.

"There you are," said Aggie.

"Hi… I let myself in. I did knock."

"Yes. Yes. That's why I gave you the key. Saves me from having to get up." She leaned in for a cigarette.

"Are you good, Aggie? After yesterday…" I studied her face. She looked well rested, nothing like the frail woman I'd witnessed the day earlier.

"I'm terrific. Never felt better. What do you mean by yesterday?"

Her eyes narrowed as if she had no idea what I'd alluded to. Either Aggie was a great actress, or she had completely forgotten my visiting her bedside.

"Can I make you a martini?" I asked, shifting my weight.

"You're being evasive. But yes, do."

"There's no ice," I said, staring down at the empty ice bucket.

Aggie was lost in her own world again, so I scurried off to the kitchen and found it bare. No food in sight. Only gleaming stainless-steel bench tops, as if it hadn't seen food or activity ever.

I opened the fridge and found it empty. I told myself that perhaps the cook needed to shop, although that did little to quell my suspicion.

Pushing the button, I held the bucket under the cascade of ice-cubes and then returned to my task of pouring spirits into the martini shaker.

Without giving it another thought, I poured the mix into two glasses. I really needed something. My nerves were on edge due to the planned meeting with Bronson later on that evening.

I still hadn't decided what I should do. A battle raged between my heart and head.

While I carried our drinks back onto the balcony, Aggie scrutinized me with alarming intensity. "You look unhappy, Ava."

Sipping my martini, I wondered if I was that transparent or whether Aggie really did possess mind-reading skills.

I shook my head. "No, I'm good."

"Tell me about that strong man of yours. Have you rid yourself of that weakling lawyer?"

Had I told her Justin was a lawyer? Having not slept well, I could hardly recall what I'd told Aggie about my personal life.

"Yes." I kept it short and sweet.

"There's no need to be coy, Ava. I like to know about you. It keeps me youthful and fresh staying in touch with the romantic shenanigans of the young and beautiful."

"It's not a game, Aggie. I'm too sensitive for that."

Wincing at my brittle tone, she replied, "Of course you are." She sat back again. "I always liked listening to stories about romance. We're women, after all." She chuckled. "And just because I'm old doesn't mean I don't feel anything."

I nodded thoughtfully. "I've had a few issues with Bronson."

"The tall, handsome, strong one. The one that's been in prison?"

I nodded. "I found something in his diary about getting back at Justin by sleeping with me."

"Mm… revenge. A natural urge."

For some reason, the icy note in her voice made me tense. "I am more concerned that he's using me as a weapon."

"Using you as a weapon? Tell me, how was the sex?"

I flinched. Was I about to share that with an old lady who happened to be my boss? My face heated up.

"Ah… that good. He made your toes curl?"

"Too much information, Aggie."

She laughed. "Monty made my toes curl."

My face turned sharply toward her. "What happened to Monty?"

"He married Penelope. But we were still together. You see, no one was as acquainted with his heart as I was." Her eyes had gone remote again. "We met, behind Penelope's back, sneaking about like teenagers." She sniffed.

"You had an affair, you mean?"

"It was never that. I hate that term," she snapped.

"I'm sorry," I said.

"You possess a curious spirit, child. I did too, once," she said in a conciliatory note. "Monty and I were together from the start. And he's still here." She touched her heart. "We'll be together again. It's eternal love."

"Do you still talk to him?"

Aggie took a sip of her drink. "Read to me. The part where Cathy's dying."

That again, I thought. I could have almost recited it by heart. The book still lay by the table where I'd left it last.

I flicked through the pages that seemed to know where I wanted to go, for the worn hardback opened on Aggie's favorite passage effortlessly.

I read Heathcliff's lines: "I have not broken your heart—*you* have broken it; and in breaking it, you have broken mine..." And once again, Aggie held her arms and rocked.

I even started to wonder whether Aggie experienced her memory of Monty through Heathcliff. From the little I'd learned of Monty, he seemed just as humorless and hardened in spirit as Emily Bronte's brooding hero.

She lit yet another cigarette and regarded me. "That's enough. Now, are you going to forgive your new man? He had every right to seek revenge from that lawyer."

"They're brothers," I said.

The fact that Aggie didn't even flinch at that comment made my spine stiffen. "Then it's only natural. Betrayal, revenge, and robbery are common among blood relatives."

Despite that grim outlook, I'd grown accustomed to Aggie's dramatic take on things.

"They're not related by blood. Bronson was adopted."

"Oh, an orphan. Clarke was an asshole," she said.

"Who was Clarke?"

"My brother. Monty, who was also an orphan, arrived at the age of five, my age." She looked up to meet my eyes. "My older brother used to lock him up. He did awful things to him. Until Monty grew up. Then he became a tall, strong man, and the tables turned. Monty had revenge sewn into his heart."

"That sounds rotten. About Clarke, I mean."

"It was more than that. It was criminal. Clarke was deranged. The horrid things he did to Monty."

"What happened to Clarke?"

"He died from alcohol abuse." She took a sip of her martini. "You'll forgive Bronson, I hope. I can understand his need to get back at this Justin, especially if he was responsible for imprisoning him."

"Did I tell you about that?"

"How else would I know?" She tilted her head. "Answer my question."

"I'm meeting Bronson later on. He just told me that..." I played with my fingers.

"That he didn't realize he'd fall so hard for you?" she asked, raising an eyebrow.

"Yes. Something like that."

"Ah..." She continued to puff on her cigarette pensively.

"He scratched our names on a tree in the park," I said.

Aggie looked pleased. "Oh... that's eternal."

A shiver ran up my spine. "Huh?"

"Initials carved into a tree will link two souls together forever. For certain. Monty and I are there." She pointed in the direction of the park.

"But you don't think it's too soon? We've only been together once." I asked.

"Darling. I saw you the day after. You were walking on cloud nine. That's love. None of this 'get to know each other and let's see where it goes' nonsense. One knows straight away. Chemistry. It's all about chemistry. It hits you hard here"—she touched her heart—"and it happens from the moment you set eyes on each other."

"But there has to be more to it. What about personality and conversation?"

"Ha... Conversation? Isn't that why girlfriends were invented? And in any case, nothing oils the tongue as does a good..." —a wicked smile formed on her face—"round of tennis."

"Tennis?" Expecting her trademark ribaldry, my voice went up an octave.

She laughed. "I'm playing. You know what I mean. In my day, that was a euphemism for fucking."

My smile lasted a second before a frown settled over me. "What about financial support and marrying for stability?"

"Who tells you that? Don't listen to that nonsense about the need to be supported by a rich man. A loveless marriage makes for a painfully dull existence."

"My mother insists that one needs a man with a good job and money."

"Tell me. Did your mother marry for love or for money?"

"For love," I said without having to think about it, considering how much my mom adored my dad.

"Is she happy?"

I nodded slowly. "Yeah. She complains about my father being a lazy so and so..."

She pointed. "There. You see. It's okay for her to marry for passion, but not for you. A double standard if I've ever heard one."

I nodded. Aggie was right. Even about Bronson. Our chemistry *was* off the charts.

CHAPTER TWENTY-FOUR

BRONSON

I contemplated the tree with our initials carved into it as I waited for Ava. She was late, which led me to the conclusion that she'd changed her mind, the thought of which added to a dull pain in my chest. I reflected on all that had happened that day, including the late phone call from my uncle telling me he'd called the CEO and that Amber Moore had been put on notice.

I hated getting people into trouble. It was, after all, just a bit of harmless flirting. That being the case, using sex as a bargaining chip was a game that lacked taste. James had been right to take it further. At least our project had generated a buzz with the consultancy firm, who stood to make a bundle should government officials sign off on it.

From a distance, I saw Ava heading toward me. I felt her energy despite the hordes of people. She was hard to miss. Her considerable grace made it appear as though she glided instead of walked.

My heart pumped harder, making the ache in my chest intensify, especially when our eyes met and her smile became mine.

"Hey." I rose and took her into my arms. A stab of pain made me start.

"Are you okay?" she asked.

Before I could reply, her eyes settled on the bandaged area of my chest.

She touched her mouth. "Oh my God, have you been injured?"

"It's okay. It's not self-mutilation. Well, maybe a little. But not by me," I said, with a half grin.

Her eyes widened. "How do you mean?"

I grinned while stroking her hair, which radiated her intoxicating signature scent of jasmine.

"Bronson, stop messing with me."

I held my hands up in defense. "Hey... it's all good. It's a tattoo."

Her forehead creased. "When did you get that done?"

"A couple of hours ago. It was a spur-of-the-moment thing," I said, taking her hand. "Come on, let's sit for a minute."

She lowered herself next to me. Her eyebrows were still drawn together. "Does it hurt?"

"A little. But I'm a big boy. Nothing I can't handle."

She nodded gently.

"I'm glad you came," I said. "I didn't think you were going to make it."

"Really?" She scrutinized me.

I stared down at my watch.

"Sorry, I got caught up with Aggie. She's responsible for me being here in many ways."

Now it was my turn to look surprised. "How?"

"She told me that revenge is a natural human instinct. And that after what Justin did to you..."

I interrupted her. "You told Aggie about me and my imprisonment?"

My rough tone made her wince. "I'm sorry. She's really inquisitive, and for some reason, Aggie draws everything out of me. I didn't mean to tell her."

The tension in my neck relaxed, and regretting my harsh response, I said, "Sorry. You probably needed someone to talk to. You said she encouraged you to meet me. What about you?"

Ava opened her hands. "I'm completely flummoxed."

"That's understandable. I'm sorry for putting you in this position. I never thought I'd fall this hard for you. It wasn't my intention."

"But having sex with me to get back at Justin was?"

I puffed out a long, slow breath. "Yeah, well…"

"Anyway, Aggie explained to me that you plotting revenge was justifiable."

My head pushed back. "This Aggie sounds pretty wise, if not a bit personal."

"She's more like a grandmother. One with a dirty mouth." She raised an eyebrow, which made me chuckle.

Placing my arm around her waist, I drew her toward me, but when her body stiffened, I released her. "Too soon?"

"Let's talk. We haven't done much of that," she said.

"I have spoken more to you than anyone else, ever," I said, staring down at my feet. "I'm not a big fan of questions. And talking never really sat well with me."

"Ever?" She turned to stare me in the face again.

I nodded. "I'm not great with words, Ava."

"You seem really intelligent and sharp to me."

A faint smile touched my lips. After a pause, I asked, "Are you hungry? We could grab a bite somewhere.

"Yeah. I could kill a burger or something fatty and disgusting."

I relaxed completely at that suggestion. "Now you're talking my language. I know just the place."

We stood and faced each other.

I brushed her cheek. "Ava, I'm happy to take this slowly if you like. We can just hang out. We don't have to…" I shrugged.

She bit her bottom lip, which made my mouth water since I wasn't sure how long I could go without tasting her again.

"What's the tattoo?" she asked.

"You'll have to wait and see. That way you'll come back and see me in a few days."

We both lingered in front of the scratched "BL loves AR" heart on the grand old elm tree.

"Aggie said that carving love declarations into trees makes it eternal."

"Then she's on the same page as me. This boss of yours sounds intriguing and scary."

Ava nodded. "You're not kidding. She's definitely a little scary."

"Do you think it means that?"

"Eternal love?" she asked.

I nodded.

Her eyes glistened under the lamplight. I wasn't sure if she was about to cry or not. But I took her into my arms anyway, and although my chest protested due to pain, I didn't care.

"It just seems so intense and somewhat rash," she said.

"Who can measure time where love is concerned?" I asked.

She pushed out my arms. "Now you're sounding like Aggie."

"What? Scary?" I asked.

"No… I mean… maybe." She looked downward.

When I lifted her chin, I was met by that searching, uncertain gaze I'd grown used to seeing. "Those notes happened before I knew you. I ripped that page out and burned it."

"Did you?" Her eyebrows knitted. "But what about the bit about clearing your name?"

"Would you accept me if I did?"

"Bronson, I accept you now."

I took her hand, soaking in her reassuring gaze. My heart thawed, and just like that, the strain of the past day vanished.

A flush of pleasure rippled through me as her rosy cheek touched my lips. "Come." I took her soft hand. "Let's go and eat something."

CHAPTER TWENTY-FIVE

AVA

Bronson stared at me without blinking. His eyes darkened, showing raw lust as he slid in. A long sigh left his parted lips as he filled me.

The extreme stretch tingled through me, sitting somewhere in that euphoric line between pleasure and pain. He was so big he stretched me to the extreme. Holding onto my waist, Bronson guided me up and down.

With each thrust, my moans deepened.

Aware of his fresh tattoo, I was careful not to rub against him, even though I really wanted to.

Slow but deliberate thrusts teased oversensitive nerve endings.

After he'd licked my pussy to that toe-curling point of no return, it had become hypersensitive.

His thrusts rubbed against what I'd discovered must have been my g-spot, because with each entry, an electrical impulse rippled through me.

My fingernails dug into his big arms, which were slippery from sweat.

It had all started with a kiss in the cab.

Bronson led me by the hand. No words. We'd hardly spoken at all. It was not easy around him. He robbed me of my senses. But it was okay. I'd grown used to our silences. It added more poignancy when we did speak. And after Justin, who babbled endlessly about nothing, it was kind of refreshing to be with someone who only spoke when something needed saying.

In any case, Bronson's body language made up for any lack of words. All it took was a gaze from those penetrating eyes or his hand in mine or that tender touch, sometimes under my skirt, regardless of location.

When we got back to his place, my body took over, dictating every move.

Although I'd never seen myself as a seductress before, Bronson had definitely fired up my sexual awakening.

Within moments of stepping inside, I removed my dress.

Before arriving to meet him, I'd chosen the sexiest underwear I could find, only because I knew that I couldn't stay away from Bronson. Whatever his motives had been, I was too weak to stay away. And like any other self-respecting hedonist on this planet, I chose to ignore the consequences of giving into blood-hot desire.

His eyes darkened as they wandered over my half nakedness. Returning the favor, I ogled Bronson when he lowered his jeans and came toward me.

I let out a deep breath. Swollen and wet, I opened my legs, and the rest was like one big lusty dream.

His finger hooked into my panties. He ripped them off and then slid inside of me while his hot mouth ate at mine.

Trailing kisses down every inch of my goose-pimpled flesh, his lips settled on my nipples. He groaned when my breasts fell into his grasp.

When his lips ended up between my legs, blood coursed through me as his tongue circled my inflamed clit. The slow, tormenting gyrations had me crying out from pleasure.

My fingers ran through his hair, nearly ripping it out due to the ferocity of my orgasm.

My body fitted perfectly into his, even with that tattoo, which I was careful not rub against. His hard cock twitched against my thigh. I ran my hands over it. Velvet and steel hard. The head dripped over my palm.

He kissed me, and I tasted my release when his tongue entered my mouth.

Desperate for him to enter me, I opened my legs wide. He mumbled something about being turned on as he stared at my drenched pussy.

Deep and hard, that first thrust made me cry out. He looked at me to make sure I was okay. Holding onto his big arms, I impelled him to continue.

Soon the pain turned into addictive pleasure, of the kind I couldn't get enough of.

I tingled all over. Each wave of heat threatened to take me far.

His face reddened as his thrusts built with urgency.

My pussy spasmed tightly around his cock until I finally surrendered to sensations of fiery waves that made me scream.

As he squeezed his eyes shut, Bronson's jaw tensed, and his head fell back. My name left his lips as he rode his climax. After that, we fell onto our backs, panting.

At that moment, while my breath slowly steadied, I just knew I was in love, even though it could have just been the flood of hormones or that heady high that comes from connecting deeply with someone through the sharing of passion. Whichever way, I gave in to that profound sense of belonging to another soul.

He'd become a part of me.

The past had turned into meaningless dust.

It was early morning when I woke. Finding the bed empty, I rose and grabbed the sheet, which I wrapped around me, and headed for the living room. There I discovered Bronson with pen in hand, writing something down.

Gazing up at me with those chocolate eyes, he looked so boyish I wanted to devour him. His naked buff chest, where my addicted fingers and lips had feasted earlier, looked tan and smooth. Bronson wore loose gray sweats that hung really low, showing off a trail that led to the promise of more sheet-gripping pleasure.

My eyes settled on *that* tattoo, which I'd been so careful not to rub against, noticing that it was exposed at last.

"Hey. I didn't wake you, I hope?" he asked with a faint smile.

As I shook my head, my eyes fell onto the mark on his chest.

I stepped closer to look at it, given Bronson had been vague about its design.

He stared back at me with that typical half grin of his that suggested so much while saying so little. His dark, thick hair, as usual, was messed up perfectly from his constant fingering.

As I moved closer to study the tattoo, my face crumpled in disbelief. "You have my name on your chest."

"I have," he said, looking pleased with himself.

He leaned back in his chair in order to study my reaction, which had gone from disbelief to tears in one breath. I'd never been such a crybaby until meeting Bronson, which was kind of embarrassing upon reflection.

Rising, he came to me. I dropped my sheet and fell into his arms, careful to place my head against the other side of his hard chest. He seemed so tall as he crouched down to hold me.

"A shower?"

I nodded and followed him as though in a dream.

"Is it permanent?" I finally asked.

"It's a real tattoo, Ava."

"A heart and a rose. My last name is…"

"Rose," he interjected. "It's a beautiful name. It suits you because you're insanely beautiful."

"Insanely?" I laughed.

"Yeah, well… I'm so into you, I've lost my mind."

"But we've only just met," I said yet again.

Testing the water first, Bronson lowered his pants.

My body nearly collapsed from an overdose of attraction. With that perfectly proportioned physique and shadowed chiseled jawline accentuating that sensuous, almost carnal mouth, I couldn't believe such a perfect specimen of masculinity could want an ordinary girl like me.

"Why are you looking at me like that?" he asked, running his hand over my breasts and drawing me close against him again.

"I'm wondering how I can keep a man like you interested."

Detaching from me, he stared deeply into my eyes in that scrutinizing, soul-reaching way that made my knees go weak. "You're a young, beautiful rosebud that will bloom and become even more beautiful. Even after a rose has died, there's a heart. Its beauty remains forever."

I melted under the cascade of hot water.

"When did you become so deep and romantic, Bronson?" A tear slid down my cheek.

A sad smile touched his lips. "I've always been on the outside. Alone in many ways. That tends to make one think about things."

He placed some body wash on a sponge and massaged it over my body. The intensity of his focus and his demonstrative body language left little doubt in my mind about Bronson's devotion to me. As he swept over my contours, Bronson expressed an appreciative groan that transmitted straight to my sex.

I touched his cock, which was steel hard. In the broad light of the morning, seeing Bronson naked pumped unbridled lust through my veins. He'd made me insatiable, which came as a surprise, given that I'd never had such a high libido before. While my girlfriends purred and gushed over the latest heartthrobs, I preferred balancing a book on my thighs rather than an oversexed frat boy.

I lowered myself to my knees. Arousal dripped saliva onto my tongue as I licked my lips.

He was so big my mouth had to stretch wide, and my jaw ached as I moved in and out. Bronson leaned against the glass cubicle, his eyes shut and his lips apart. His extended groan encouraged me to continue moving my mouth up and down his shaft.

Sore jaw or not, I kept going until his distended veins pulsated on my tongue. My lips pursed and gripped his thick length.

"I'm going to come," he said in a strangled tone.

On a mission to take all of him, my tongue flickered away at the creamy head, sucking him dry as hot, thick cream shot to the back of my throat.

Bronson tried to pull away, but I remained steadfast.

After he returned to the land of the living, he took me into his arms again.

The water went cold, and we both jumped out.

"I have to move somewhere with a better hot water system," he grumbled.

I responded with a giggle as he dried me vigorously and slapped my bottom in the process.

While I dressed, Bronson made us coffee and toast.

As I entered the living room, I found him walking about with a towel around his waist.

"I can do the rest while you change," I said.

Placing a plate of toast in front of me, Bronson said, "You don't like a half-naked man serving you?"

"I like it very much. Too much." I chuckled. "You're like a male supermodel."

He sniffed. "Not with my record. I'm nothing."

Searching for a glimmer of a smile, I stopped buttering my toast. Instead, his serious, almost cold expression sent a shiver through me.

Softening my tone, I said, "Hey, I'm sure you'll clear your name somehow."

"I don't know how. All I've got are photos."

He went off to the bedroom, leaving me to deal with my jarred nerves. Bronson's mood shift had taken me by surprise.

A few moments later, having changed into jeans and a worn-out gray T-shirt, Bronson returned, still in a dark mood.

"What photos?" I asked.

He picked up his cup and took a sip of coffee, he replied. "I've got some images of Justin doing blow."

"Cocaine?"

Biting away at his lip, Bronson nodded.

A picture of someone who would never rest until he'd walked somewhere dark suddenly appeared before me.

That alone should have made me run.

Crime, retribution, drugs were all the subjects I enjoyed in books or even films, but in real life, I was out of my depth.

Bronson gathered his designs and placed them in a portfolio, reminding me that he wasn't just some twisted guy in search of trouble but a uniquely talented individual.

He stopped what he was doing, and his gaze bore into me again. It was unnerving, making me shift in my chair.

"Am I too dark for you?" he asked. His forehead lowered.

"A little," I said.

"Then why are you here?"

I met his glare in the hope that he was kidding. Instead, my heart clenched.

"I... want to be here." My voice was thin and jittery. "What are you doing, Bronson?"

He held my gaze, steady and tight, but then his eyes softened, and he came to me and held me close.

My chest collapsed, and I started to cry.

"I'm sorry, angel. You're too good for me."

I pulled away. "Are you trying to find an excuse to leave me?"

He combed through his hair with his fingers almost violently. "No fucking way. I want you." He pointed to his tattoo.

"Then why say that to me?" I asked.

"Because I want to fucking shine for you. Make you proud of me."

"I already am. Your drawings, your talent. You…"

He cupped my head with his hands, and his lips took possession of my mouth again.

It was a passionate, hungry kiss as his tongue tangled with mine.

Just as his hands caressed my breasts and his mouth ate at mine, the phone went off.

He ignored it. A few moments later, it sounded again.

We separated. "I should take that," he said.

I covered myself with the sheet again. Bronson kept watching me as he spoke on the phone.

After he ended the call, Bronson said, "I'm sorry for being a fruitcake." He let out a deep breath. "I should probably see a shrink. I had a few sessions in prison, and that kinda helped."

"You can speak to me about anything, Bronson." I nodded reassuringly. "I'm part of you, and you're part of me. We're in this together."

His face cleared, and his eyes flickered with warmth, something I'd grown so needy for that I would have done anything just to keep seeing him like that.

Touching my cheek, he leaned in and kissed me tenderly. As he drew away, his eyes shone with sincerity. "Marry me."

I stepped back, my eyes widening in shock. "Ha?"

"I've never been more certain of anything in my life. You're breathtaking, Ava."

"It's way too soon, Bronson. Let's get to know each other first. You don't really know me. I'm actually quite a boring person."

"Bullshit. I love listening to you talk. You're intelligent. You never bore me. You're exciting to be with." He held both of my hands. His eyes had a hint of vulnerability. And again, Bronson reminded me of a lost boy.

"But that's only because I'm new."

"New?" His eyebrows met. "You've been here all my life." He touched his heart.

I shuddered because that reminded me of something Aggie had said about Monty.

"Bronson. I'm new. We've only slept together twice."

"Don't you feel it?" he asked, his eyebrows knitting.

"Of course, I do. I wouldn't be here, otherwise. But your intensity...."

He stepped back. "I frighten you, is that it?" Bronson's face had gone dark again. He let go of my hands and raked his hair.

Not waiting for my response, he turned his back and moved about, clearing things away.

As I followed him around, I answered, "No." But then he turned to look at me. And when I saw that dark, restless need in his eyes, I confessed, "Maybe you do a little."

Bronson rubbed his neck. Eating me alive with his gaze, he just went stone cold and looked away.

"Bronson, look at me," I asked, my voice cracking.

He pointed to the door. "Leave."

I froze. "What?"

He turned his back to me again, and tears streamed down my face. *How did we get to this?* I wondered. A moment earlier, it had been undying love.

In a daze, I dressed quickly and left.

My legs trembled as I leaned up against the elevator wall. I was relieved to be alone because tears poured down my cheeks.

I reached the ground floor and drifted through the glass doors back onto the street like a ghost. Stepping onto the pavement, I nearly ran into the crowds going about their busy morning.

Drowning in a whirlpool of emotion, I moved forward slowly. After I reached the end of the block, I sensed someone close behind and turned.

Bronson touched my arm, his mouth wide open from puffing.

It seemed as though we were in our own little bubble standing there staring at each other. At that time of the morning, when people had to be somewhere, the masses moved around us.

After what seemed like ages, I collapsed into his arms. I had to. It would have seemed cruel to do otherwise. Bronson looked so broken.

"I'm sorry, angel."

After we unlocked arms, words escaped me. Incoherent from the deluge of emotion swamping me, all I could do was stare down at my feet.

CHAPTER TWENTY-SIX

BRONSON

"Don't leave me, Ava. That was my fucked-up head in there. I promise to work on myself." I couldn't believe those words actually left my lips. I'd never heard myself pleading like that before. It seemed as though years of pent-up emotion spewed out of me, as though a demon had taken over me.

And I hated myself for it.

"You're the one that threw me out," she said at last.

I shook my head, trying to make sense of myself. "You had this look on your face."

"What look was that?" Ava challenged.

As I visualized her shocked grimace, I tried to find the right words to describe it.

Ava interjected. "It's just that it threw me, I suppose. That tattoo… you asking me to marry you…"

"Would you have preferred I didn't get the tattoo?" I asked.

"No… but you had it done while we were broken up. That I don't understand. You must have been seriously confident that I'd take you back."

"It was nothing like that. It was just a spur-of-the-moment thing. I passed a parlor and…" I shrugged. "Hey, let's not talk here." I pointed over to the park.

Ava allowed me to take her hand. When I felt how cold and shaky it was, I hated myself even more for throwing shit into what should have been a great morning.

My chest relaxed when we hit the avenue of trees, a path I normally jogged on to sweat out my rage.

We found a bench and sat down.

I turned so that I could stare Ava straight in the face.

"Even if you hadn't taken me back, I'd still carry that tattoo with total conviction. Because for me, Ava, it was love at first sight." I took a breath as I drank in her eyes pooling with tears. "I want you so badly it hurts."

"But it shouldn't hurt, should it?" she asked, taking a tissue out of her bag.

"It did when you left me. It cut deep. In many ways, that tattoo helped mask the pain I felt. And you're wrong about me. I've never been confident about anything. I got that tattoo more for myself, as a testimony to true love. Whether it's one night or an eternity, I know I found that with you, Ava."

"I feel the same, Bronson," she replied with a breathy voice that made me want to kiss her passionately. "I had a terrible time of it, too. And after you told me to leave earlier, you may as well have dug a knife into me."

"I'm sorry, angel." I stroked her damp cheek. "I'm defensive and suspicious to a fault. I jump to conclusions all the time about everyone. Especially those closest to me. Ava, you've got to understand that being left alone in that crib has made it difficult for me to believe that I'll ever be worthy of anyone's love."

Having never voiced that before, I hated how pathetic it sounded. Ava's response was pity as her limpid eyes drowned in tears, causing people's heads to turn as they went about their "normal" lives.

I didn't give a shit, even if displaying emotion in public challenged my private inclinations. But I'd changed. That last admission had come out of nowhere before I'd had a chance to stop it.

If anything, it exposed how fucking weak I was.

"God, Bronson... Shit... I'd never do anything to hurt you. I want to be with you. It's just that marriage at this stage is a bit too rushed. Maybe if we were seriously drunk in Las Vegas or something, you know how you hear those stories of dwarfs marrying people, or Elvis impersonators acting as priests."

If she was trying to make me laugh, she succeeded. A raucous eruption from my chest left my lips. When it settled, I replied, "Ava... if and when we marry—that's if you'll forgive me..." She squeezed my hand, which answered that very nicely for me. "There won't be a dwarf or an Elvis impersonator within sight."

"Now you're being dwarfist," she said, cocking her pretty head.

"That's so ridiculous I won't dignify it with a response," I said, returning her smirk.

She looked up at me, and her smile faded. "I now understand why you kicked me out."

I stroked her thick, brown hair, which glistened with red highlights in the morning sun. Her crookedly buttoned blouse brought a glimmer of a smile back to my lips. She was even more beautiful for it.

Ava gazed up at me with that uncertain, shy smile. I rolled my tongue over my lips so that I could make a meal of hers.

I towered over Ava more than usual because she wore flat shoes.

"I want to protect you. Not push you away with my crazy shit."

Before she could respond, I took her into my arms.

We kissed as passionately as if it was our first kiss.

Because it was a sunny morning, there were dog walkers, joggers, and every other type of humanity crowding the park, but I didn't care. Kissing as if it were midnight in the middle of the morning owned its own special magic.

"Are we good?" I asked, my chin touching my neck as I studied her face.

She nodded with a smile. "Yeah. I get it, Bronson. You've had a difficult time."

"I don't want your pity, Ava. I couldn't stand it."

"What about empathy?" A curl came to her lips.

"I think I can handle that." I brushed her cheek. "Tonight?"

She nodded with a sweet smile.

As I wiped the sweat from my brow with the back of my hand, I let out a long, slow breath. I'd nearly fucked up the most important thing in my life.

After a final kiss, I stood there and watched Ava walk off into the morning light. Her shapely ass with that natural sway made me hot again.

When I got back, I returned a call I'd missed from James.

"Hey, Bronson, I got a call from Caswell's Consulting."

"And?"

"There's a formal event tomorrow night. They've invited us so that we can rub shoulders with a few of the councilors, who are on the same page as us with regard to this project."

"Do I need a tux?"

"You do. It's a dinner. You can bring someone. I've invited your mom."

"I'll ask Ava, then." An uncomfortable knot formed in my gut. "I hope Mom will be cool, considering Ava was with Justin only a few weeks ago."

"She knows."

"You told her?" I asked.

"Alice was worried she hadn't heard from you, and Justin was acting all weird on her about things, so I told her everything. She's with me now, Bronson. We have no secrets."

"Yeah. Sure. I'm good about that. Ava's part of my life. Mom had to know sooner or later, I guess."

"Then get out your swankiest suit."

"Do you think it's a good idea? Aren't you the front man? The clean guy."

There was a pause. "Look, Bronson, the designs and ideas are all that matters. Even though I'm bankrolling it, we're in this as a partnership."

"If someone asks what I've been doing for the past year, I'll tell them I've been making furniture. Which is kind of the truth." I chuckled.

"It will be fine, Bronson. The designs speak for themselves. People aren't as interested in what one does in their private lives as you may think, especially where there's a buck to be made."

A tight breath left my lungs. "Send me the details. I'll be there."

I got off the phone, changed into my work gear, and headed off to the site.

"I'd love to see you in that pink dress you wore to Marc and Cassie's engagement party," I said, watching Ava swan about in her tiny apartment clearing away clothes as she looked for something to wear for my business function.

Having always been a clean freak, I found sitting amid her mess challenging.

The interior, at least, wasn't half as bad as the exterior.

From the moment I'd arrived at her apartment's ground-level entrance, which didn't require a key or card, I'd started to worry. As I stood before the non-descript seventies building that would have been cheaper to bulldoze than to renovate, I checked out the dirty neighborhood. It was packed with lowlifes offering everything from cheap blowjobs to drugs. For a moment there, I even forgot that I was visiting the flower that was Ava, and that I was back in prison, considering one scumbag was like any other in my book.

When I finally made it to the fifth floor, I had to take a moment to steady my breath, given that the elevator didn't work, after which I told Ava that I hated her living there.

She led me inside and let me kiss her, or I should say devour her lips. They were hot and moist and filled with so much promise that I instantly forgot about everything else.

Ava said, "I'm moving soon."

"Why don't you move in with me?" I asked, stepping out of her way as she cleared some room for me to sit on the couch.

A frown touched her pretty brow. "Look at all my stuff."

I stretched out my tired legs. It had been a big day on the site. Every day was.

My eyes did a sweep of her space. She had a point. I couldn't even find the wall, there was so much stuff strewn about.

"Are you a collector?" I asked, looking at the bookshelf that not only held countless volumes of hardback books but all kinds of bric-a-brac. It was too much for the eyes to take in.

She laughed. "No. But I don't like getting rid of things."

I nodded pensively. *Opposites attract*, I thought to myself.

"I can live with that. I could always get a cleaner," I said as my eyes wandered into the kitchen, settling on the stacked-up dishes.

Ava looked embarrassed. "I've been busy writing and working. And I'm shit at dishes. Sorry."

"Hey, it's all good. I love doing dishes. Here, I'll do them for you."

"What?" Her eyes widened in disbelief. "No you won't. I didn't invite you here to wash my dishes."

"Then why did you invite me?" I raised an eyebrow and smirked.

Her cheeks reddened slightly, which made heat travel down to my groin.

I patted the couch for her to sit.

From there, it got seriously dirty as my hands crept under her bra and unclasped it. I let out a deep sigh as I caressed her soft, full breasts. My mouth watered at the thought of her erect nipples. I'd been dreaming about this moment all day.

Her nipples spiked against my tongue as my fingers walked up her velvety thighs, where I felt a moist wonderland of womanliness.

My chest collapsed with desire. I needed to smell her, taste her.

She wriggled out of my hold. "I haven't showered."

I took her back into my hands. "All the better."

Before she could respond, my tongue licked slowly over her bud, and after a tiny bit of tension, she surrendered by allowing me to make a meal of her pretty pussy.

I clasped her ass and held her close to my face as she gyrated through a release. Her breathy moans sent my cock into a frenzy.

Remaining with her legs apart, Ava began to close them, and I shook my head. "Please don't."

My cock went blue as I eyed her creamy pink opening, which was slick with a mixture of saliva and cum.

She remained there all rosy cheeked and heavy-lidded as she looked at my cock, which throbbed impatiently.

"You look so fucking hot, Ava," I said.

"So do you," she said with a breathy voice.

"Sit on my lap," I said.

I held my cock so she could lower slowly onto it. My chest collapsed from the fiery pleasure of her tight, wet opening.

Ava was hot and responsive. I'd never felt a woman like her before.

Her breasts fell onto my face. I'd always loved big breasts, and Ava was stacked. They were natural and soft. Sheer perfection.

I moved her up and down slowly at first. Her hair was loose and wild.

Ava's eyes had that sexy glow of lust as my unshifting gaze remained on her pretty face, while blood pumped furiously down to my groin as her tits bounced up and down.

Her hips gyrated in my hands as I held on. The friction from our frenzied pace took me over the edge. Ava's lips parted, and her eyelids fluttered as her pussy went into a spasm and squeezed my cock senseless.

I blew with such intensity that a loud groan left my lips.

"You're mine," I gasped, holding her tightly.

CHAPTER TWENTY-SEVEN

AVA

Bronson turned heads as he entered the room. It wasn't just his six-foot-two frame but that he radiated charisma. Self-effacing to a fault, Bronson was totally unaware of his charms. He wasn't exactly the most affable person, more bad boy than anything else. But for some reason, probably to do with primitive urges, women went gaga over raw testosterone. And Bronson had plenty of that.

The fact that he looked ridiculously handsome in that snug black suit that fitted his body in all the right places, made it impossible not to stare.

I forgave all the women in that room for ogling him despite a little jealous muscle tweaking within. That was new. I'd never been jealous before. But then, I'd never felt that type of profound attraction before.

Dressed in the classic pink gown that Aggie had given me, I felt out of place, given that most of the women wore tiny bits of fabric exposing plenty of flesh.

Bronson clutched my hand almost possessively. I didn't mind. If anything, I gloated at the envious pouts directed my way.

"I feel old-fashioned in this dress," I said.

"You take my breath away. You look beautiful. Like a princess." He kissed me on the cheek. "A sexy one."

His hot breath caressed my ear. "And you fill that suit in ways that are making me melt. Women keep looking at you."

"They don't even register, angel."

His eyes held a sweet twinkle, which I'd never noticed before. Bronson seemed relaxed. He was nothing like the tense person who'd faced me a few days back. Not that I'd forgotten that bone-chilling moment he'd turned antagonistic within a breath. But I could do little but stay close. I couldn't run away from him.

The tattoo had touched me profoundly, even if it did also freak me out. Cassie's jaw had dropped when I told her. She even admitted to feeling jealous at how intensely romantic my connection to Bronson had become.

The function was in full swing when James came to join us with Alice close by his side, who cast me a reassuring smile. It did feel rather awkward considering that she'd met me when I was dating Justin. But then she whispered, "Life is strange like that. In some families, love can sometimes be shared."

I returned a faint smile. Her comment reminded me of Aggie and her romance with a half-brother, which seemed incestuous, even if they weren't related by blood.

James said, "Bronson, there are a few people I'd like you to meet."

Bronson squeezed my hand. "Back soon."

"I've never seen him look so happy," said Alice.

"His designs are visionary," I said.

Alice nodded. Her eyes filled with admiration. "As a boy, Bronson spent most of his spare time making things. He made us so much furniture. All very useful and well made. He was a good boy."

Visualizing a scruffy dark-haired boy, I smiled. But as I observed him across the room with that tall, almost noble bearing and his hair with enough product in it to make it look suave, Bronson could have made a perfect James Bond. And it was patently obvious that every female there seemed fixated on him. I couldn't help but notice their eyes following him with unshifting attention.

"It's a shame about what happened."

I looked at her. "His imprisonment, you mean?"

She nodded grimly. "Yeah. It's broken him. I saw the same desperate look on his face when he came to us as a five-year-old. He just covers it up well by showing a tough exterior. But when no one's looking, he reverts inward again."

I'd seen that remote expression on many occasions. Although it made me recoil, it also made me want to take Bronson into my arms and hold him all night long.

"Do you think he suffered?" I asked.

"In prison? Or as a child?"

"As a child," I answered.

"He did. For the first year, he screamed at night and slept with us. That was when Justin's resentment began. I had a hard time convincing Justin that I loved them equally. I don't think he could ever come to terms with the fact that we'd let someone else into our inner sanctum."

"Do you regret it? I mean, it sounds like it caused problems."

She shook her head. "No. Elliot, Bronson's father, was also adopted. And he wanted to help make a difference for one of those little lives. Those places aren't nice."

"No." I thought about a young Bronson and those remote looks I'd grown used to. "Bronson speaks often of his need to find his biological parents."

"I know." A sad smile cast a shadow over her face. "All that was found in his crib was a memento. No note."

"A memento?" I asked.

"A cameo. It's beautiful. Bronson would often spend hours looking at it as a child. It broke my heart. He has such a sensitive soul underneath that tough-guy exterior. I just don't know what to do about Justin," she said, frowning.

"How do you mean?" I asked, uncertain whether Alice knew of Justin's drug issues.

"He's now with Candy, as I'm sure you know. He seethes at the mention of Bronson."

My legs tensed. "Is that because of me?"

"That, among other things. He's become aggressive and difficult to talk to. He keeps accusing me of favoring Bronson, something that he always did as a child. Mainly after I'd reprimanded him for misbehaving. He was out of control as a child. I think he may have suffered from attention deficit disorder. Justin could never focus on one thing for too long."

He still suffered that, I thought. "But he became a lawyer," I said.

"He did. I think that cocaine is a form of medication for Justin."

"Oh, you know about that?"

"Of course. I also suspect he was responsible for Bronson's incarceration."

My eyes widened. "Have you told Bronson?"

She shook her head. "What good is it going to do? It will destroy Justin's career. And I'm frightened to think of what Bronson will do to him."

"Bronson's obsessed with clearing his name."

A deep sigh left her lips. "Don't I know it." She looked at me with a mock smile of resignation.

James and Bronson came to join us.

"It looks like the sky's fallen. What are you two discussing?" asked Bronson, scrutinizing us both.

"It's all good," said Alice. "We were discussing what a handsome figure you cut in that suit."

A half grin claimed his face, which was always Bronson's response to compliments. For a seriously handsome guy, he didn't have a vain bone in his body, which was another thing I loved about him.

"That went really well," James said, looking at Bronson.

Bronson nodded before casting his attention to me. "With a bit of luck, this time next year, I'll be a rich man, and then we'll be set."

Alice looked at James and then at Bronson. "Is there something you're not telling us?"

Bronson took my hand and kissed it. "We're good."

That question came flooding back to me.

Was I ready to marry Bronson?

After his meltdown, warning bells had rung in the distance, even though the throbbing of my heart whenever he looked at me or stood close drowned them out.

It was midnight when we got back to Bronson's place. Watching him pacing about restlessly, I asked, "What's wrong?"

"Nothing." He combed through his tousled hair, which I was dying to do too. A glimmer of a smile chased his frown away. "I love you in that dress."

I rose from the couch and held him. "You seem a little tense."

He kissed my neck. "Not when you're close. I need you close all the time, angel."

"I'm not going anywhere," I said, looking into his eyes, which had gone black in the night.

"Then why will you not give me an answer?"

"It seems too soon. We've only been together for less than a month."

He nodded with that remote, glazed look.

"Is that why you've gone all moody?" I asked.

Bronson exhaled. "I'm pissed off that I can't stand proud and own my project because of that fucking conviction. That's all."

It was a stalemate. There it was again. Always the same ball and chain. I wished I could find a way past it for him.

"James will do the right thing by you, Bronson."

"I'd trust him with my life. It's not that. I would have loved to have registered the company in my name. I'm a lone wolf in many ways. Always have been."

"I'm here," I said with a tight smile.

"That's different. I need you like I need air."

I collapsed into his arms, and our lips met in a tender kiss that quickly turned hot and devouring.

He tilted my head back so his tongue could enter deeply.

His hands stroked my breasts, and he said, "I need you naked."

Bronson removed his jacket, and I loosened his tie.

Standing back to watch him, I indulged in some blood-pumping arousal as I undid a couple of his buttons. His tanned face stood out against the crisp white collar.

He lifted a layer of my silk dress. "I don't know why, but seeing you in this dress makes me feel safe."

"Ha?" My brow puckered.

"You look so familiar to me. Like I've known you forever," he said.

My mouth opened, but no words followed.

"Dance for me," said Bronson.

I was still getting over the earlier comment. "I'm not sure if I can."

"And all those years of dance classes, then?" He cocked his head.

His smile was so encouraging, I spun around, becoming lightheaded and giggly while my skirt swished about, floating in the air.

I stopped. "I need music to dance."

Bronson went to his laptop and pressed a few buttons and the song "Happy" came on.

A big smile filled my heart. I loved that song. Dancing wildly suddenly, I let myself go, performing all the moves I'd collected—some silly, some really practiced. Spinning then shimmying my shoulders and moving my head side to side, I clapped along just as the song told me to. Because I was happy, all right.

Looking amused, Bronson sat with his long arm stretched out over the top of the couch. I crooked my finger, and taking him by the hand, I coaxed him into joining me.

At first, he stood there with that sultry grin. Then his shoulders moved ever so slightly in a sexy shimmy. Oh, my God, he was such a stud, he made me go dizzy with desire. He lowered his head toward my face. Our foreheads were close to touching. His hips moved slowly and sensually like they did when he entered me. Bronson looked so bashful and manly at the same time that I wanted to eat him.

Holding onto my waist, he lifted me up and swirled me about, making me giggle like a child.

When the song ended, I fell breathlessly into his arms, and he carried me to the bedroom. There, Bronson sat back watching my slow, sexy striptease. The dark, lusty glow in his eyes made the whole performance worth it.

Especially a few moments later when, unable to wait, Bronson was so hard he entered me in one hungry thrust and sent me soaring.

It was still dark. I was on my back panting after Bronson had hit g-spots I didn't even know existed, making me scream through one orgasm after another. Beneath me, the wet sheet stuck to my sated body.

Bronson rose from the bed. His long muscular and athletic legs flexed as he strode about naked looking like a god. He then opened a drawer and brought out a box.

Propping myself up, I asked, "What are you doing?"

Bronson came back to the bed. He opened the box. Inside sat a silk scarf wrapped around something. He unraveled it, and under the lamplight, I saw a carved white pendant with a coral background and recognized it immediately as a cameo.

He handed it to me. And as I took the striking pendant, I shook my head, almost speechless. "It's beautiful, Bronson."

Despite recalling Alice telling me about it, I feigned surprise. I was uncertain how Bronson would take our discussing his sad beginnings.

"I want you to have it."

"But… isn't it valuable?" I asked.

CHAPTER TWENTY-EIGHT

BRONSON

That cameo was the most valuable thing I owned, sentimentally speaking. "Hold it up against your neck so I can see how it looks. I've never seen it worn by anyone."

She gazed up at me in wonder. "Really?"

"No one has even been allowed to go near it. I would have killed them."

The way her eyes shone with alarm made me regret that last comment. I normally hid those dark thoughts.

"Bronson, that's kind of scary."

I lifted a hand in defense. "Hey, just a figure of speech. I'm trying to say that you're the only person that I could ever allow to touch it. And now I want you to have it. As proof…"

"Proof of what?" she asked, studying me with those searching eyes.

I touched my heart where that tattoo sat. "Of my undying love for you."

She bit her lip, and her eyes watered.

"Will you keep it?" I asked.

As she fell into my arms, Ava's wet cheek touched mine.

After that, we lay in each other's arms tightly all night, and I fell into a peaceful sleep, my body wrapped around Ava's.

The following morning, after we'd fucked to the state of rawness, I sat back and watched Ava place the cameo in front of her swan-like neck.

"It's beautiful, sweetheart." I smiled.

It was Sunday. Since it was a day of rest, I lounged about shirtless in my favorite sweats. Ava kept groping at me. I loved that her shyness had relaxed, and as her hands crept into my pants, she stroked my cock, pumping blood down to my groin.

Wearing my shirt, she looked so sexy I wouldn't let her change. She was free of underwear just as I loved. My hands returned the favor by traveling up her thighs.

I licked my lips and then ravaged her again.

She wiggled in my hold. "Bronson, we're supposed to have breakfast."

I lifted my head to look at her. "That's exactly what I'm doing. You're delicious. And anyhow, you started it by touching my cock."

She laughed and surrendered to my tongue as her supple thighs opened wide.

The large block, which had once been a munitions facility, was cordoned off with barbed wire. Harry stood by my side as we studied the vast expanse of land. I'd decided to bring him in, given that he had the workers. I liked his no-nonsense approach, and he had an abundance of knowledge and experience.

And he also got me.

"What do you think?" I asked.

He nodded slowly. "It's flat. We won't have to cut into it, which will speed things up."

"The contract's signed. All we're waiting on is the check."

"What's in the ground?" he asked.

"All kinds of nasties. Seeing that it once was an armament's plant I imagine there's lead, cadmium. All your regular heavy industrial metals."

"No mines or unfired grenades, I hope," he said with a smirk.

Harry had been in the army before setting up a building firm. He was one of those tough guys who didn't let emotional scars slow him down. Always joking around, he'd helped me a lot, not only by giving me a job but also because he accepted me for who I really was. He didn't see me as some nobody who'd done time.

"Before we get started, the area will have to be decontaminated. I'm sure once they've been through it, we'll be able to grow organic tomatoes."

Harry's eyebrows contracted. "Farming's not part of the plan, is it?"

I chuckled. "Just pulling your leg, pal."

"You never joke, Bron. What's got into you?"

"I don't know. Life's starting to feel a little better." My mouth curled up at one end. "Especially since I met this girl."

He nodded. "Uh… It always comes down to the fairer sex, doesn't it? A good woman and life's great again."

A faint smile crossed my face.

He clasped his hands. "So we're, what, six months away?"

"Maybe. Depends on that check. We've got contractors ready to move in."

"Good. This is going to be big. It's a great location. Close enough to the main town. How did you swing it?"

"Luck. I guess that was the only positive thing about being locked up. I had plenty of time to read. I stumbled upon a trade magazine and read that the government was offering grants to revitalize industrial land in return for affordable housing."

Harry looked impressed. "So we're basically creating a small village?"

"Yep."

"Have you got a name for it."

I nodded. "Avahart."

"Mm… nice, after your girl?"

"Yeah," I said.

"She's really gotten to you."

"She's made me a better man."

"That's the sign that you've met the right woman," he said with that deep drawl of his. He patted me on the shoulder. "You're going to do good." He nodded with belief etched into his eyes.

For the first time in my life, I had a spring to my step. All those hours of devising and drawing had finally started to come to something.

After I left Harry, I headed back home. Having not slept much after four hours of slow and intense lovemaking, I needed to sleep.

But first, I returned a call I'd missed from my mother. "Hey, Mom."

"Darling. Are you good?"

"Yeah. Really good. The project's up and running."

"James told me all about it. I'm proud of you, son."

Her loving support made me gulp back a lump. "Is this about the dinner?"

"It is. James and I felt it would nice to have a few friends around so that we could share our news."

"Justin?"

There was a pause at the other end. "That's what I need to talk to you about."

"You want to invite him? With Candy?" I didn't hide my surprise.

"I'm not sure what to do. He's my son."

"Do what you feel is right. What about James? How does he feel about Candy being there? I hear she's trying to sink those fake talons into his fortune."

She sighed. "I'm not inviting her. But I feel I have to invite Justin."

"I suppose I can sit somewhere far away. But Ava will be there. Close by my side."

"That's the thing, sweetie. Maybe it would be better if she didn't come. That way it doesn't descend into chaos. You know how Justin is after a few drinks."

"I won't be there, then. Ava's part of me."

"I can't imagine you not being there, Bronson."

"Without Ava, I'm not going anywhere, Mom."

"Okay, darling. Leave it with me. I must admit James isn't big on Justin at the moment, either. Oh, why did he turn out this way? He was always a troubled child." Her voice trembled slightly.

My heart sank. "I'm sorry. The last thing I want to do is cause you pain. Perhaps you should have a word with Justin alone."

"I've done that. He's all pent up. Angry. Blames you. No, he blames your father for…"

"For adopting me?" I asked.

"Don't listen to that, darling. Your father loved you both equally."

"Then why did he cut me out?" I asked.

I'd promised myself to keep money out of it. But it hurt, knowing that my late father had written me out of his will. It would have made sense if everything had gone to my mother.

"I don't know what happened there. I looked at the original will. It distinctly expressed a three-way split. The lawyer told me that he'd drafted another one. Elliot never told me he'd devised a new one. He just reminded me, while he was in the hospital, where the documents were. The same documents that I still possess, which now, apparently, are null and void."

Gripping my cell tight, I smelled a rat. "Then something doesn't sound right, does it?"

She let out a long, ragged breath. "I spoke to James about it. He brought it up. He'd been concerned about it for some time. I just don't know what to do."

"I'd say Justin's a good place to start."

"Leave it with me. I'll arrange a dinner for just you and Ava, along with Marc and Cassie."

"That sounds good. I know Justin's your one and only, but something's not right. And he is a lawyer."

"He's not my one and only. You are just as precious to me, Bronson. Remember that."

"I will. Love you, Mom."

I ended the call. A dark cloud just floated over me. Yet again, fucking Justin. I needed to get a good lawyer to go over that last will with a fine-toothed comb.

CHAPTER TWENTY-NINE

AVA

As much as I liked taking the elevator in order to ply Charlie with questions, I needed the exercise. Before arriving for work, I'd met Cassie to discuss her upcoming wedding. While talking about my role as the maid of honor, I stuffed my face with delicious donuts and then begged Cassie not to make me wear a dress that resembled a wedding cake.

We giggled raucously while joking about the kinds of outrageous gowns we both could wear, and three donuts later, I waddled out of the café feeling sorry for myself.

After running up the stairs, I leaned against the wall puffing. A few moments later, I wiped my brow and then unlocked the door.

Nothing too surprising had happened that week, only Aggie talking about her life growing up, interspersed with heart-wrenching passages from *Wuthering Heights*. Always the same pages over and over— Heathcliff and Catherine's declarations of love while repeatedly mentioning death and hell. Emily Bronte, who had died at a young age, seemed obsessed with the darker side of human nature.

When I discovered that Aggie wasn't in her normal spot on the terrace, I fell into the floral armchair and distracted myself by looking at all the beautiful bric-a-brac, particularly the Art Deco lamps with figurines holding moons for light shades. Original paintings depicting flowers in vases, women in bright flowing gowns, and Impressionist landscapes all battled for space on the pink walls. But it was the lack of family photos and the way the room seemed barely lived in that struck me as odd.

Five minutes later, I became concerned about Aggie's well-being, so I decided to visit her bedroom.

Up the snaky, mahogany staircase I went. My hand slid along the smooth wood that framed black filigree railing. One step at a time, my feet landed on the red floral Persian runner.

Having arrived on the landing, I was again met by the chilling stare emanating from young Aggie. Except for that expression, she looked like me, and that, once again, freaked me out.

Noticing her bedroom open, I entered, taking small, hesitant steps into the darkened room. There, I discovered Aggie in bed, lying on her back.

As I approached more closely, I noticed her eyes were wide open.

Is she dead? I wondered.

"Aggie," I whispered.

"Who's that?" She turned but didn't seem to see me.

"It's me, Ava."

She looked in my direction and waved her hand for me to come forward.

"Are you okay? Do you need a doctor?" I asked.

"No doctors," she said.

Aggie pointed to the lamp by the bed. "Turn it on so I can see you."

I switched on the carved red-glass lamp and remained standing by her bed.

"Sit," she instructed.

Noticing a chair in the corner, I brought it over and lowered myself onto it.

Studying Aggie's blank, pale face, I asked, "Are you not well?"

"I'll have no questions. Just sit."

I nodded hesitantly. Her scraping response added to my growing tension.

Pointing, she looked at my neck. "What's that?"

"It's a cameo that Bronson gave me."

She crooked her finger. "Come closer. Let me see it."

As I leaned in, her eyes widened slightly, and her mouth dropped open. "It can't be."

Shaking my head, I asked, "What?"

"Take it off. I must look at it under the light. Now!"

My hands trembled as I unknotted the velvet ribbon holding the cameo against my throat and handed it to Aggie.

She rubbed her fingers over it the way a blind person would read braille. "This is a genuine piece," she muttered. "A flashlight. I must have a flashlight."

"Um… where will I find one?" I asked.

"In that drawer. There." She pointed to the chest of drawers beside the bed. I opened the top drawer and saw a box with a key, hankies and a flashlight.

I brought it out and fumbled with the switch to turn it on.

"Not on my face," she grumbled.

I apologized before passing it to her.

Mystified and bewildered, I watched Aggie's forehead scrunch as she scrutinized the cameo as a scholar might a rare relic. She looked up at me. "But this cannot be."

"What?"

"This belonged to my mother."

My muscles gripped. "How can you tell?"

"This marking, right here." She ran her fingernail along the back.

I reached out to take it, but she held onto it, almost possessively.

"It was originally my grandmother's. My grandfather had it carved for her in Naples. On the back, it's engraved. Here." She passed it to me. The item shook in my trembling hand. "Read what it says."

Taking the flashlight, I shone it onto the transparent pink back. There, I read, "Alan with a heart…"

"Joan," she uttered, finishing it for me.

My breath hitched. "It must be a coincidence."

"Where did he get it? You must tell me." The desperation in her tone made the hairs on my arms stand up.

"Um… he said it was the only family memento he owned."

"The *only* memento?" She whispered. Her forehead wrinkled as if she was trying to solve a puzzle.

Clasping the cameo, which was damp from my sweaty palm, I asked, "When did you last see it?"

"It disappeared along with Monty. The family accused him. And to be honest, at first, I refused to believe it. But when he returned, a year later, with that horrible wife and money in his pockets for the first time in his life, I did wonder."

"But then he would have sold it?"

"He insisted he hadn't. I asked and asked. Monty was a proud figure. Secretive to a fault. He rarely revealed what was in here." She touched her heart.

"But what about his undying love for you?"

"*That* was all he revealed."

"Then he must have sold it, and whoever gave it to Bronson purchased it from a secondhand shop or something."

"You said earlier that a family member gave it to him?"

"I think so." I bit my lip. I couldn't bring myself to reveal that the cameo had been found in his crib. It seemed so personal.

"You must find out. I need to know." She sank back under the covers again. "Go. I need to rest."

"Aggie, I'm worried about you. Can I call someone? Or wait here to watch over you?"

"No, child. Be gone. I'm well enough. I need rest. Go. Please."

I ran down the stairs as if I'd seen a ghost.

An inner voice kept repeating, "It's a coincidence, nothing but a coincidence." But something screamed louder at the back of my head.

After I raced out the door, I stood before the elevator, which was closed. I placed my ear against the wooden door but couldn't hear the cables operating. In fact, I'd never seen it in operation up at that level. Only on the ground floor. As if waiting for me.

CHAPTER THIRTY

BRONSON

Ava sounded so desperate to see me that I dropped everything and promised to meet her by our tree in the park.

I arrived to find her looking pale. Sitting down close to her, I took her hand and kissed her cheek, which was as cool as her palm.

"What's happened, Ava? You're freezing."

"That's because I'm chilled to the bone."

I began to remove my hooded jacket, but she stopped me.

"No. I'm not cold in that way."

"Ava, will you stop playing with my head and tell me what all this is about?"

She rummaged in her bag and brought out the cameo.

"Why aren't you wearing it?" I asked.

She stared at me square in the face. "Where did you get it? Tell me exactly."

"I've already told you. That cameo was the only thing they found in my crib." Admitting that sad little detail never got any easier, and seeing Ava studying me as if trying to understand how such a thing could happen felt like icy fingers walking up my spine.

"It belonged to Aggie's family," she said.

My jaw dropped. "What?"

"Aggie recognized it. Apparently, her grandfather had it made for his wife. Look…" She turned it over and pointed to faint carving. "She quoted it exactly. Without even looking at it."

Having seen it on numerous occasions myself, I too didn't need to study that inscription. I grabbed my cell out of my pocket.

Ava asked, "Who are you calling?"

Before I could answer her, my mom picked up. "Darling, how are you?"

"I'm okay." I pushed back a strand of hair from my damp forehead. "Mom, that cameo, how did it come about? I need the truth."

"There's nothing to tell. Only what you already know, Bronson. It was found in your crib wrapped in a handkerchief."

A loud breath left my dry mouth. "Are you sure?"

"Of course. We would never lie. I unraveled the cloth it came in. That was all we got from the orphanage."

I stared at Ava long and hard. "Some new information has come to light to do with the original owner."

"Really? Then follow it up, son. There could be the answer you've been seeking all these years. How odd. You'll have to tell me all about it."

"I will. Catch you soon." I ended the call and turned to Ava. "Take me to Aggie."

Ava bit her lip. "I'm not sure if she'll like that. She's pretty private."

"Then I need to go snooping around. I'll employ a detective to look into her past if I must. Are there photo albums, pictures? Can you get access to anything like that?" Words poured out faster than I could think.

Ava replied, "I suppose I could look around. I was in her bedroom earlier today. That's pretty empty, which is kind of weird, to be honest."

"Why?" I asked, suddenly obsessed with the eccentric lady that I'd heard so much about.

It suddenly occurred to me: Aggie might have even been my biological grandmother! The thought fired my veins with an impatient need to meet her despite a sudden prickle of discomfort. Because if we were blood-related, I would find it hard to look at her in face for abandoning me.

"There are no images of family. Except…"

"Except what?"

"Just that there's a painting of Aggie when she was younger…" Ava's stammering made me hold my breath. "She happens to look like me."

"Is this some kind of weird shit going on?" My voice had turned stony.

"What?" Her face contorted in alarm. "Are you accusing me of setting this up?"

I took her hand. "Hey. No. And even if you did, I'd still want you."

Her mouth pulled a mock smile. "Gee, thanks."

"Oh, come on, please, Ava. Don't…" I ran my hands through my hair almost violently. "Hey." I brushed her cheek and stared straight into her eyes. "I'm sorry, okay?" She nodded, appearing just as spooked as me. "But it *is* fucking weirdly coincidental," I had to add.

She nodded. "You're not kidding."

"Tell me, how exactly did you get this job?"

She bit into a nail. "Through an agency."

"That's pretty random."

"It is. Only… they asked for photos of me."

"Is that standard practice?" I asked.

"I haven't been asked for one before, not that I've gone for many jobs that way. After I lost my job, I wasn't sure what to do. Cassie suggested an agency, and they asked for my photo. After that, I got the job."

"Did you ask Aggie why?"

She nodded. "She said she wanted someone pretty to look at."

My head pushed back. "She's not like that, is she?"

"No… she's a fully-fledged man lover. She's pretty frank when it comes to her dalliances as a young woman."

Grabbing Ava by the hand, I said, "Come on, we're going there now."

Her eyes shone with concern. "I just left Aggie in bed."

I looked down at my watch. "It's only seven o'clock. You can introduce me to her. Explain that it's about the cameo…" My words raced along with my heart. "Damn it. Just tell her the fucking truth, Ava."

"Aggie could receive a shock if we turn up like this," she said.

I took a deep breath. Ava had a point. We should respect Aggie's age and need for privacy. "Then tomorrow, take me with you."

The following day, I met Ava at our regular meeting spot in the park. I'd been nervous all day about visiting Aggie.

As I took Ava into my arms, I kissed her and drew in the fresh, fragrant scent of her hair, which always filled me with hope and positivity. Despite our having spent the night together, she still managed to take my breath away.

Whatever this was, Ava was still the prize.

"Are you okay, baby? You look pale."

"I'm just a bit spooked," she admitted.

I lowered my head to look at her properly. "I don't believe in that stuff. I'm sure there's a reasonable explanation. And I *do* plan to get to the bottom of it."

"But there are so many weird aspects to this. I googled Agatha Johnson, researching the social pages of old *Vogues* and *Cosmopolitans,* but there was nothing about her anywhere."

I shrugged. "It's not like today where everyone's profile and image are locatable via popular media. Maybe Aggie was also private back then."

Ava nodded vaguely. "Let's do this, then."

When we arrived at the gray-stone Art Deco building, I almost forgot about the strange mission ahead of me and whistled. "I love this era of design. Very elegant."

Ava squeezed my hand. "Me too. It's a weird scene in there, though. There's no one around except Charlie. Let's ride the elevator so you can meet him."

The elevator was open, but there was no Charlie.

"Where is he?" asked Ava.

"Maybe it's his day off," I said, leading her in.

"But he's always here." Ava's voice rang with disappointment. "I so wanted you to meet him. He's like something out of a 1930's movie."

When we stepped out of the elevator, I had to adjust my eyes to the dark, moody lighting, which only added to a ghostly vibe.

I looked about me, and with each step, a strange feeling that we were being watched cast a shadow over me.

CHAPTER THIRTY-ONE

AVA

Bronson stroked the walls. "Silk wallpaper. No cost has been spared here." He pointed to the ceiling. "I love the geometric design. The detail is incredible."

A smile helped ease the tension that had followed me into that building. When no response came to my knock, I unlocked the door, and we stepped into the Aggie's opulent home.

Roses arranged in crystal vases filled the air with a pleasant scent. The fact that they hadn't been there the previous day indicated that someone had visited, bringing me relief. I hated the idea of Aggie being alone.

Assuming that Aggie was upstairs, I whispered, "Come with me."

We both looked up at the imposing staircase. Bronson ran his hand over the polished wooden balustrade, as I'd done the first time ascending that grand old staircase.

I spoke into his ear. "I don't want to frighten her. So don't follow me into the bedroom until I say."

When we reached the landing, Bronson stopped to look at the large portrait on the wall.

I whispered, "Who does she look like?"

His scrutiny shifted from the painting to me and back again. "What aren't you telling me?"

"I've already told you. I have nothing to do with this."

The way his eyes narrowed chilled me. I stared straight at Bronson in a bid for him to look at me, but his attention went straight to the open door leading into Aggie's bedroom.

Instead of embarking on an argument, which was what I wanted to do, given this sudden lack of trust, I headed into Aggie's bedroom.

She seemed asleep, so I crept in slowly and wavered while I stood by her bedside. It always felt intrusive being there.

I looked around the room, and a closet caught my eye. I snuck over and tried to open it, but couldn't.

I returned to Aggie's bedside, where Bronson now had joined me. We both jumped when Aggie murmured something. Noticing her eyes shut, I decided it must have been a dream.

Grabbing a chair, I sat down. Looking over at Bronson, I cocked my head toward the closet. My heart raced as I watched him tiptoe over to it. Just as he was trying to turn the handle, Aggie stirred and opened her eyes.

"Who's there?" she asked.

"It's Ava," I said, unsure whether she could see me.

"Oh… but you're not alone…"

At the sound of her voice, Bronson was by my side again. And before I could reply, she lifted herself up and craned her neck.

"Aren't you going to introduce me?"

Stepping closer, Bronson came into the light. It took a moment for her to focus, but when she did, Aggie touched her mouth. Her eyes widened, and a cry left her lips. "Monty! Oh, my soul… Monty! Am I dead?"

Then, just as I took her hand, it became limp. She'd passed out.

I panicked and looked to Bronson, who felt her wrist for a pulse before placing his hand under her nose. "She's breathing."

"She's had a shock," I said. Leaving him there alone with Aggie, I ran to the kitchen and bounded back up the stairs with a glass of water, spilling some of it along the way.

I found Bronson holding her hand, while Aggie smiled lovingly into his face.

Bronson turned to look at me, widening his eyes in puzzlement, as I handed Aggie the water.

"Have a drink, Aggie. I'm sorry to have shocked you this way, but Bronson…"

"Bronson?" A deep line grew between her eyebrows. "This is Monty."

He turned to me and responded with a subtle shake of the head.

"My darling Monty. I always knew you'd come back."

I lowered my voice. "Aggie… This is not Monty. It's Bronson."

"But he is his image. How can this be?"

"He gave me this cameo." I removed it to show her again.

Aggie studied Bronson. "You stole it, didn't you, Monty? I suspected you did. Is that how you came into that money? And to think, I defended you after Clarke pointed the finger at you."

Aggie's heavy breathing made it difficult for her to talk. I looked at Bronson and whispered, "Let her rest."

Just as he rose from the chair by her bed, Aggie grabbed for his hand. "Don't leave me again, Monty. You can have the cameo. I won't tell Mother." And then she dropped back onto the pillow and closed her eyes.

After making sure Aggie was still breathing, I led Bronson out of the room.

"She's delirious. I don't think you're going to get much sense out of her. And with her thinking you're Monty, that's only adding to her excitement," I whispered.

"Who the fuck's Monty?" Bronson asked, looking pale and bewildered.

I crooked my finger. "Let's go and get a drink. I could really use one. And I will tell you all about Monty. Or at least what I know."

"There's that closet," said Bronson when we were back on the ground floor. "We need to look inside it."

As I followed him to the lobby, that was all that he'd said. Bronson looked pale and unrecognizable as if he'd seen a ghost. I supposed that was probably how I looked too. At least I could now share the strangeness of this experience with another, I thought.

Standing before the glass doors, looking out onto the busy pavement, I couldn't help but wonder at the stark contrast between the empty, old-world foyer that seemed to trap time and the endless parade of humanity pushing time along. Holding cells to their ears, they pounded the pavement in a very different world from the one I was just in.

We finally settled for a quiet bar only a few doors up from Aggie's. I ordered a martini, of all things, while Bronson went for a double shot of bourbon.

Taking a sip of the calming drink, I said, "Bronson, I'm not involved in any kind of crazy scheme here. I hope you realize that."

He gulped down half a glass of liquor. "What do you know about that painting? She looks a lot like you."

"So you keep saying," I responded coolly.

He touched my hand, thawing the chill that had settled there. "I don't think you cooked this up to lure me, Ava. It's just fucking strange."

"How do you think I felt when I first saw it? I obviously look a lot like Aggie did when she was my age." I knitted my fingers together. "It's a coincidence, I suppose." That last comment lacked conviction, given that coincidence seemed too lame an excuse for the conspiracy theories I'd come up with.

"I don't believe in the supernatural, Ava." Bronson's intense gaze bored into me.

"Nor do I, Bronson. If you keep implying that I've got something to do with this, I'm going to leave right now." My quivering words were fueled by the fiery liquid that slid down my throat.

Shaking his head vehemently, Bronson grabbed my hand and leaned forward. The intensity of alarm emanating from those dark eyes caused the hairs on my arms to spike. I was witnessing firsthand what the fear of abandonment looked like.

An audible sigh left me. Locking eyes with my intense boyfriend, I gulped down my martini as though it were lemonade.

Having already finished his drink, Bronson beckoned the staff.

When the waiter arrived, he collected our empty glasses, and asked me, "Another?"

I nodded.

After the drinks arrived, Bronson said, "You promised to fill me in on Monty."

Brevity was not one of my virtues when it came to the retelling of events. That being the case, I ended up relating everything I'd heard and experienced during my visits to Aggie. Given that his DNA was potentially woven into the story somehow, I had Bronson's unflinching attention.

"Then Monty must be my relative," he responded after a long period of reflection. "I'm too young to be their love child. Do you think Aggie's my grandmother?"

I responded with a decisive shake of the head. "Impossible. Aggie never gave birth. She did tell me, however, that Monty married Penelope, who then became pregnant."

"Then Monty must be my grandfather, I suppose," said Bronson.

"I'd say so, going on Aggie's reaction. You're his double it seems."

The more I thought about it, the more I saw how ridiculous the whole situation looked, so much so that I started to laugh.

"Why are you laughing, Ava?" His serious glare only added to my dark amusement, which I couldn't help, because I kept seeing Aggie lunging for Bronson.

Bronson's features softened a little. "I suppose I'd laugh too if I were watching it play out. She did look like she was ready to pounce on me."

"You do have that effect on women, Bron," I said.

"Bron?" His lips curled with a hint of a smile.

I responded with a smirk. It was either that or lose my mind. "Can't I call you that?"

He stroked my hand. "As long as you let me rip your panties off, you can call me whatever you want."

"Then we better get back to your place, Bron," I said, playing with his fingers and relieved to have a break from what had been an intense couple of hours.

As we were leaving, Bronson said, "You do realize I have to get to the bottom of this?"

I stopped walking and said, "I wouldn't expect anything less from you. In any case, my curiosity's piqued big time."

"I need to get into that closet," he said.

As that same thought crossed my mind, I remembered that key in the drawer by Aggie's bed.

CHAPTER THIRTY-TWO

BRONSON

I clasped my beer as if it was my last drink. James had a dramatic expression on his face. And suddenly I expected that he was about to tell me that the project had stalled.

"What's up, James? You've just downed that shot like your life depended on it." I watched him toy with his bottle of beer. A shot in the late afternoon, followed by a beer chaser suggested something was eating away at my normally moderate uncle.

"Marc had a big night out with Justin two nights ago. It was Justin's birthday."

I remembered that dirtbag's birthday like I remembered all my family's dates. For some reason, I had a good memory for birthdays.

"That must have been a lonely affair." My dry tone made my uncle's mouth curve at one end.

"Your mother arranged a dinner for him. I didn't go, because Justin had insisted on taking Candy."

I sniffed. "Mm... why does that not surprise me? He only ever thinks about himself."

James sipped his beer. His eyes plowed into me.

"Okay, out with it. The short version. I need to meet Ava soon." My foot tapped impatiently against the bar stool.

Since meeting Aggie, I hadn't had a moment's rest. Questions swirled like a kite battered in a storm. Even Ava's sudden presence in my life perplexed me. Other than her calling me that first time, I had to keep reminding myself that I'd been the one doing the chasing.

James said, "Justin dragged Marc out for a big night on the town. You know Justin, always looking for a party." He circled his bottle slowly while collecting his words. "Look, Bronson, he admitted to it."

"What?" I studied him intently.

"He admitted to stashing the coke in your room."

"That's old news. Except…" My mind started to tick away. With those photos I had of Justin doing powder, coupled with a testimony from Marc, it would be enough to crucify him.

"Would Marc testify?"

James shrugged. "It's very complicated. None of us are surprised. But it would mean Justin being struck from the bar."

"I don't give a fuck about that. He's ruined my reputation. I lost one year of my life because of that prick."

"Alice has already spoken to Justin. Today, I believe. He's come out swinging. Saying that it's all bullshit and that there isn't any proof."

"I could make this dirtier if I want. I've got a photo of him snorting coke," I said. "With Candy."

His brow moved. "You have?"

I nodded.

"Then, there's something there. It will kill Alice."

My poor mother. I hated having to put her in the middle of our battle. "There's another way," I said.

"What's that?" he asked.

"The will Justin cooked up."

"You believe Justin forged your father's will?"

I cocked my head. "What do you think? I'm sure Mom's told you about the original will she found. The one that Dad, with his last breath, spoke about."

He nodded solemnly. "Something doesn't smell right for sure. He's getting around in that flashy red BMW, and he's just splashed out on some swanky penthouse on Park Avenue."

My knuckles had gone white thinking about how much Justin had fucked me over.

"I've got another matter to deal with that's pretty out there in the priority department. But I'm determined to get my hands on that last will."

"You mean to contest it, then?" he asked.

"What would you do, James?" I raised a brow.

He sipped his beer pensively, and then looked up at me and nodded slowly. "Yeah. Sure. I'd be walking into that attorney's office and demanding the details. Your mother has the right to do that."

I let out a deep breath. How I dreamed of being on a beach somewhere with Ava dressed in a skimpy bikini, away from all the crap.

Rising, I patted him on the shoulder. "Hopefully next time we can talk about the project. But thanks for the update. I'm glad you're on my side."

"I always have been, Bronson. Elliot thought the world of you."

I swallowed a tangled lump of emotion at the mention of that great man that had been my father. Who said one needed to be related by blood to love a parent?

Ava looked pretty in a flouncy blue blouse that echoed the light in her eyes. I loved that she was feminine and subdued and didn't flaunt her perfect curves to the world. A tingling sensation surged through my veins, making my strides quicker as I approached her.

"Hey, pretty girl," I said, kissing her rosy cheek.

Her smile slipped and a cloud crossed her face. "Are we really going to do this?"

I took her hand. "I've got you."

"I know you have, Bronson. It just feels so sneaky."

"I have to know, Ava." We stood in the middle of Fifth Avenue. A busy afternoon crowd moved around us. Their lives seemed so normal, while ours was anything but. "For us," I added.

Ava remained frozen on the spot, devouring me with a questioning gaze. "What do you mean?" she asked finally.

I took a deep breath and bit my lip. Articulation having never been my strong point, hijacked by emotion, I became speechless.

"Do you think that I am part of some conspiracy to bring you here?" Ava asked, resentment coating her words.

"No. But this is fucking strange. The coincidence is too weird. It's almost freaking supernatural."

She sighed with resignation. "There's a fine line between coincidence and the supernatural, you know."

Ava's matter-of-fact tone did little to quell my unease. If anything, it only stirred things up. "So you think that Aggie's a ghost?" I asked. When she didn't respond, I protested, "But that's fucking preposterous."

The crowds were so distant that it seemed as though a plate of glass separated us, like some kind of warped parallel universe, despite our shoulders nearly rubbing with those rushing by.

I took hold of both her hands. "All I know is that I love you, Ava. If you have come to me through some ghostly process or whether it is just plain outright coincidence, it doesn't matter. You're a part of me." I touched my heart.

Her eyes softened, and then we fell into each other's arms and forgot about everything else.

My mouth ate at her fleshy lips with feverish need.

Ava pulled away and looked at me, her eyes sultry and aroused. But then she blinked, and an earnest frown washed over her again. "I'm worried about Aggie. I should call a doctor. That's knotting me up the most, to be honest. But she won't let me."

"Come on, let's go and visit Aggie."

Ava studied me again.

"What's that look?" I asked.

"Just you calling her that. It sounded familiar on your lips."

"Ha?" My brow scrunched. "The only thing familiar to my lips…" I touched her mouth and pointed down to her groin."

She giggled. "You've got a one-track mind, Bronson."

"I haven't heard any complaints," I replied dryly. "And in any case, it's a two-track mind."

"And the other?" she asked.

"Finding out who I really am."

"Is that an existential or ancestral quest?"

"Both, Ava." I drew her close to me.

The marble floor in the lobby had a mosaic that I hadn't noticed before, mainly due to the rush of emotions last time I'd visited that attractive building.

Grabbing my phone from my pocket, I took a photo.

"It's gorgeous. I've been admiring it from the first day I arrived," said Ava, watching me.

I nodded. "I have this thing for mosaics. In another lifetime, maybe."

She smiled at me again.

"What?"

"You're so cute when you drop that intensity."

"Okay. I'll bear that in mind and look for more mosaic floors."

She hit me gently on the arm and giggled.

That was just what we needed to remove the edge of what was about to come because something told me we wouldn't be doing much laughing up there.

Ava pulled a face when we discovered the elevator empty again, disappointed that the character she'd met was nowhere to be found.

We stepped in and rode up to the tenth floor, and I stroked the walnut walls.

"Is that all you can think of?" asked Ava.

I grinned at her glower. Even pulling faces, she was beautiful. "Apart from your body, I'm kind of obsessed with stroking wood for some reason."

Ava took my hand and smiled.

When the elevator arrived at the top floor, we stepped out into the hallway and walked over to Aggie's door.

Watching Ava knock on the door, I asked, "Don't you have a key?"

"I have, but I like to alert Aggie that I'm arriving."

After what seemed a long time to wait, I became impatient to enter, so I cocked my head toward the key, and Ava opened the door.

Like the first time I'd visited, the room was clean and pristine, in that unlived in way.

"Aggie must be upstairs," whispered Ava.

When we got to the top, I had to pause at the painting of Ava's look alike. This time I inspected it closely. The frame seemed recent. The wood had that fresh look about it.

"Why are you smelling that?" she asked.

"Because it's only recently been framed. I know fresh wood when I see it." I ran my finger over the oil painting. That too had a bright sheen to it. It didn't seem worn with time as a fifty-year-old painting would be. My suspicion was confirmed by the painting hanging at its side, which looked dull in comparison.

"Do you think..." Ava was interrupted by a voice in the distance.

"Who's there?"

Ava headed straight to the door of Aggie's bedroom.

"Is that you, Ava?"

"Yes, Aggie." She approached the bed while I hid at the entrance.

"I'm glad you're here. Come sit."

Ava picked up a chair and lowered herself onto it.

"I saw Monty the other day. He had the cameo. I think he did steal it after all. I'm sure Mother will understand. He's made good. Moved up in the world and beautiful. So handsome."

I stepped back into the hallway, even though I was dying to charge in and ask questions. It was obvious that Aggie was either out of it or a better actress than Meryl Streep.

"Aggie, I'm worried about you. Are you eating? Can I get you something? I really wish you'd let me call a doctor to see you. I worry about you when I'm not here."

"No doctor," Aggie snapped. "But a martini would be nice. Anyway, Louisa's been here. She made me eat this mushy horrid stuff. Don't worry about me. I have a button somewhere that I can press."

Ava looked around and found a beeper hanging by the side of the bed, placing it close to Aggie.

"I'm not in any pain. Now go and get me that martini."

"But is that wise?"

When Aggie sighed dramatically, Ava rose.

I followed her downstairs.

We entered a kitchen that looked as if a meal had never been cooked in it.

"How am I going to get into that closet?" I asked.

"I don't know. We're going to have to improvise. Aggie's in and out of delirium. She seems to think you were an apparition, but just now, she was lucid."

We returned to the living room, where I watched Ava concoct a martini like a professional bartender.

She looked up at me with a nervous smile while shaking the silver receptacle. "Why are you looking at me like that?"

"At least I know where to go if I ever get a taste for those."

"One of my many skills," she said, raising an eyebrow.

"I look forward to discovering more. I've already stumbled upon a few," I said, pinching her ass.

She jumped back. "Not here."

"Why not?" I asked. "From what you tell me about Aggie, she wouldn't mind."

Ava smiled and continued to pour out two martinis.

"Are you making her two?" I asked.

"No, one's for me. Aggie always insists I join her. Do you want one?"

I rubbed my neck. "I could use a bourbon." My eyes went straight to a bottle of Bulleit. "She's got good taste in liquor."

I poured half a glass and drank it as if it were water.

CHAPTER THIRTY-THREE

AVA

The martini was just what I needed to take the edge off my nerves. Taking little sips, I sat by Aggie's bedside, hoping she'd soon drop off, while Bronson waited in the hallway.

Noticing Aggie's eyelids lowering, given she'd just drained half of her martini, I pounced on the opportunity to get to that key I'd spied earlier in the drawer.

My heart pounded against my rib cage. With one eye on Aggie and the other on the drawer handle, I pulled on it slowly.

The key stared back at me, and just as I clasped it, Aggie stirred.

"What are you scouting around for?" she asked.

"Just looking for a hanky," I said, grabbing a white fabric square with lace corners.

"There are plenty in there. Help yourself," she said.

After managing to grab the key, I removed a hanky and wiped my nose.

Painful seconds ticked away.

Then Aggie asked me to read to her, so I headed downstairs to grab a copy of *Wuthering Heights*, passing Bronson the key along the way.

He followed me downstairs again and headed straight to the bourbon, taking a swig out of the bottle.

The sinews in his forearms swelled as he lifted the bottle. His dark eyes brushed over my face, easing into a tender smile as he wiped his lips.

I responded with a tense smile. Even with all this cloak-and-dagger stuff, my body, with a mind of its own, melted over Bronson. That moment of arousal was short-lived, though, because as I peered up at the stairs, fear gripped me again.

A touch of guilt streaked my spirit. Sneaking around left a bad taste in my mouth. But the force of nature that was my lover, coupled with my own thirst for knowledge, had taken control.

When I returned with book in hand, Aggie was fast asleep.

I tiptoed out and gestured to Bronson with a hasty nod.

With Bronson by my side, my fingers quivered as I unlocked the closet door. Forgetting to breathe, I quietly opened the door, whose squeaky hinges were in desperate need of oiling, which didn't help my jumpy nerves.

Upon opening the door, we discovered not a closet but a small room.

Bronson cocked his head for me to remain on watch.

When I heard Aggie snoring, I allowed curiosity to get the better of me and followed Bronson in.

Bronson stared at something that had stopped him in his tracks.

Adrenaline charged through my veins. *This was not the time to linger,* I thought.

I tapped his shoulder gently as a gesture for him to do something, but then my eyes landed on the object that had captured his attention.

Time stretched into a gaping hole.

My jaw fell open, and a silent gasp scraped at the back of my throat. The need to maintain silence made it even more painful, for what I really wanted to do was scream.

Instead, I placed my hand in front of my mouth as my eyeballs stretched out of their sockets.

To my horror, floating in a jar filled with liquid, was a pink fleshy object. The ridiculous notion that it might be an alien, or something else that shockingly unreal, formed in my brain, because to my imagination's defense, it did look like some kind of disfigured embryonic form. In many ways, I wished it had been. Because an otherworldly explanation for that ghastly floating thing would have almost seemed easier to swallow.

Although this discovery had made my veins turn to ice, I had to understand what the hell that thing was.

Meanwhile, Bronson lifted the jar and turned it around to study it closely. The pink, fleshy thing seemed to pulsate.

A gasp left my lips. *Was it alive?* I wondered.

He turned to look at me with a stupefied frown that I was certain mirrored the one carved on my face. "What the fuck?" his lips mimed.

Harnessing as much inner strength as I could muster, I forced myself to study it a little closer, only to discover that the bulbous pink object had what looked like a large scar.

I murmured, "Fuck!" It finally dawned on me that the thing in the jar was a heart.

My lunch made its way to my throat and I had to turn away from the ghastly sight.

"Is that what I think it is?" I whispered.

Bronson nodded, and a grim expression shadowed his face.

After studying it a little further, he placed it back on the shelf.

Next to the gruesome jar stood a photo in a gold frame housing an image of a blond woman who looked like a younger Aggie and a man who looked exactly like Bronson. Although he wore gray, high-waisted, loose slacks and was not as buff, the face was Bronson's.

The resemblance made my knees weaken.

That was Monty with Aggie. And more significantly, she didn't look like me. Although I should have been relieved by that knowledge, it only fueled more questions.

Who was the woman in the painting, then?

Even though it had been a matter of minutes, it felt as if we'd been in there for hours. Aggie's heavy breathing in the background allowed me time for a few steadying breaths of my own.

Gripping the photo, Bronson leaned against the wall, his eyes glued to the image. He seemed lost in a world as distant in time as our ability to make sense of it.

Aggie groaned and then started to mumble. Our heads turned sharply toward her bed.

Closing the door to hide the light, Bronson signaled for me to go and check on her.

After I was satisfied that she was fast asleep, I returned to find Bronson peering into a shoebox that contained photos and other odds and ends.

All the while, I had to stop myself from looking at the corner where that ghastly jar with that heart stood. Morbid and terrifying as it was, I bore witness to a woman's obsession, as I could do little but conjecture that the scarred organ had belonged to Monty.

How it had gotten there bothered me the most.

Sweat shone on Bronson's brow and his hands trembled as he rummaged through the box.

There was so much in there that he tucked the box under his arm.

"You can't take it," I whispered. "Aggie may look for it."

Bronson looked as if he'd been to the other side. He took a deep breath and nodded.

He settled on a few photos, all of Monty. Bronson placed one in his pocket and continued to look through the contents of that box.

An envelope addressed to Aggie Johnson, with "personal and private" stamped on it, fell into his hand. He took that and tucked it into his pocket too. There was nothing else in there of interest, although I noticed Bronson revisit some of the photos of Monty. The one that he'd tucked into his pocket was an image of the dead man's face.

The face that Bronson shared.

I went on before him to check that the coast was clear. As Aggie's snores filled the air, I gestured for him to follow.

When we got to the landing, I noticed he had the jar in his hand.

"You've brought that with you?" I asked. I couldn't stand the idea of being anywhere near it.

He pointed for me to descend the stairs.

Once we were in the living room, out of Aggie's earshot, Bronson put the jar down and studied it again.

He ran his fingers through his mess of hair. "That's a freaking human heart."

Unwilling to look at it for any longer, I said, "Are you sure?"

"Of course, I'm sure. And what's more... Look at the scar," he said, pointing at the jar.

Unlike me, Bronson didn't seem the least bit squeamish.

Taking a quick peek, I had to swallow back a deluge of revulsion, as though it was a big fat hairy spider in there.

"That's a stab wound. That's how he must have died. Stabbed in the heart."

Flinching at the graphic description, I asked, "What are you going to do with it?"

Having gone pale, Bronson set it down. "I don't know. But one thing's for certain: here are the remains of a murdered person."

"Do we call the cops?" I asked.

"I don't know." Bronson wiped the jar with his T-shirt.

"I think you should return it to where it was while we think this through properly."

He ran his tongue over his lips and held my gaze for a moment. I could almost see his mind ticking away. "That's probably the sensible thing to do."

After sneaking the jar back to where we'd found it, we sprinted down the stairs.

I puffed in a bid to keep up with Bronson, who seemed like he was on a mission to get somewhere fast.

He took me by the hand when we reached the street. "Let's grab a cab. I need to get home."

That remote, intense expression had returned.

Thinking he'd want to be alone, I asked, "Do you want me to leave you to it?"

His eyebrows indented sharply. "Are you kidding? I need you there with me. Please, Ava…"

Bronson's chocolatey eyes gazed down at me, making me melt into his arms. "I just thought you would need some space."

"I've had space all my fucking life," he said.

He grabbed my hand, and while that comment stormed through my emotions, I followed along.

When we arrived back at his apartment, I fell onto the couch and started to breathe properly again. All the earlier oppression had slowly started to thaw away. I felt safe there, even with Bronson and his edgy vibe, as he continually ran his fingers through his hair and paced about.

On our way home, Bronson hadn't spoken a word. He'd just kissed my hand and then spent the entire trip staring out the window. I thought he would have at least read the letter he'd taken from the box.

That was to come. The delay was justified after we discovered its content.

Bronson flicked his laptop lid up.

"What are you doing?"

"I need to see how big the human heart is."

"Do you think it's Monty's?" I asked, already knowing the answer.

He puffed out a breath. "That's the logical conclusion."

"She must have murdered him."

Lost in thought as he studied the screen, Bronson nodded slowly. "Yeah. I agree. What's Monty's last name?" He asked.

"Are you going to check for any unsolved murders?"

He nodded.

"Aggie's surname is Johnson. Her maiden name, which I can't recall, would be the same as Monty's."

Bronson's head pushed back sharply. "Huh?"

"They were siblings." I grimaced. "Not by blood, though."

"Fuck. How twisted," said Bronson to himself.

"Hey... I think Aggie's name's written on the inside cover of the books I've been reading for her," I said.

He nodded slowly. "Good. That's a start."

"When I visit tomorrow, I'll look for it."

Bronson continued to type on his laptop.

"So why would she have murdered him?" I asked.

"My grandfather, you mean," said Bronson, staring at the letter that he'd taken from his pocket.

"You're convinced that he was that?" I asked, knowing it was a stupid question.

"You saw Aggie's reaction to me." He removed the photo from his pocket and studied it closely before handing it to me.

As I took the worn crumpled photo I said, "I hope Aggie doesn't notice it missing."

That same penetrating, intense stare reflecting off the black-and-white photo dispelled all doubt that I had Bronson's relative before me.

I looked up at Bronson. "The likeness is incredible."

Lost in deep contemplation, he bit his lip. A few moments later, he rose and headed to the fridge. "Wine?"

"Yes. Please."

After pouring a glass of chardonnay, Bronson twisted off the top of a beer and came back to join me, handing me the glass.

He continued to pace about.

I patted the sofa. "Sit here, and relax for a moment, Bronson. You've had a big shock."

Clutching onto the envelope he sat down and placed his bottle onto the elliptical-shaped table that he'd made from gnarly wood that as a child had reminded me of eyes.

Bronson studied the handwritten page that sat flat on his hands. Every now and then, I glanced at his face, noting that the furrows on his brow had not smoothed.

When he finished reading it, he placed the letter on his knees, and it wafted to the ground. As a result, I bent down and picked it up.

Bronson had entered his own little world, which I recognized well enough, for his eyes had gone black and remote— a look I'd never seen on anyone else before.

He went over to the balcony and looked out.

Staring down at the letter, I murmured, "Do you mind if I read it?"

He shook his head while continuing to sip his beer pensively.

I took the letter into my hands and read:

Agatha,

I can't bring myself to call you dear, because you are anything but that to me. By the time you read this, many years would have passed, and I will be dust. That said, my ghost will continue to haunt you. Especially if you fail to do what I ask.

As no doubt you will have noticed, this letter is postdated. I have given strict instruction to my attorney to have it delivered to you when my son turns twenty-one, or in the event that you fall ill before he turns that age.

Sadly, you were the only living relative. Not that I thought of you as that, given that you were not my father's real sister, a small blessing, I suppose. Otherwise, the incestuous nature of your affair would have been too difficult to stomach, even for someone like me, who's seen it all.

Being myself an orphan, I toyed with the idea of leaving my child with you to raise. But knowing how twisted, conceited, and shallow you are, I couldn't bear the idea of entrusting the soul of an innocent little boy with you.

No. That child can never be yours to care for because I don't think you have a caring bone in that skinny body. I've decided to leave him at the hospital.

Not long after, I expect, I'll be on my way to hell.

In the hope that he manages to survive the jungle that's life, given his lonely entrance into the world, I have written to make you aware of his existence.

Because I have no knowledge of the child's real father, I ask that you find it in your conscience to make him your sole heir. The boy is, after all, my father's grandchild.

You have no heirs, due to being childless. And the fact that the boy shares my father's blood should, I dearly hope, appeal to any semblance of regard you may still hold for my late father.

I ask that you leave everything to my son.

It's no secret that I hated you. My mother's disgust and loathing toward you affected me while I was growing in her stomach, and then there was the heavy drinking that she drowned me in, before and after. She would stare alone at the walls crying, while my father, your lover, spent all his time with you.

He didn't even hide it. That's how blatant his obsession for you was. I recall as a young girl smelling the same scent that wafted in with you on my father.

When he disappeared without a trace, my mother became so bitter and broken, she took her own life. I hated my father for what he did to my beloved mother, who couldn't find enough love in her heart for me to keep living, thereby turning me into an orphan at thirteen.

Call it weakness of spirit, but my heart broke that day she died. Never to heal.

I had little choice but to walk on the wild side, being my only escape from the pain that you'd wreaked on my family.

I don't know what became of my father. If I had been a doting, loving daughter I would have moved mountains to find him. For all I know, he may still be hidden somewhere away with you in that mansion of yours.

I can't forgive him for what he did. Why he married my beautiful mother, I'll never understand.

Discovering that I was pregnant crushed my already broken spirit. I'd planned to end my life, but couldn't, not with a life inside of me.

I'm not sure which of the brutes I'd bedded was the father. All of them were like me, creatures of the night—zombies who'd lost their way.

That dark cloud has consumed me at last. It followed me through this sad journey, and has, at last, extinguished that fire that raged within me. As a child, I hated with such passionate force I couldn't even be around other children. I hated so much that I spent my hours coming up with ways to murder you. But, sadly, courage was never a strong point.

So now in my last hour, I write this in hope that when you read it, you will understand you have an obligation to my son. For it was you that tore the very fabric of this family apart. My broken spirit and mangled soul will travel with me to the other side, where I will watch your every move.
Marion Black

CHAPTER THIRTY-FOUR

BRONSON

Rotating around and around like a film with no beginning and end was the story of my mother drowning me, her son, in drink and sadness. I stood on the balcony, regretting my decision to give up cigarettes. But that was when the tide had turned. Now all I saw was a gray, bleak sky threatening to do its stormy worst.

I went back inside and pulled out drawers, the contents of which spilled all over the place while I searched desperately for a pack of cigarettes.

Ava looked up at me. The sadness written on her face chilled me.

The last thing I wanted from her, or from anyone else, was pity.

I felt naked. My ugly past had burst into my life. Being blissfully ignorant made perfect sense because I would have preferred to have remained just that.

There were so many questions running through my head, like the voices of mad people, lots of whispering underneath one loud and clear voice repeating that same tragic lament—*I was not important enough to justify my mother's existence.*

I grabbed my jacket.

Ava flinched when she saw the keys jangling in my hands.

"Where are you going?" Alarm rang in her voice.

"I need cigarettes," I mumbled.

I stood at the door and hesitated, then turned. A shivery sensation flushed through me, as I uttered, "Why are you still here?"

The voice didn't even sound like me.

Her face crumpled in dismay. "Because I want to be."

"You should go, Ava. I'm no good. I come from shit."

She rushed over and grabbed my hand.

I couldn't look at her. Burning shame overtook my whole being. I needed to do something— scream or punch a wall even, something destructive.

I removed my hand.

"Bronson, please, let me be here for you." Her eyes pooled with tears.

Pity.

Always fucking pity.

I'd seen it all my life.

I recalled that same expression on my mother when she thought I wasn't looking.

"I don't want you to feel sorry for me, Ava."

"I don't!" she cried.

I stared at her for a long while, my mouth open, but no words formed. "I have to go and get this rage out of me. It will eat me alive otherwise."

"I'll get smashed with you."

I nearly laughed. Ava the angel. What I should have said was that I wanted to go somewhere rough and dangerous and get my head smashed in.

Even though I wanted to hold her, I knew that tangle of raw, hardwired emotion would unravel and a bomb would go off within, destroying everything closest to me in its wake.

My eyes started to blur.

I was a man. A tough man. Not a pussy. I needed to run.

"What can I get you?" the bartender asked.

"Bourbon," I said.

He studied me for a moment. Compared to the lowlifes around me, I looked a picture of cleanliness, even though I hadn't showered or changed my sweaty T-shirt. I'd gone for a long run, and it was stuck to me. Instead of going home, I'd jumped in a cab and headed to the grimiest place I could find, somewhere I could rub shoulders with other abandoned souls.

Considering how sorry I felt for myself, the last thing I wanted was to be around bright and happy people living happy lives.

I craved darkness.

I needed to see how those who had walked on the wild side of life were doing. Having come from that same source of struggle, I was one of them. They were more comparable to me than any well-adjusted person.

Evident by the row of lonely men with heads down, staring solemnly at their drinks, the bar had seen its share of sorrow.

The barman returned with a bottle and poured some into a glass.

"Leave the bottle," I said.

The older man studied me for a moment. I tossed a card at him and after he swiped it through the machine, his mood lifted. I'd made his night big, it seemed.

What a week. What a year. What a life.

I lit a cigarette and hated the flavor of it, but as the nicotine hit my lungs, my head started to spin in a pleasant kind of way.

By my third shot, I started to unwind. My shoulders released some tension, and the voices in my head started to dull.

"You're not from here," I heard over my shoulder.

I turned and looked at the shabby excuse for a man by my side. I shook my head and continued to puff away.

"Can I have one of those?" he asked.

I passed the pack of cigarettes over to him.

"Take them," I said, pushing a lighter toward him.

His eyebrows drew in slightly. Something told me he wasn't used to receiving things for nothing. "That's okay. We can share."

I continued to stare into space, enjoying the emptiness of the moment, for amnesia was one thing I extracted from alcohol. And boy, did I need to forget.

"Woman problems?" he asked.

"Nope." I stared down at my glass of amber fluid. "Mother issues."

"Oh..." he rasped. After a few puffs, he added, "I never knew mine."

My head turned sharply to study him. Of an indeterminable age, he could have been in his mid-thirties or in his fifties. Wearing his battles on his face, he was that guy society had forgotten about.

I grabbed the pack and took another cigarette out. As the smoke left my lips I said, "You too."

His bloodshot blue eyes narrowed. "A woman can rip at one's heart, but a mother rips deeper. At one's very fucking soul."

I shrugged, even though that was probably closer to the truth than I chose to accept.

He held out his hand. "Sam."

"Bronson," I said, taking his hard, calloused hand.

"You're a builder?" he asked.

"That I am. The hands, ah?"

He flashed his yellowing teeth. "Me too. Twenty years on a site."

"Are you still working?" I asked.

"No, man. Fucked up my back. I'm injured. I can't work."

I looked at his glass, which had been empty for a while. He noticed and said, "It's all right. I just like to sit here because it's warmer and a little safer than the park." He chuckled.

"You're sleeping rough?" I asked.

He opened his hands. "Yeah, I suppose I am."

"Can I buy you a drink?" I looked behind the bar to see if there was any food and noticed sandwiches in plastic wrap. "Something to eat?"

"Hey, man, I don't expect it from you. The cigarettes are good."

I summoned the bartender. "Get Sam what he wants. Keep them coming. And a few of those sandwiches. Are they fresh?" I asked, suddenly feeling hungry after having not eaten all day.

The bartender passed the tray over. "We have ham and roast beef."

"I'll take a roast beef." I looked over at Sam. "Take whatever you want. Take a few. For breakfast too."

His eyes shone with genuine gratitude. "That's really kind of you. Only if you can. I don't like to impose."

"It's all good. I've got a job. And pretty soon, when my life sorts out the shit that's just floated in, I'll be rich. And I'll make it so that guys like you won't have to live on the streets through no fault of your own."

"Well said. Are you going into politics?" he asked.

I studied him to see if he was joking, but he had an earnest, hopeful shine in his eyes that made me wonder if indeed I needed to do more to help the Sam's of the world.

"Nope. I'm not smart enough for that," I said with a tight half smile.

"It doesn't take intelligence, just ambition, ruthlessness, and rubbing shoulders with the right guys," he said.

I sniffed. "Yeah, well, that's not me." I shifted on my barstool. "How is it you didn't know your mom?"

"I was one when she died."

Noticing his glass was empty, I gestured to the bartender to top him up. Sam played with his fingers. "My old man killed her. I had what's commonly known as a tragic beginning." He took a gulp of beer, wiping his mouth with the back of his hand. "It was on the news. I even have an article about it back with my possessions."

"You kept that?"

"It's the only photo I have of my mom."

Hell. The emotion that his expression stirred. He wasn't looking sorry for himself, not like me earlier. There was something almost noble in the way he'd grown to accept it. He'd had the time to adjust, I told myself.

How long did it take to accept the devil in one's bloodline?

"Shit, man. I'm really sorry," I said, draining my glass.

I lifted the bottle. "Do you want a shot?"

He nodded. "Sure, why not." He studied me for a moment. "What's a guy like you doing in a hole like this?"

"I'm not much different from you, Sam. Only that I was lucky to be adopted by an affectionate father and mother. My adopted brother was a different story. But that's one for later."

"Then life's been a little kind, even if you're sad about your real mom."

"I just found a letter she wrote. Today. That's why I'm here. It's fucked my head up big time." I took a deep breath. "She killed herself just after giving birth to me." Downing a shot, I said, almost to myself. "She must have really fucking hated me."

He studied me for a moment. There was no pity in his face, which I appreciated. "Hey, man… she gave you life. She must have been fucking sad and lost, but she put up with her suffering. She gave birth to you first. That says something to me."

They say that during those big moments, things move in slow frames, which help you assess your life. That was exactly what happened as I navigated Sam's unwashed, craggy features. The sincerity that shone from that reassuring flicker in his eyes made me think through what had been my life. When I landed in the present, Ava and her shining light came before me.

The beautiful girl that was Ava, who'd come into my life and was waiting for me.

She didn't run away.

I ran away.

I had given her space so that she could run away without feeling obligated to do the right thing by me, an emotional invalid.

I took out my cell and turned it on. There was a bank of messages, most of which could wait, but from Ava, there was only one.

Scrolling down, I read, "I love you, Bronson, unconditionally. I'm not ashamed of who you are. If anything, I'm proud of what you've become."

CHAPTER THIRTY-FIVE

AVA

My cell pinged. It was from Bronson. A loud "at last" left my lips. The text read, "I'll be home as soon as I can hail a cab. I love you with all my heart and soul."

It was two in the morning.

He'd been gone for five hours.

So many times, I had begun to leave. But as I stood at the door, I just couldn't. It was as though some hidden force held me there.

I'd pulled one of his worn shirts out of the laundry and slipped it on. As I lounged about, his addictive scent flooded my senses, that same dizzying blend of cologne and sweat that I drew in deeply when lying in his arms with my nose buried in his warm neck.

I'd been a sagging mess ever since he'd walked out. I understood Bronson's need to be alone. He was a proud man. The dramatic details of his entrance into the world were so tragic that as much as I tried, I couldn't stop tears of pity.

I wanted to be strong for him. But my heart had shriveled when I witnessed that lost, broken expression in his eyes after he'd set *that* letter down.

Just as I poured hot water into my umpteenth cup of herbal tea, guaranteed to keep me peeing all night, the door opened.

Hearing voices, I put the kettle down.

Bronson was not alone.

When I entered the living room, a rank odor hit my nostrils with such force I had to take a step back.

Bronson had brought home a hobo.

I couldn't tell who was more surprised, the stranger or me.

Standing there with my mouth slightly agape, I nodded a quick welcome. Realizing I was naked underneath Bronson's shirt, I excused myself and headed for the bedroom.

Bronson followed me.

He gazed at me, and before I had a chance to speak, he took me into his arms and held me tightly. It wasn't in his normal passionate-bordering-on-groping way, but as if we hadn't seen each other for months and needed to be reacquainted.

"I'm sorry," he said with an uneasy expression.

He'd been drinking heavily, for he had that glazed look in his eyes. But with that stubble on his face, his boyish chocolatey eyes, and sensual lips moistened for a kiss, I wanted so much to push him against the wall and have hard sex without any rules.

I unraveled from his clasp and slipped on a pair of jeans.

"Who's that?" I asked.

"Sam. Come on. I'll introduce you." He grabbed me by the hand. I'd never seen him like that. He was almost like a teenager bringing home a new pal.

"Bronson, he needs a shower," I whispered.

He held a finger up. "Okay, then. Back in a minute."

I heard mumbling, and then Bronson returned to grab a towel from his closet.

It was extraordinary what a few drinks could do for one's mood, given that Bronson was the most relaxed I'd ever seen him.

While we sat on the bed, he told me all about Sam. And that he'd offered him the couch until he could find him a place to live.

A spark flitted over his eyes. "What about your place?"

"Where am I to live?" I asked.

"Why, here, of course. With me." He smiled sweetly. It was as if he'd forgotten about what had happened that day.

I hadn't. That heart in the jar hung around like some festering wound.

"Let's talk about it tomorrow," I said, looking over his shoulder at Sam, who was rubbing his washed hair with a towel.

"Hey, I hope you don't mind me intruding like this, I…"

"It's all good, Sam. Ava understands."

Despite a ton of questions banking up, I smiled sweetly and left them on hold for when Bronson was sober.

It was late, and when Bronson fell onto the bed after what had been a *big* day, he fell into a deep sleep with his legs and arms wrapped around me.

The following morning, I woke to find the bed empty. After dressing, I discovered Bronson in the kitchen waving a spatula over a pan of fried eggs and bacon.

I rubbed my eyes and greeted Bronson's new pal, Sam, who was sitting at the table with coffee in hand and a big smile.

"Hey," said Bronson looking up at me with a sultry smile.

"You've been up a while?" I asked.

"Uh-huh. Are you hungry?"

I nodded. "Sure." I studied Bronson. "For someone who had a bit to drink, you seem pretty bright."

"I don't do hangovers," he responded. "Come and sit here." He pointed to the table, where he'd placed a plate with fried eggs, bacon, and tomato. "I'll pour you a coffee."

Where was the Bronson I knew? I asked myself. This new version was either in denial or had found God. As he moved about playing mother, host, and waiter, I decided I preferred the brooding, silent version.

I looked over at Sam, who seemed to have a permanent smile etched on his otherwise scraggy features.

"I hope you don't mind me invading your space," he said.

"No, of course not," I replied, flickering a questioning stare at Bronson since I did wonder what the plan was.

The food was exceptional. Bronson was great around the kitchen, it seemed, which was handy, considering my lack in that area.

Wiping my mouth, I asked Bronson, "So, what are you up to today?"

"I'm going to buy Sam some clothes, and then after that, I'm off to the building site to see if Harry can give him a job. And then we'll look into finding him somewhere to stay until your place becomes available."

I nodded slowly. "Bronson, can I have a word?"

He followed me into the bedroom.

"What are you doing?"

"About what?" he asked, taking me by the hand and sitting next to me on the bed, where he proceeded to play with a strand of my hair.

He stroked my cheek, and I fell into his arms. "I miss the old you, Bronson."

"I'm still here," he said, lowering his chin to stare into my eyes.

His eyes darkened. "I don't miss the old me. Do you know how hard it is carrying around a shitload of bitterness? How it eats away at one's gut?"

"It's just that we haven't even held each other today. And you're acting differently."

"I'm holding you now." He pulled away and studied me. "Is this because of Sam? I just want to help the poor guy. He's unable to fend for himself." His unshaven face tensed, and again, a shadow fell over his handsome features.

A thought suddenly occurred to me. "You see yourself in Sam."

His eyes held mine. "Maybe. Not that I've thought about it that way, but had I not been adopted by a good family, that could have been me."

"But it's not you, Bronson. You undervalue yourself. You have so much talent, drive, and intrinsic understanding of human nature, beyond your years. You're an old soul," I said.

"Does that make me a dirty old man?" His eyes flickered with dark amusement.

Instead of frustration at his banter, I smiled and fell into his arms again.

Our mouths met in a tender kiss that quickly heated when his tongue entered deeply, making me shudder with pleasure.

That was the erotic version of Bronson I craved, as his hands indulged on the swell of my breasts.

He stood up and lowered his jeans.

I sighed as I saw how his considerable bulge stretched out the cotton fabric of his white briefs that made his skin appear deliciously tanned.

He lowered them as a lusty moan left my lips. He parted my legs roughly, for the hunger in his gaze showed he couldn't wait.

As he thrust hard into me, he looked deeply into my eyes.

My hands pressed his firm ass toward me as I arched my back to meet his thrusts all the way. It was rougher than usual but devastatingly arousing. With each entry, I gave way to explosions of delicious heat.

His eyelids became heavy, and his breath gusted over my neck.

"I need you to come for me, Ava." His voice was tight and shaky.

The friction, the intensity of his gaze, those full, sensual lips open and gasping with arousal only added to the rippling heat tearing through me, until the build-up was so unbearable that I let go. My toes squeezed tight, and I moaned into his neck as I drew in his testosterone-infused scent.

He shuddered through a release. His jaw tightened, and his head dropped back.

After a few moments, we came back to life.

Aware we were not alone, I said, "I hope we weren't too noisy."

"I'll find somewhere for Sam today. That will give you time to give me an answer." He pushed back a black curl that had fallen over his forehead.

I studied him for a moment. "Do you really want to do this?" My eyes landed on the heart tattoo with my name on his chest.

That was a "forever" act if I'd ever seen one.

Noticing my focus, Bronson cocked his head. "What do you think?"

CHAPTER THIRTY-SIX

BRONSON

Harry found some menial tasks for Sam in return for a basic wage, giving him enough to survive. As it turned out, Harry had a bungalow at the back of his house that he offered Sam at a low rent. That was why I liked Harry. He had a heart of gold when it came to those who'd fallen on hard times.

It was a big day at the site. I had a kitchen to oversee, which involved carting around heavy bits of wood. At least that was one thing about being a builder: I didn't need a gym in order to get fit.

I had to meet James to discuss the project and to talk about Justin, who, having not covered his steps well, left little doubt that he'd forged the new will. Although my fucking brother was the last thing I wanted to visit in my already heavily occupied mind, a wrong had to be addressed. It also meant that I'd be able to buy a large house for Ava and give her everything her heart desired because I wanted nothing more than for her to live like a princess.

As the jar with the heart entered my thoughts for the millionth time, my cell buzzed. I saw Ava's pretty face and picked up. "Hey, sexy."

"I'm sorry to call while you're working," she said, sounding formal, despite me having explored every delectable inch of her naked body only hours earlier.

"Anytime, Ava. I love hearing your voice. Especially when it's in my ear."

"I love your voice, too," she said with a breathy sigh. "My mother insists on meeting you. I told her that I was going to move in with you."

My chest expanded. "Oh, angel, that's a yes then?"

"Yes. It was always going to be that, Bronson. I can't imagine being without you."

"I need you too, Ava." I paused. "So, I'm going to meet your parents. Shit. That's scary."

"No, it's not. I mean, my mom's a bit scary, given her annoying tendency to ask lots of questions. You'll have to find a way to deal with that. I still struggle with it, I have to admit."

My smile faded as quickly as it had arrived. "What am I to say about the one-year stint in prison?"

"I've told them."

"Really?" I asked.

"Mom's a bit tense about it. But Dad's cool. He's great. You'll like him. He's a retired carpenter."

"Really? He's like me, then," I said, releasing some tension.

"Well, not alike in personality. But he did work with his hands and spent most of his life in the shed. Probably to get away from my mom." She giggled.

"She sounds formidable."

"No more than any other ambitious mother."

"Shit. An ambitious mother, in my book, means a go-getter that judges a person by where he's been in order to determine his worth."

"Don't worry, I'll be there to shield you from her."

I couldn't tell if Ava was kidding.

"When's the inquisition?" I asked, not hiding the gloomy note in my voice.

She laughed. "Oh, Bronson, you make it sound like a trial."

"Well it is, isn't it?"

"It's tomorrow night. I'll take the night off from Aggie's."

Cold water that had just been poured over my head at the thought of meeting Ava's mom had turned into a deluge at the mention of Aggie. "Are you there now?"

"I'm on my way," she said.

"Are you going to talk to her about *it*?"

"The heart?"

I sighed loudly. My day had just gotten bleaker. "Yep. Fuck, Ava. It's back."

"What is?"

"This fucking nagging question of whether we should be calling the cops," I said.

"Yeah. Me too. I'm plagued with the same thoughts," she said.

"You realize we've become accessories if and when that thing's found."

"Not you Bronson, more like me. I'm the one that goes there."

"Ava, there are such things as CCTV sprinkled everywhere. I'm sure the cops would see us entering that building at some point. Considering the place is deserted, it won't be hard to question those who come and go."

"But she's got staff, too."

"Have you seen any of her staff?" I asked.

"No... But I've got a plan to go in early tomorrow because I need to get to the bottom of things. There's so much that just doesn't add up. And I need to know if she's a ghost."

"What? But you said you don't believe in the supernatural. And I as sure as hell don't." The sinews in my forearms throbbed as I clasped the phone tightly.

"I know. But here I am standing in the lobby. It's empty. Why would a beautiful building like this be empty?"

"Ava, have you thought that Aggie may own that building and want it all to herself?"

"Hm... I haven't. But that's plausible, I suppose. She is seriously private and strange about people."

"There are no fucking ghosts, Ava," I said emphatically. I thought I needed convincing because I was creeped out by that place just as much as Ava was. But I needed to man up by removing doubt.

"Okay. Best go. I'll see you tonight?"

"Sam's staying at Harry's, so we can play. I need to get a bit dirty." My pants tightened at that fantasy. The one remedy for my troubled mind was hardcore sex with my curvaceous, ripe, and delicious girlfriend.

"That sounds promising. I'll have to remember to wear my nice underwear."

Her giggle made my cock lengthen. "Not too nice. I plan to rip them off and make a meal of you."

"Mm… that sounds yummy," she purred.

"Bye, angel."

I climbed into my car. And with Dire Straits blaring away, instead of grumbling at the bumper-to-bumper traffic, I sang.

CHAPTER THIRTY-SEVEN

AVA

Resigned to the fact that Charlie was no longer employed there, I rode the elevator alone.

After I entered, expecting Aggie to be upstairs. Standing at the bottom of the stairs, I heard her calling out from the balcony.

The pretty terrace with the mosaic floor, housing terra cotta pots with roses creeping up on trellises, belied the existence of ghosts. If anything, the place was bursting with life.

"There you are," she said with a sunny smile.

"I'm surprised to find you up and about," I said.

She leaned over and grabbed a cigarette. "I've had a few bad days. But I'm better today. Taken a few pills that the doctor prescribed."

"Oh… a doctor's been here, then?" I asked.

"Yes. Yes. He came snooping around yesterday. Louisa called him. I'll be alive for a few more martinis." A throaty chuckle mingled with the smoke that exited her lips.

"Does he know you smoke?" I asked.

"Now, don't go all censorious on me, and make me that martini," she said in her typical gruff manner.

When I returned, I placed the glass by her side.

Noticing her hand tremble more than usual when she picked it up, I said, "Aggie, I worry about you."

She waved her hand. "Yes. Yes. Now stop making a fuss and tell me about your love life."

I wondered if she remembered Bronson, or whether she still believed that she'd dreamt up Monty.

"You've met him," I said.

Her eyes met mine. There was something lost in them. I couldn't tell what she was thinking. "I don't recall."

"He came upstairs. He's the one that gave me the cameo."

"Monty stole that cameo. I now know why. I forgive him," she said.

I asked myself if Aggie was being evasive, or just off with the fairies.

Extracting some courage after taking a few sips from the large martini I'd made myself on purpose for the difficult discussion that lay ahead, I said, "Aggie, there's something I need to ask you?"

"I don't like questions, Ava. That was the agreement."

Slumping back on my chair, I took a deep breath. Her pale face and tremulous state stopped me from pressing further.

"You haven't answered my question," she said. "How is your love life?"

"It's great."

"You're no longer with that awful lawyer, I hope. You're with the tall, dark, and handsome one, then?"

"Yes. I'm with Bronson." I couldn't recall if I'd described Bronson like that.

"Good. Very good." She fell back on her chair as if allowing distant memories to invade her thoughts, for I lost her after that.

The relief on her face, however, was not lost on me.

Why would Aggie be so happy to know about my relationship? Why did that matter to her?

Those same questions revolved in my head the next day when I visited my neglected apartment to find something to wear to dinner with my parents and Bronson. In what was a sad testimony to my disorganized life, I stood by a pile of clothes at my feet. Indecisive as always, I'd also managed to bury my bed in potential outfits.

The thought of my mom meeting Bronson had me on edge.

It had to happen. If we were to take the relationship to that next stage, my parents needed to meet him. I just prayed my mom wouldn't ask after Justin, who'd charmed the pants off her with his endless babble and self-confidence.

They say one can't choose their parents. In many ways I took solace in that adage, considering how shallow and social climbing my mom really was. Her only redeeming feature was that she married my sweet father. If it weren't for my dad, I may have even tried to keep my contact time with her down to those routine occasions like Christmas and birthdays.

Settling for a pink shirt, I stood before the mirror and buttoned it up. My hair hung with sad neglect. A frustrated sigh left me at the thought of ripping through it with a brush. I wondered if Bronson would still like me if I cut it. Running my fingers through the knots, I decided to tie it back into a ponytail. Cutting my hair was another thing my mother kept on at me about. But then, nothing I did seemed to please her. Perhaps it was because I was an only child.

Was it too soon for us to move in together? Where would all my possessions go? Maybe I'd store them at my parents', I thought. They had plenty of room there. Bronson's apartment was too small for everything. I would need my books, however.

My thoughts kept buzzing about like bees trapped in a hive, colliding with each other.

Aggie, Bronson, my mom, my possessions, my hair, my life…

"Stop!" I screamed. With my head in my hands, I allowed things to settle. The buzzer at the door made me jump.

I opened it, and Bronson stood before me. His scent hit me first, which made my body tingle, especially as my eyes feasted on him. Gone was that bedroom tousle. In its place, Bronson's hair was neatly combed back with product, his natural wave sitting at the perfect height for his high-cheekboned features. He wore a tan sport jacket with cream-colored chinos and a white shirt. I could have eaten him. Bronson looked like one of those hunky guys one saw on the cover of a men's magazine.

With that natural sultry stride, he entered my messy apartment and sat down next to me. Like magnets, we were drawn to each other. Had it only been morning when we had last seen each other?

I buried my nose in his warm neck, sucking in his scent as if starved for it.

He kissed me tenderly.

When we separated, a roguish smile touched his lips as his eyes swept over me. "You look beautiful."

"Not as beautiful as you," I countered, stroking his jacket.

"Is it okay? I paid a pretty sum for it."

"It's really stylish, and it suits you," I said.

He rose and headed to the kitchen.

"Please, don't go in there," I warned. I hadn't had a chance to clean for a while.

"Why? Is there a dead body in there?" His eyes lit up with dark amusement.

When he saw my lips forming a tight line, recalling that dreaded heart in the jar, he added, "Maybe not a good choice of words."

"What are you looking for?" I asked.

He rubbed himself against me. "You."

Bronson seemed more relaxed than me as we drove over the George Washington Bridge. I looked behind me at the sleepless city that was my home. The farther we traveled, the lights blurred and shimmered resembling an abstract work of art rather than a metropolis.

"I haven't been out of the city for a while," I said.

"We're only heading for Jersey," he said.

A confident driver, Bronson wove in and out of the traffic, putting his foot down when needed. Normally a jumpy passenger, I felt at ease with him at the wheel.

He stole the occasional glance at me. "You don't seem yourself, Ava."

"I'm nervous."

"About me meeting your folks?"

I sighed. "Uh-huh… Dad's great, but my mom's hard work. She'll ask a lot of questions."

"So you've mentioned."

Just as we left the bridge, Bronson slowed the car down. Finding a spot on the side of the road, he stopped.

Turning to look at me, he became serious all of a sudden.

"Ava. Do you want to do this?"

"I want to be with you."

The tightness in his face faded into a faint smile. "Then I can take it if you can."

Every time I looked at Bronson, my desire for him intensified. I wanted to lunge for him, but instead, I indulged in holding his hand, which seemed to fuse us together, for it felt like a pleasant current running through me.

My mother, who did not possess a subtle bone in her body, tried to keep her cool as she scrutinized the living daylights out of Bronson, while my father was his usual affable self. He became more so upon discovering that he and Bronson shared many things in common, especially a love of wood.

While Dad showed Bronson around his workshop, my mom led me into the kitchen, where a thousand words a minute poured out of her mouth.

At the end of it all, she asked, "What happened to Justin?"

"What don't you like about Bronson?" I asked.

"He's dishy, that's for sure. Very good looking in that troubled way."

My eyebrows drew in tight. "What are you talking about?"

"He's been locked up, darling." She knitted her fingers.

"Falsely. That was Justin's doing, I might add."

"You haven't got proof."

"Oh, Mom, get over it. Justin's not an option." Frustration fired my speech. "Bronson has just had a housing development he designed approved. That should please you, seeing you're into real estate."

"Hm…" She began setting the table.

"Do you need a hand?" I asked.

"Bring out that tray of roast potatoes."

When Bronson and my father returned, I heard my father ask, "Can I get you a beer?"

"No." Bronson looked at me. "I'm driving. I'm good."

After we settled at the table, with the meat carved, and our plates full, my mother remarked, "You're Justin's brother, I believe."

Bronson nodded. "Not biological brother." He looked at me. "I met Ava at a family function."

"That must have caused a stir," she said.

"Mom…" I interjected.

Bronson touched my hand and gave me a subtle nod. "Justin and I don't talk."

"Ava tells me you're working on a housing development."

"I am. We're building smaller-sized homes on vacant industrial land. It's what's known as an affordable housing project."

"Oh." She paused for a moment. "This is a bit soon between the two of you. Ava tells me she's moving in with you."

"I can understand your concern, Mrs. Rose." His eyes met mine. "I'm in love with your daughter."

As I placed my hand in his, tears pricked my eyes.

CHAPTER THIRTY-EIGHT

BRONSON

Apart from sharing the same stunning looks, Ava was nothing like her mom. Thank God for that. Because even with her awe-inspiring beauty and curves, I would never have fallen for Ava otherwise.

Ava was more like her father, who was a gentleman in the true sense of that word. His vast knowledge of woodwork impressed me so much that my jaw dropped at how similar our approach to working with the grain of timber was. There was definitely potential for a friendship there since I could imagine us spending time together in his workshop, sharing tips over a few beers.

As we were leaving, I kissed Laura Rose on the cheek, which left a cold tingle on my lips. John stood quietly beside his wife. I figured that was why they'd stayed together. If one was to survive the force that was Laura Rose, a man would need to agree to everything.

In any case, Ava's father took me aside and whispered, "It's all good. Don't mind her. She's a bit of a ball-breaker. Underneath it all, she's one hell of a woman." He nodded and returned a smile as he patted me on the back. "It's been great meeting you, Bronson. I look forward to seeing some of your pieces."

When we were in the car, Ava said, "That went well." Her sardonic tone summed up my state of mind entirely.

Remaining quiet, I drove to the next street and parked the car.

Ava turned to look at me. "Why are we stopping?"

"Did you ever love Justin?" I turned to face her squarely.

Ava looked as though I'd flashed headlights in front of her.

"Um… no." A line formed between her eyes. "Why are you asking me this? You know how I felt about Justin and how much I hate him now."

A rough breath left me. "I don't think I'm going to measure up. I'm not good enough for you."

I hated how pathetic that sounded, but a churning of insecurities surfaced suddenly.

"I warned you about my mom. She's like that with most people unless it's a client that she's trying to sell a house to. That's her way. She's a go-getter. And she's always been like that about me. I disappointed her a long time ago."

Ava grabbed my hand and gazed at me with such love that she could have melted the polar ice caps.

"Fucking parents… without them, we're lost; with them, we're never good enough," I said running my fingers through my hair, which returned a sticky stain on my palms. "And I hate fucking hair products. Shit."

I rubbed my hands on my pants.

Her lips twitched into a smile. "I prefer you with messy, just-fucked hair anyway."

Ava rarely swore, but hearing that coming out of her pretty mouth made my pants tighten all of a sudden.

"I was just trying to make an impression," I said.

"You and Dad got on really well. He really likes you. That says something, and you share a passion. I love that about you both. Give me a creative man, anytime," she said.

As much as I loved hearing that comment, a dark cloud continued to fog my head. "Did you ever love Justin? Did he make you come?"

"What? No. I mean… we hardly ever did it."

Ava's eyes glistened with outraged confusion. I shouldn't have gone there. The past was the past. She hadn't asked me about all the women I'd fucked. There'd been so many I would never have been able to put a number to it. A fact I wasn't proud of, and therefore grateful that Ava had never asked me about it.

I puffed out a long breath. "I'm sorry, Ava. Your mom seems stuck on Justin. One would need to be brainless not to have noticed the disappointment on her face after she met me."

"Listen to me, Bronson. You're the love of my life. We've been together for one minute, but yet I feel as if we've known each other for a lifetime. I want to live with you, even though your potential OCD will creep me out over time."

"Huh?" I studied her to see if there was a smile or a joke brewing. "OCD? I don't suffer that."

"Um… Hello… I've watched you fold your clothes neatly while you're ripping off my panties with your mouth."

I laughed at that ridiculous picture. "Now you're exaggerating. I'd need four hands to do that."

"But jokes aside, Bronson. We live differently. I'm messy to a fault. I'm almost allergic to washing dishes. That's why I chose to live alone."

"I hate where you live, amongst druggies and thieves," I muttered. The tension that had been eating away at me dissolved into dull background noise as I stroked Ava's smooth arm. "Am I really the love of your life?"

"You are, Bronson. As much as I've tried to take it slowly, it's hard when I'm around you."

"Yeah, you got that right. It's always *hard* when you're around me," I said with a flicker of a grin.

She tilted her head and smiled. "Well then, Mr. Clean Freak, let's get back so I can see just how hard it is to resist your animal charms."

Starting up the engine, I laughed for the first time in days.

I pressed the play button, and "Born To Be Wild" came on—hard driving just like me. Moving my head back and forth to the driving rhythm, I tapped the steering wheel.

"My dad loves this kind of music. I grew up with it," said Ava.

"At least we can escape into his workspace. I can see why he needs to hang there for long periods."

"He loves my mom. And she loves him," Ava defended.

"Then why is she trying to foist a dirtbag lawyer onto you? That's hypercritical, isn't it?"

"When have you ever noticed humans not being that?"

"True. Wise, beautiful girl." I flashed a smile.

Tension, it seemed, where Ava was involved, generated such an insatiable need in me that we barely made it to the door. Her bra was already unclasped. After seeing her nipples prickling through her blouse, I crept my hand up while we rode the elevator. Just as her full breasts fell into my palms, another person jumped on. I took a deep breath in order to still the charge of blood heading for my groin.

When we stepped out of the lift, my mouth ate at hers with such ferocious need that I nearly fell against her on the wall. While my tongue burrowed deep into her mouth, I reached for my keys.

With one arm around her waist, I pushed open the door, and we fell into the room. The lights from the street gave us just enough to see as we made it onto the couch.

I pulled off her jeans and ran my fingers up her sticky thighs.

Lowering my face onto her pussy, I caressed it while ripping off her panties. By now, Ava was used to my need to taste her. I preferred her at the end of a day for some reason. Her flavor was sharper, sexier.

My tongue fluttered over her bud. Arching her back, she responded with an elongated sigh. Her clit swelled against my tongue as I licked up and down and around until she wiggled in my hands and came loudly.

I undid my trousers. My cock throbbed with such intensity it hurt.

As I clasped her firm, curvy butt, her hot tight muscles flooded my finger as I entered, while Ava managed to undo the buttons of my shirt and ran her hands up and down my torso.

I opened her legs and thrust deeply into her.

Her eyes hooded and lips parted as my cock was met by a contracting wet mass of hot, tight muscles.

"Ah…" left my lips, while my heart thumped against my chest as blood raged through me.

"I need to take you from behind," I said, squeezing her ass.

We fell onto the rug, and she positioned herself on all fours. I lifted her hips and entered her deeply.

While our heavy breathing filled the air, I pumped into her, my hands cradling her heavy tits. As with each time we fucked, it was so sensual and erotic that I found it difficult not to blow quickly.

"I need you to come for me, Ava," I rasped.

CHAPTER THIRTY-NINE

AVA

"Ah…" left my lips. The friction caused that delicious climb to the top as one wave of sensation overtook another. Overwhelmed with arousal, my sex convulsed around him, making him feel so large that he stretched me beyond bliss. His hot breath gusted over my neck between bites. With each entry, a burning throb threatened to finish me off.

Every inch of my skin tingled, and I was showered by one euphoric wave after another until an almighty eruption brought tears to my fluttering eyelashes.

Digging my nails into his hard biceps, I cried out.

His body shuddered along with a loud groan. He injected deeply into me as if aiming his seed into my brain.

Taking a moment to get my breath back, I remained on my back, waiting for the stars to fade away.

Bronson turned to face me. His lips curved, making his cheeks dimple and giving him that irresistible boyish charm that made my heart bubble over.

"What?" he asked as I smiled back at him.

"I'm just thinking how sweet you look after an orgasm."

"It does have a purging effect on me, I suppose," he said.

"You make it sound like a laxative."

He laughed. "In a way, it's an emotional one, I suppose. I always feel light and fantastic afterward. Only with you.... have I..." He pushed back a curl from his forehead.

"Only with me, what?" I asked, leaning up on my elbow.

"I feel safe. I know that sounds weird. But before you, I lacked grounding. I couldn't imagine ever belonging to anyone."

"You belong to me, Bronson. I've got you." I nodded.

"And I've got you, angel. I'd kill for you."

His eyes, having gone a dark shade of intensity, sent a shiver through me.

"That's hopefully not going to be necessary," I said, trying to make light of something that was anything but.

It was my second visit to Aggie's that day. After Bronson departed for work, I'd decided to pay a visit so that I might speak to her staff in the hope of gaining some fresh insights.

That hideous thing in the jar was foremost in my mind, as it was in Bronson's, given the family connection. In any case, he wasn't going to allow the mystery to remain unsolved. And after that hair-raising comment stating that he'd kill for me, I knew that Bronson had a closer relationship to the darker side than I could ever have.

On my first visit to Aggie's, I stood before the locked entrance scratching my head. Everything within and around it seemed so lifeless it was as if the building had been condemned. Not that it was run down. If anything, the pretty gray brick building shone like a jewel among its sharp-edged glass-walled neighbors.

When I arrived at my regular hour, later that day, the glass doors, as always, opened as I pushed on them.

I rode the elevator and entered with my key. This time, I didn't knock.

Determination fueled my steps. Questions were going to be asked regardless of Aggie's rules.

Now that a connection between Aggie and Bronson had been established, coincidence was too lame an explanation for why I'd been employed there in the first place. I left the supernatural speculation for the story I was writing, which seemed to offer more answers.

I was relieved to find Aggie up and not bedridden.

"Ah… there you are. Good. Take a seat," she said.

"You don't want a martini?" I asked.

"No. I'm not in the mood today," she said, looking pensive. Noting my mystified frown, she added, "I'm not a complete dipsomaniac, you know."

"I didn't think you were," I replied, settling down at my regular spot by her side.

After engaging in some small talk, I took a deep breath. "Aggie, I need to speak to you about something."

"Out with it, then," she said. Her scraping tone sent my nails digging into my palms.

"I arrived earlier today to pay you a visit, and found the entrance doors locked."

Her eyebrows moved in sharply. "Why did you even come here?"

"Because I wanted to meet Louisa and Charlie."

"Charlie? Why he's been dead for years."

"What?" My heart thumped hard. "But I've met him in the elevator plenty of times. Not lately, though."

"It's an illusion, darling. I have them all the time. This place is strange like that."

"I don't believe in the supernatural, Aggie. There's got to be a better reason for all of this."

"I'm flesh and blood if that's what you mean."

"Aggie, why did you employ me? Why does the painting upstairs look like me?"

She took a deep breath. "That painting was placed there to do just what it's done."

"To attract my curiosity, you mean?"

"Yes. Got it in one. You're too inquisitive for your own good, though. One thing I learned later in life that might be worthwhile adopting is not to ask too many questions. Everyone has a skeleton or two in the closet. If you poke around long enough, they'll fall out, and what good will that do in the end?"

I sat forward. "That's a timely analogy for what I'm about to say," I said with a grim smile. Before Aggie could respond, I launched straight in. "The other night, Bronson was here. You were upstairs asleep, and we opened the closet in your room."

Her inscrutable stare burned holes into my brow, for suddenly I felt a headache pounding. "After you connected the cameo that Bronson had given me to your family, he naturally couldn't wait to meet you. I mean it wasn't completely instigated by him." I bit my lip. "And you were being so evasive with this no-question-rule of yours."

She waved her hand. "Continue."

"Anyway, I found the key in your drawer. And after we opened the closet, we discovered a jar, a box with pictures, and a letter."

"He found the letter from Marion?" Her voice resonated with dread.

"The letter from his mother, you mean? Yes." I couldn't believe she hadn't even winced at the mention of the jar.

Aggie placed her hand over her mouth, and her eyes filled with dread and sadness. "You must bring him here. I need to speak to him."

Noticing that the blood had drained from her face, I became alarmed. "I can do that tomorrow, if you like."

"No... now." Her urgent and forceful tone made me stir. "I'm not sure if I'll be here tomorrow," she added almost to herself.

"But you seem well today," I said.

"That I was until a moment ago. Please get me my pills." She touched her heart.

I ran upstairs and picked up the packet of pills by her bed.

When I returned, Aggie had her eyes closed. My heart thumped against my chest. What had I done? *Did I tip her over the edge?* I asked myself while I studied her intently in the hope that her chest moved.

"Aggie," I said, standing by her chair. She opened her eyes slowly. "Are you okay. Should I call 9-1-1?"

"No." She held out her hand, and I passed her the pills and a glass of water.

I sat and waited.

"Well, are you going to call him?" she asked.

I rose and took my phone into the other room.

Bronson picked up right away. "Hey, angel."

"Hey. Um... Aggie wants to see you."

"Is she ready to talk about the heart?"

"We haven't got to that as yet. But I did mention the letter, and she nearly fainted. It had a profound impact on her. She wants to see you urgently because of that."

"I'm at the lawyer's with James. We've just uncovered some of Justin's dirty work. But I can leave James to it. I can be there in about thirty minutes."

"I'll see you when you get here, Bronson."

"Sure." There was a pause as I held on. "I love you," he murmured.

"I love you, too," I replied with a quiver in my voice.

That was a first for me.

Not for Bronson. Whenever we made love, it always spilled out on his breath on climax.

CHAPTER FORTY

BRONSON

Aggie kept looking at me with those cool, faded blue eyes that stripped me bare and chilled me at the same time. Shaking her head in disbelief, she said, "My God, you are Monty's double. All the way to that dark, all-consuming look he got when something ate away at him."

I thought Aggie was about to cry. It wasn't an easy place for me. I'd never been good around people who expressed deep emotion, especially strangers. And although I couldn't exactly think of Aggie as a stranger, we had never technically met.

"When I received that letter four years ago, it was like being stabbed in the heart and jolted simultaneously. Learning of Marion's suffering and how my actions may have contributed to her suicide made me retch. You see, we were meant to be together forever, Monty and I. I should never have married Ashley." She touched her chest. "I loved your grandfather with my soul. After I read that letter, I knew I had to find you. Then I discovered you were in prison thanks to a private detective I'd hired to look for you. That broke me, knowing that you'd fallen on the wrong path. But then as I got my P.I. to dig deeper, he came back with the disturbing news that you'd been imprisoned falsely and that you'd been set up by that nasty half-brother of yours. By golly, I had to act. I delayed my death because of you."

"What do you mean by that, Aggie?" asked Ava.

"That's my business." Her dismissive, cutting response made me wince.

"You knew about Justin before I started working here?" Ava asked.

"Yes. Why do you think I employed you?"

"Ha?" Ava's mouth fell open.

Aggie's focus returned to me. Pointing at a floral chair, she said, "Sit here, by my side. Let me look at you."

I lowered myself onto the chair and crossed my arms. I wasn't used to that type of searing scrutiny.

"My dear boy." She continued to study me closely, almost like a doctor would, as if looking for markings or something.

A faint smile touched her lips, which gave me some space to breathe. "When I received that letter," she continued, "it brought me great pain and joy in equal measure. You see, I never knew you existed. Monty died when Penelope was pregnant. Therefore, I didn't even know Marion, your mother, existed."

"Penelope was my grandmother?"

Although she nodded, Aggie seemed distracted. "Oh my, you even sound like him."

"My mother wrote that you killed my grandfather," I said. The earlier pity I'd felt for Aggie vanished.

"Yes… But it was an accident. A horrible, horrible accident." Her eyes pooled with tears.

"Were the police involved?" I asked.

She shook her head. "It was cleaned up. One could do that back then with the right sum of cash."

"Then the heart in the jar belongs to Monty?" asked Ava.

Aggie's head turned sharply to Ava and then back to me. "You've seen it?" Her eyes searched deeply in a bid to read me.

Catching a glint of deep pain and sorrow, I saw the pathetic image of an old woman gnawed by regret.

"Yes," I replied. "And I've also seen the scar, which suggests a knife wound." My heart started to race.

I couldn't quite fathom how that shadow of a woman might be a murderer. Sickened at the thought of interrogating her, I would have preferred not to have found that heart at all.

She looked at Ava. "I think I need that drink now."

Standing up, Ava looked at me. "Do you want one, too?"

I nodded. "Bourbon."

"That was Monty's favorite drink. Ava tells me you're a talented designer and that you create beautiful furniture," she said with an almost childlike twinkle in her eyes.

That jarred. I was not in the mood for light and sociable conversation. "I do." I shifted in my seat. "Anyway, you were saying?"

She picked up her cigarettes and offered me one. Despite wanting one badly, I declined.

I watched her smoke in silence. Respecting her need for a drink, I waited patiently until Ava returned with a long-stemmed glass for Aggie and a tumbler half filled with bourbon.

With the thirst of a sailor, I gulped back half of it before returning my focus to Aggie.

After a couple of sips, Aggie cleared her voice. "Monty came to me one night, as he always did. You see, we were virtually living together. Here."

"Did he work?" I asked, not wishing to learn of their twisted relationship. I just wanted to know something about my real grandfather.

"Oh, yes. Monty was a hard worker. He started off as a laborer when young. That was when we lived in the same house growing up as teenagers. Not related by blood. Nothing like that. He was an orphan. My father, kind man that he was, brought Monty home when he was just five."

"And they say history doesn't repeat itself," I said almost to myself.

Aggie continued, "Your grandfather was a great man. He started with nothing. A strong man who could carry a lump of steel in his bare hands. He wasn't frightened of work."

"Did he set up his own company?" I asked, stunned by the parallel between his life and mine.

"I suppose he did," said Aggie. "You know, nobody really knew how Monty made his money. I was too deeply in love with him to talk about mundane affairs. I'd lived a privileged existence." Her face changed as she looked out into the distance. "I used to visit his worksite when I was a young woman so that I could ogle his beautiful male form"—she chuckled—"but we never spoke about his business interests. My father left him a nice chunk of money, though. Clarke, my brother, died young. Monty and I were the only heirs to a fortune."

Aggie shook her head as she studied me intently. "I can't believe how alike you are. Even your bodies. Tall and well built. Men. Real Men. None of that sissy-boy shit."

A faint smile formed on my face.

Now that I saw the woman who I'd heard so much about, I wasn't sure how I felt about her. Pity was the biggest impulse, but then, she'd also wrecked a family. A family that could have given me a normal life. Whatever that meant, given that apart from Justin, my adopted family had furnished me with nothing but love and affection.

"Aggie, how did he die?" I asked, returning to the grim presence of *that* jar upstairs.

"After Monty cited Penelope's pregnancy as a reason for not going ahead with our plan to run away together, I lost it. I'd been drinking. Seeing him late at night wasn't enough for me. I needed him all day, all night. We were soul mates, you see." She paused to take a sip. "When he came here that night, explaining that we'd have to wait until the child was born, I went crazy. I wanted to kill myself."

Clasping the stem of the glass with a tremble, she sipped her drink before continuing, "I grabbed a knife and went to cut my veins. Monty, who'd also been drinking, lunged to take it from me. We tussled, which made me stumble. When I fell on top of him, the knife went straight into his heart." Her head moved from side to side as she gripped her arms. Tears splashed over her withered cheeks.

Ava rummaged in her bag and brought out a packet of tissues. She passed one to me, and I handed it to Aggie.

"Can we get you some water?" I asked, unsure how to navigate the emotional storm erupting both within me and in front of me in the shape of a haunted old woman.

"A drink," she murmured, barely able to speak.

"Bronson, maybe we should allow Aggie some rest."

I stared at Ava and nodded.

"No. I want to finish this story. It's been a cancer eating away at me all my life," Aggie said, gesturing for us to remain still.

I looked at Ava. "Perhaps that drink, then. I wouldn't mind another. That's if you don't mind." I mustered a tight smile.

Ava returned with our drinks. She placed the martini beside Aggie and waited for her to replenish her strength. If that was what one got from martinis. For me, it was slurred words and a shocking headache the morning after. But Aggie seemed like a force of nature where liquor and cigarettes were concerned.

"Did you call 9-1-1?" I asked returning to the gloomy task of establishing the truth about my grandfather's death.

"He died in my arms. It was a matter of seconds," she murmured. I had to lean in to hear. It seemed a struggle for her to speak. "His last words were: 'Take my heart.'" Aggie choked back tears.

"And you did," I said, gulping back my bourbon. "So, you cut it out, then?"

"No…" She looked straight into my eyes. The faded blue irises floated in tears. "Charlie did that. He cleaned everything up. Charlie was my champion. He looked after me."

"Is that Charlie from the elevator?" asked Ava.

Aggie nodded. "Yes. Charlie was buried not so long ago."

"While I've known you?" asked Ava.

"I don't know. Time is confusing. Yesterday seems like fifty years ago, and fifty years ago seems like yesterday."

"Your bodyguard cleaned it up. Is that right?" I asked.

She nodded.

"Was my grandfather's body ever found?"

"That wouldn't have been possible." She turned toward me. Her eyes had a cold sting in them. "He was cremated."

"But how did you get that cleared without a death certificate?" I asked.

"If one's got money in this town, one can do anything. Charlie arranged it. He knew someone working for the Mafia who had contacts, that's it. Nothing else to say. And now… I need you both to leave because I am…" She slumped back in her seat and closed her eyes.

"We should leave her," said Ava, turning to the older woman. "Aggie, let us help you up to your bed. You won't be able to climb the stairs otherwise."

"Leave me. Go." She waved her hand.

Rising, I hesitated. I'd never felt as indecisive as that moment.

Aggie's eyes opened slightly. Her wrinkled, cold hand touched mine. "I am so happy that you've found a good woman. Marion, your mother, got it wrong when she said I would have hurt you. If I had known about you, I would have smothered you with love and given you everything and more. I would have cared for you with more love than I'd ever given anyone, even Monty. I need you to know that. Your mother was wrong to believe that I would have hurt you. It was her final act of revenge against me, and it worked, because after I received that letter four years ago, my life became a living hell. No… not four years ago, but from the moment your grandfather died in my arms." She fell back into her chair.

CHAPTER FORTY-ONE

AVA

It had been a week since I'd visited Aggie. She kept paying me nevertheless. I'd attempted to address that since it didn't seem right, but I couldn't get through the front doors, nor did anyone ever pick up the phone when I tried calling. I'd even contacted my bank, who had nothing to offer, only what I already knew. They did, however, mention that it had been made a permanent ongoing deposit. Four thousand dollars a month.

That meant I could live my dream of writing without having to work.

As comforting as that was, I couldn't help but wonder what had happened to Aggie.

Bronson had been even more difficult to deal with. Although he still smothered me with love, I gritted my teeth whenever his brooding silence created a chasm between us. He wouldn't share his thoughts about Monty and Aggie, even when I asked.

In my arms, Bronson was hungrier. He seemed driven almost by an animal lust that always began tenderly enough with tender kisses and caresses but invariably descended into a hotbed of deep and hard fucking that ended with the scattering of my senses.

I tapped away on my laptop. The story, which had started as a novella, had turned into a novel. Although I'd never believed in the paranormal, since I'd started working on my story, the actual process of writing bordered on that, for my fingers moved around the keypad forming words before I'd had a chance to conceive them.

The story revolved around an old woman who was manipulating a younger woman onto a path that she wished she had taken. They could even be the same person. I left that open to interpretation. Commercial imperatives no longer mattered, because I soon discovered writing stopped me from losing my mind.

I was meant to be packing boxes for my move to Bronson's, and I'd started, but got distracted by the need to write when a knock came at the door. Expecting it to be Bronson, I opened the door, only to find a dazed and disheveled Justin standing before me.

Before I could slam the door in his face, he shoved his way in.

"You can't barge in here uninvited," I said.

"I can fucking do what I like, bitch."

I'd never seem him like that, given that Justin took pride in his appearance. The dark rings under his saggy eyes showed he hadn't slept, and he reeked of liquor.

The malevolent flicker in his gaze and sinister curl of his lips told me this was not a friendly visit. The closer he approached, the more my heart raced, and a breath became trapped in my throat.

He pushed me down onto the couch. "Sit." A menacing snarl left his lips.

"I'm expecting Bronson soon, Justin," I said.

"Oh… Mr. Everything. The man of the moment."

"You shouldn't have cooked up that will, Justin."

"How do you think it felt sharing what was mine with a fucking intruder? It should have just been me and my mom and dad. But my father, harboring some kind of twisted social obligation, brought home an 'unwanted.' And what's more, that fucking piece of shit has taken everything away from me. I've been disbarred. I've become a nobody, which is what Bronson was when he invaded my life."

"You should never have set Bronson up. That was a mean act, Justin. At least he hasn't dredged that up. He could have."

"I don't give a fuck. You know what I hate the most about that asshole?"

I remained silent.

"He took you away. That's right, look at me with fucking pity. I fucking loved you, bitch."

I clenched my jaw. "There's no need to be like this."

"Even when you refused to blow me, and when you went all frigid on me and wouldn't let me fuck you, I was still fucking smitten."

He lowered onto the couch next to me, and his hands grabbed at my breasts.

"You've got these fucking tits that make me so hard." His hands squeezed my breasts.

"You're hurting me, Justin."

"Oh, I plan to fuck you until you're red raw, and then you're coming with me."

"Justin. You can't do this. You can't force yourself on me like this," I cried.

He ripped open my shirt, and his mouth landed on my neck as he clawed away at the clasp of my bra.

Just at that moment, a knock came at the door. I was certain that it was Bronson this time. And such was my relief at being rescued that I pushed Justin off me.

I ran to the door, screaming, "Help!"

Justin pulled me back by my ponytail. "Come back here. You're not letting that asshole in. If you do, he'll get this." He pulled out a gun.

While Bronson thumped at the door, I was so gripped with fear that a scream froze in the back of my throat. "Ava!" came from the other side.

When I screamed again, Justin hit me, which made me fall back onto the sofa. In the background, Bronson continued to kick and bang at the door, while Justin virtually sat on me to keep me still.

"You can't do this, Justin!"

"Shut the fuck up," he spat.

Listening for Bronson's steps, I knew that he'd return, so I relaxed as Justin's sweaty face remained close to mine while he unzipped my jeans.

"Take them off. I'm going to fuck you and then shoot that fucker."

"Justin..."

The next few minutes played out frame by frame. Bronson burst through the door wielding a large metal implement. Wearing a fierce expression, he resembled a predatory animal about to pounce on his prey.

Justin lifted his gun and placed it against my head. "Come any closer and I'll shoot her."

Trembling as the icy metal chilled my temple, I saw my parents' faces contort with pain upon learning of my death and Bronson lifting my cold, inert body into his arms. I also told myself that at least I'd experienced the kind of heart-melting love that I'd thought unattainable and only invented to ravage the imaginations of hardcore romantics.

"What do you want, Justin?" asked Bronson.

"I want Ava back. She acts like Miss Fucking Frigid but put a cock in her and she goes all soft and creamy."

Bronson's knuckles looked as though they would pierce through his skin.

"You fucking touch her," roared Bronson.

The brothers glared at each other with such mutual hatred that the atmosphere thickened with testosterone and adrenaline.

Time played tricks, as it was known to do in potentially fatal situations. Justin's thick, heavy breath invaded my hearing, while the gun shook in his hand. He resembled an atrocious, sweaty beast.

"Now look, Justin," I said with my softest, calmest voice. "It's not worth it. You're young. You've got your whole life in front of you."

"Bullshit. Not since that asshole imposter, posing as a fucking brother, dug up shit on me. There's nothing out there for me."

"You're rich, Justin. Richer than most at your age," I said.

"Not for long." He stretched his arm and pointed at Bronson. "You stuck your greasy fucking nose where you shouldn't have. That fucking money was my blood right."

"I'll withdraw my claim. You can keep your money. Just drop that gun and get out of here," said Bronson.

They say that in dangerous situations, our instincts heighten. As adrenaline raged through me, in an act that was risky at best, I pushed off the couch with all my strength, hooking my shoulder under Justin's armpit. In so doing, I jolted his hand toward the ceiling.

As I jumped away, gunfire sounded.

Running to the kitchen, I hid behind the island, my legs frozen with fear.

I heard scuffling, and as I peeked over the table, I saw Bronson squeezing Justin's wrist so tight that he released the gun. It clanged to the ground.

Running over to the weapon, I kicked it away before picking it up.

Eyeing my phone on the table, I managed to grab it and dial 9-1-1.

"Help," I said in a loud whisper. As I spluttered the address through shallow intakes of breath, I watched in horror as Bronson, whose face had gone deep red, pummeled Justin.

Blood splattered the walls. The sound of cracking bones and cries woke me from shock. When Bronson placed his hands around Justin's neck, I knew that if I didn't intervene, he'd kill him.

"No!" I screamed. "The police are on their way. Just hold him down. Don't kill him! It's not worth it."

Bronson looked up at me, his face fierce and sweaty.

He released Justin's neck and planted his knee on his chest to hold him in place.

"Have you got any string or, better still, electrical tape?" he asked, looking up at me. With that sheen coating his face and droplets of blood on scratched skin, Bronson looked as though he'd been in a war zone.

I rummaged through drawers, and after tossing their contents onto the ground, I stumbled upon some tape.

Grabbing a pair of scissors, I cut a long piece.

Having suffered what looked like a broken nose and in obvious pain, Justin lay there groaning.

Turning Justin onto his stomach effortlessly, as if he were half his size, Bronson, whose veiny biceps bulged as he took control, wrapped tape around Justin's wrists.

"Ouch! Call a fucking ambulance." Justin writhed in pain.

"Just stay still," demanded Bronson. "They're on their way."

Hearing sirens down below, I ran to meet the police.

"We need an ambulance," I said to one of the uniformed men.

After speaking on his phone, he asked, "What's the state of the victim?"

"He's injured. He tried to rape me and then placed a pistol to my head."

He nodded, then looked away to speak into his cell, giving directions, after which, along with a colleague, he followed me up to the crime scene that had so recently been my home.

CHAPTER FORTY-TWO

BRONSON

Just how far I might have gone frightened the hell out of me. If Ava hadn't stepped in when she did, I would have killed Justin. It was as though I'd become possessed by some external force because I could have punched a hole through a brick wall, such was the strength flowing through me.

As my hands crushed his neck, seething animosity filtered through my veins. Reliving our life growing up together, I summoned up all the humiliation Justin had inflicted upon me. The numerous times he'd locked me in the cupboard, disabling my future with claustrophobia so suffocating that in prison, I'd had to breathe into a fucking paper bag.

As I continued to crush his throat, I recalled the jibes, the nasty bullying and how at school, Justin told the other kids that I wore a diaper because I pissed my bed every night. Even though it was bullshit, they believed it anyhow. Then, as a teenager, he'd steal money from my mother's purse and lay the blame on me. The cocaine in my backpack was the last straw. As my knees pushed deep into his groin, I would have killed the dirtbag were it not for Ava.

After the police took Justin away, and we'd made our statements at the police station, I placed my arm around Ava. "You were amazing in there. Trained men, double your size, couldn't have pulled that off."

Her body stiffened in my arms. I drew away. "What is it, Ava?"

"You would have killed him if I hadn't stopped you."

I wiped my brow. "Something came over me, that's for sure." I stared into her eyes. "The way he looked at you with that self-entitled smirk of his just set me off. It's not me. I'm normally passive."

"Passive? You're hardly that, Bronson. You're intense."

I studied her for a moment. "Ava, please, don't do this." I took her by the hand. "Come on, I need a shower, and then we can talk about it."

She removed her hand. "No, Bronson. I need some space."

Her face had gone pale. I stared deeply into her eyes, looking for the love that had been there earlier, but instead, I was met with emptiness.

"I need time alone to think. Bronson. Please." Ava turned her back and walked away.

As I watched her deliberate steps, I waited, hoping that she'd turn and come running back to me. Instead, Ava kept walking while blood drained out of me.

"You're not going to press charges?" asked James as I sat in the sunny courtyard by his swimming pool.

I'd been staying at James's house for a few days, as the site I was working at was not far away, and I needed some time away from the craziness of the city, which had Ava written all over it. Besides, I thought having nature around and hearing birds sing would offer me some respite from depression.

"Nope. It's over. The funds from Father's original will have come through. I'm wealthy," I said, soberly. "I can pump more into our project. Build myself a nice big home out here somewhere and live a sad, lonely existence."

"Bronson. You're too popular for that," he said with an encouraging smile. James looked increasingly like my late father, the more I hung out with him.

A flicker of a smile came and went. "I don't know where I'd be without you, James. You've been a tower of strength."

"Anything to help. And it needed to come out. At least now you'll have cleared your name. You have a clean slate, so to speak."

I sighed. "Yep. That's a good thing."

He noticed my downturned mouth. "No word from Ava?"

A tight breath left my lungs. I shook my head. It had been two weeks. The pain generated by the sound of her name burned like a knife into a wound.

"She thinks I'm a monster. A potential murderer."

"Seeing a man in blind rage can be disturbing." He paused for a moment. "I don't blame you, though. Anyone would have snapped after how Justin treated you over the years."

"But why can't Ava see that?" I asked, looking up at my uncle.

Shrugging, he said, "Give it time. She's been through a lot. And the story of Aggie and how you've located your real grandfather through her is nothing short of astounding."

"Isn't it?" I puffed out my cheeks and exhaled slowly.

After James left me, I lounged back and closed my eyes, enjoying the sun on my skin despite my blood remaining frozen. It seemed that even the heat of the day was incapable of warming my veins.

Having never experienced a broken heart before, I suddenly understood the dramatic lengths people went to in order to escape themselves. There I'd been, like some sad, neglected dog, standing outside Ava's apartment every day, during which time I only ran into her once. Her long and drawn face told me that Ava wasn't having a great time of it either, despite shooing me away as if I were a pest.

CHAPTER FORTY-THREE

AVA

Yet again, Aggie asked me to read the passage in which Heathcliff visits Cathy just before she dies. After I finished, I asked, "Do you see Monty in Heathcliff?"

"I see Monty in everything. He's always with me. No matter what I'm doing."

A faint smile washed over me. Bronson had affected me that way, too. He was everywhere—in my dreams, my thoughts, my daily activities. I found myself often wondering what he'd think about this or that.

Aggie studied me. "What's happened to you, Ava? You're not yourself. Being loved by a devilishly handsome man like Bronson, you should be constantly bubbling with that edgy sense of excitement."

What an apt way to describe the constant state of arousal I'd been in around Bronson. *But that was in the past,* I thought with a silent sigh.

"I've left him." I shifted in my seat.

"What?" The dramatic expression in her face made me wince. "But you can't. You have to be together. Otherwise, what's all this been for?"

I frowned. "What do you mean by that?"

Aggie looked away.

"Why did you employ me? You mentioned you designed it that way. Why?" I asked, determined to get an answer this time.

She held her hands up in defense. "So many questions."

"Aggie, why am I here?"

"Because I wanted to get back at that horrible Justin. I wanted to see what you were like and whether I could push you toward Bronson as a way to get back at that conniving rat."

A frustrated sigh deflated my chest. "Aggie. You've been playing with people's emotions."

"So what if I have?" She tilted her head slightly. "I've addressed a wrong. I needed a way into Bronson's circle somehow. Now enough of your moaning, and tell me why you're no longer together. Bronson is absolutely besotted by you."

Despite the flooding warmth, I felt from that observation, I continued to grill Aggie. "Where's Charlie?"

"Oh my God, why him again?"

"I met him in the elevator, and he spoke about you and the past. And then there's the painting that looks like me. Why?" My nerves had been strung so tight that they were about to snap.

"Is that why you left Bronson? Because of all this mystery?" She waved her hand about.

"No!" I took a deep breath to steady myself. "I lost myself to him. Then when I saw him almost murder Justin… His rage frightened me."

Aggie studied me with a puckered brow as if trying to understand me. "Let me see, Bronson was protecting you?"

I nodded sheepishly. "Well, yeah, but he would have strangled Justin."

"You care that much for Justin?"

"Of course not. He's one of the worst people I've ever known."

"Then?"

"Aggie. There was murder in Bronson's face."

"So that's put you off him? You no longer have feelings for him? You've stopped loving him?"

"No. No. And no. I can't eat. I can't sleep. I have no energy. I'm lost." My face crumpled in dismay while tears threatened to erupt again.

"Ha… That spells love to me," said Aggie.

"Enough of Bronson. Why all of this? Why the game, Aggie? I have to know."

"As I've already said, this so-called game was designed solely to bring Bronson to me." She sat back and took a breath. "I needed to meet him. If I'm to give Bronson everything, it's vital that I see what kind of man he is."

"But why draw me into it?"

"Because I wanted to know you. At first, it was a form of revenge on that cad, Justin. Then, as I got to know you, I discovered you were overly curious, so I designed it this way so that you would continue to visit. It was fun, too, in that potentially supernatural way." She chuckled.

"Fun? My God, Aggie, it's been keeping me up at nights."

"Then I'm sorry." A glimmer of sympathy washed over her eyes. "Even though it wasn't my initial plan, but the more I got to know you, I could see that you'd make an ideal partner for Bronson. You're both suited to each other. And because of that, you'll have a steadying influence on him." She paused to take a breath. "I see so much potential in Bronson. However, in the wrong hands, he could fall, just like Monty did. If I had married Monty, he would have had a great life. I don't want Bronson ending up with a bad woman, because when one chooses poorly, it destroys one's life."

"But how can you tell that we're well suited?" I asked.

"He has a sparkle in his eyes when he gazes at you." Aggie stared away into the distance. "I recognized it well. His grandfather had the same look whenever his eyes met mine."

A tear fell down my cheek, and I quickly wiped it away. I'd cried so much in that two weeks that my emotions were raw. As I wiped my nose, a thought suddenly occurred to me.

"Are you reliving your romance with Monty vicariously through Bronson and me?"

"Maybe. Who doesn't like watching an exciting romance unfold and see themselves in the position of the heroine?" She raised her eyebrows.

While I sought a response, she waved her hand. "Now, off you go. I'm tired."

"But you haven't answered me yet. And it's only six o'clock."

"Please. Don't tax me. Tomorrow."

Reluctant to go back to my empty place, I decided to go for a walk in the park, specifically to the tree with our carved initials, which was a place I'd visited regularly during the last two weeks.

Entering the pretty tree-lined path, I drifted along while inhaling a heady mix of earth and grass. The space that I'd craved had turned into a black hole of nothingness. I'd lost my heart to Bronson. And as much as I thought I could regain it by being alone, the only insight I'd gained was how lonely, sad, and empty life seemed without him.

Soaking in the late afternoon sun, I watched beams of light shimmering off delicate green foliage. Wind rustling through the branches whispered hope in that same way a wise, gentle-voiced friend would.

Bronson's face kept appearing before me. Awake or asleep, I summoned up his crushing love and unwavering desire, to have, hold, and possess me.

The possessive part was intimidating.

As much as I'd grown seriously fond of if not addicted to his strong, virile body, I also needed to be with a partner that I could realize my full potential with. Equality and independence were musts. I could never be that little wife in the suburbs.

Would Bronson enable me to be that?

He was definitely driven. My heart melted at that image of Bronson on the couch, barefoot and shirtless, in deep concentration with pencil in hand, drawing and tilting his head from side to side while assessing his work.

The fact that Bronson hadn't called me for a few days weighed heavily on me. I'd grown needy for those messages in which he'd pause between words with nothing but a breath for me to listen to.

How would I live without him? He'd become a part of me.

As I crossed into the avenue that housed our tree, I saw a familiar figure ahead. Sitting on the bench, Bronson had his arm stretched along the back of the seat. His head was half-cocked as he stared at the tree.

Even from afar, Bronson radiated charisma. His legs were slightly splayed with that devil-may-care body language that made my lips curl.

I had just hidden behind a tree to help steady my heartbeat when a pretty girl stepped before him.

What did she want? I asked myself. Was she a date? The fact Bronson hadn't moved a muscle suggested disinterest on his part. That helped me relax.

She persisted, though. I couldn't blame her. Hot and seriously sexy, in a worn T-shirt that showed off those big tattooed biceps and with that tousled dark hair, Bronson had "bad boy" written all over him. He was the type of hunk that women dropped their panties for even before a "hello" had left their lips.

As she sat down, Bronson moved along to make room for her. A sinking feeling overtook me. She turned to face him square on and then moved her hands about as if expressing something that needed saying. And she kept at it. The pretty blonde girl seemed to talk endlessly.

Observing Bronson's disinterest, I suddenly found myself admiring him for being haughty.

There was only one thing to do.

With a deliberate stride, I headed toward him. That was after I undid a couple of buttons to reveal some cleavage, untied my ponytail and fluffed out my hair.

After I'd taken only a few strides toward him, Bronson must have sensed my approach, because he looked up, and the bored expression in his eyes faded away.

Meanwhile, turning to see who had taken her conquest's attention, the girl looked me up and down with cold disregard.

"Excuse me," Bronson said to the girl, who continued to yammer despite his obvious disinterest.

He rose and came to me. "Ava." His lips twitched into a half smile.

"You've got company, I see," I said, keeping it cool, even though I was anything but. My heart was in my throat, blocking speech. My timidity seemed ridiculous, considering I'd lain with him upside down with my legs in the air, taking every delicious inch in deep.

The longer I studied his face, the more I noticed what a wreck he was. Who would have thought dark rings under one's eyes could make one still look sexy as hell? He was dressed in his favorite pair of worn, ripped jeans that he'd owned for years and not paid a month's salary for.

"I don't know her," he said, quietly.

From the corner of my eye, I noticed her slink off.

He ran his hands through his hair, which ended up in a mess of waves that always managed to sit in all the right places.

As Bronson's gaze burned into me, his serious expression eased into a tender smile. "I wanted to call you so many times."

I lowered myself onto the bench and placed a little distance between us. Bronson moved closer to me, which tipped me over the libidinous edge, especially when a gentle breeze wafted his blend of cologne and maleness up my nose.

Almost banging heads, we both turned at the same time. He said "Ava," over my "Bronson."

I giggled nervously, and he sniffed.

His gaze burned into me. "I've missed you so much it fucking hurts. I didn't even want to get out of bed."

"I haven't changed the sheets," I added, softly.

The way his brow puckered as he studied me made me ask, "What?"

"That doesn't surprise me," he said with a cheeky grin.

"What do you mean?" I thought about it and realized he was poking fun at my untidiness. "I'm into doing my laundry if that's what you're referring to." I hit his big arm. And he smiled.

"What brings you here, Bronson? Are you waiting for pretty girls to hit on you?"

He turned sharply to look at me. "Are you fucking kidding me? Do you think I'm that fucking shallow?"

Ouch. That was like a slap. His eyes had gone so dark I fell in again. Taking a moment to rise to the surface, I replied, "I'm sorry. I was just kidding."

His eyes softened. "I'm sorry for the overreaction. I've had a shit time. My project's floundering because I can't even face people."

I played with my fingers. "I haven't been in a good place, either."

"What do you mean?" He tilted his head slightly.

"Just that, I suppose." I shrugged. "I'm glad that you didn't press charges against Justin."

"I did it for my mother. If it were up to me, I would have gone out of my way to have his ugly ass locked away." He paused to gauge my reaction, but I remained blank. "He won't come near you again. Apparently, he's moved to LA. That should suit him. The land of endless cocaine parties and plenty of stray pussy."

I rolled my eyes with a mocking grin.

He shook his head. "What?"

"I was just thinking how coarse you are."

"It's who I am," he said, raking through his hair. "Do you want me to change? I will. If it means you'll come back to me." A glint of vulnerability reflected off his gaze.

"I don't need you to change. If anything, I kind of find your rawness hard to resist. Pure animal charm, I'd call it."

He stroked a strand of hair that had fallen over my arm. "And you look so beautiful. You resemble an angel."

"That's unsexy," I said.

His eyes landed on my cleavage, and for some reason mine landed on his crotch, where a bulge grew before my eyes, setting off a pleasant pulse between my legs.

"My God, Ava, if only you knew how damn sexy you are. I can't even look at other women. That girl, for instance, was a weed compared to you, a beautiful rose."

How could I not smile at that? Bronson's eyes wandered over my face and body and back, leaving a trail of heat as I moistened my lips unconsciously.

"You're the most beautiful woman I've ever seen or known for that matter. From the moment I saw you." He stroked my cheek.

I swallowed. What was I to do? My body was a fireball of need. My heart took over as my overactive mind retreated.

I rested my head on his shoulder as he continued to stroke my hair.

"You're a part of me, Ava. That tree there knows it."

I sat up. "Ha? You're sounding surreal, like this whole crazy story of us and Aggie."

He sniffed. "It's kind of magical, isn't it?"

I nodded. Bronson was right. Life was there for surprises and miracles, which pretty much summed up our relationship.

He rose. "Come on. Let me buy you some dinner."

"All right, then," I said, as a smile grew and remained there for the first time in weeks.

CHAPTER FORTY-FOUR

BRONSON

"Ava, can you do me a favor and do up a couple of your buttons?" We were sitting at a busy café. Discovering that my appetite had returned with a vengeance, I salivated as a sizzling steak was lowered in front of me.

"Why?" she asked with that sweet smile of hers that made me want to devour her lips.

"Because I'm about to break that guy's arm if he keeps greasy eyeballing you."

She looked over my shoulder and giggled. "You really are an alpha male."

"How else am I going to protect what's mine?"

"Is that what I am to you? A possession?"

I studied Ava for a moment. "You possess me."

She stared at me as if trying to find more in my words. "After that pretty girl tried to hit on you, I wanted to show you what you'd been missing out on."

"Oh, God, Ava. Trust me. I don't need to see your spectacular tits to be reminded of how hot you are. Only that I'd prefer it to be for my eyes only."

She did up her buttons. "There."

I nodded. "Better. Now I can concentrate on my steak."

"Is that all you wish to devour tonight?" she asked with a sweet grin.

"Trust me, Ava, my appetite at the moment is so damn huge that I've got the whole night and morning to fill." I emphasized "fill" and raised an eyebrow.

After I paid the waiter, I took Ava by the hand, and we walked back onto the main drag to hail a cab.

One arrived straight away, and I opened the door for Ava to climb in first.

It wasn't until we hit the Williamsburg Bridge that I drew her in close and, unable to hold back any longer, my lips landed on her soft, moist mouth. My chest released as her flavor filled me with the promise of something that was both sweet and dirty. If we hadn't been in a cab, I would have entered her there and then. My hand managed to sneak into her wet panties as she sighed deeply into my mouth.

Ava pulled away. "Not here, Bronson."

When we arrived at my place, I paid the driver and virtually carried Ava in my arms. Leaning against the wall of the elevator—which was full, much to my disappointment—I managed to squeeze Ava's curvy butt, making her giggle. A content sigh left my lungs. All the pain and emptiness of the past two weeks vanished from the moment Ava's pretty blue eyes smiled at me.

After arriving on my floor, we barely made it through the door as we fell onto the couch and held each other close. Our lips fused and our tongues tangled, expressing the same hungry need to devour.

The following afternoon, Ava and I rode the elevator to Aggie's apartment. We'd received a message earlier that day calling us in, which surprised Ava given that Aggie had never sent her a message before. She wasn't even sure if Aggie owned a cell phone.

"I have the strangest feeling about this," said Ava as she leaned against the wall of the elevator.

Under the soft light with her thick, chestnut hair waving around her beautiful alabaster skin, I didn't have a care in the world. For the first time in my life, I found it hard not to smile.

"Why are you looking at me like that?" she asked.

"Because every time I look at you, your beauty grows, and I want to ravage you again."

"Bronson, I'm sore down there."

"Your pussy, you mean? Say it."

"My pussy is sore," she repeated with a shy lilt that made my cock stiffen.

I drew her in close and devoured her soft lips.

"After that break, my appetite is off the charts."

"Mine too," she said, and her large eyes had that twinkle of mischief that made me hard again.

"The scratches all over my shoulders and arms are back. I like them there. You're very responsive, angel."

"That's because you feel amazing. And I'm in love with your tongue."

"Only my tongue?" I said.

"And this." She grabbed my cock, making it throb again.

"Maybe we should stop the lift," I said.

She giggled. "You're a sex maniac."

"Only for you, Ava."

Falling into my arms, Ava stood on her toes, and our lips fused.

The elevator reached Aggie's floor, and we untangled ourselves. I let her exit first and had a feel of her ass in the process, which returned a sweet peal of laughter from Ava.

Although I felt lighter now that Ava had forgiven me, that violent episode with Justin reminded me how close that dark side lurked. If Ava hadn't stepped in, I might actually have killed him. The thought that made me break into a cold sweat.

After spending one year in prison, I'd become jumpy, especially if someone shadowed me. In the earlier days, after my release, I'd even believed I was being followed. The few visits to the shrink hadn't helped. There were too many questions about feelings. I'd never been great at talking about that deeper side of me. I didn't understand it. So how the hell was I meant to articulate that to a stranger?

With Ava by my side, all of a sudden, things became clearer, and the tension that I'd carried all my life dissolved. Only the important things mattered, like having a plan, getting ahead in life, and marrying Ava.

I'd become stronger because of Ava.

The door opened, and a seventyish man with a paunch asked us to enter.

"Charlie!" exclaimed Ava.

"No. I'm David. He was my twin."

She looked disappointed for some reason. "Oh… Aggie mentioned he passed away. I used to like chatting to him on the elevator."

As we followed David into the pink living room, he said, "Charlie loved wearing his uniform. He lived in the past and was convinced that the ghosts of residents still rode the elevator. We'd humor him. Charlie was a little different." He raised his eyebrows as if letting us in on a secret.

"Is the whole building vacant?" I asked. "We never see anyone."

"Aggie purchased the building following Ashley's death and decided to keep it unoccupied. She was a very private woman in many ways."

"Was?" asked Ava.

He stretched out his arm. "Please, take a seat." He lowered himself into a pink, embossed silk armchair. "I'm afraid Aggie passed away a few days ago."

A line formed between Ava's brows. "What? But she seemed so happy when I last saw her."

"She passed away in her sleep, peacefully," he said in a gentle tone.

"But there are still so many questions…"

David handed her a letter. "Here. Hopefully, that will help you understand." He nodded with a reassuring smile. "I'm Aggie's attorney. I have some legal matters to discuss."

He picked up a folder sitting on the table at his side and turned to face me for the first time. The flicker of surprise in his eyes when he looked at me sent a shiver through me.

"One of the reasons Aggie went out of her way to find you, Bronson, was so that she'd have an heir." He pointed to the walls. "Along with this building, Aggie left you properties in the

Hamptons and a substantial share portfolio. All told, you're now a very wealthy man."

Before I could respond. He continued, "Ava, Aggie wanted you to have her entire wardrobe of designer dresses, artwork, many of which are originals, and a monthly stipend of ten thousand dollars for the rest of your life."

Ava stared at me, looking stunned, which summed up how I felt too.

"There is a caveat, however." David held up a finger. Noticing my eyebrows move, he clarified, "A condition."

"I know what caveat means," I replied, sitting forward. "Please, go on."

"All of Aggie's estate becomes yours when you marry. And only..." He paused.

"And only?" I asked, casting a sideways glance at Ava, whose mouth had remained open.

"Only if you marry Ava Rose."

CHAPTER FORTY-FIVE

AVA

I studied Bronson's face for signs of dread or misgiving. Instead, I encountered a smile that grew at the side of his lips. Whereas for me, rebellious at heart, my initial response was to protest at being dictated to. But as I opened my mouth, nothing exited. It was Bronson, I told myself, not some detestable male who I couldn't even relate to, let alone have sex with. I wasn't having a hairy old man foisted upon me for his family spoils. Or having my virginity offered on a platter to an obese distant relative in order to empower a dynasty.

It was Bronson.

Could I spend my life with Bronson? I asked myself as I battled a maelstrom of inner voices.

"Why the games?" I asked.

"That letter will probably explain that to you," David replied.

"What about the heart in the jar?" I asked.

"Yes… Aggie mentioned you'd learned of its presence. That was placed in her hands before she was cremated."

"How could you manage that without questions?" I asked.

"Aggie was very rich, therefore able to manage anything she liked, including that."

"Has there been a funeral? Can we attend?" I asked.

"I scattered her ashes in the Hudson yesterday. Aggie's instructions were to keep it private. She never liked attending funerals and therefore hated the idea of anyone attending her own."

A deep feeling of loss and sorrow hit me all of a sudden. Putting aside Aggie's acerbic tongue and saucy intrusiveness, not to mention this devious plan she'd cooked up to ensure Bronson married someone she approved of, I'd found Aggie kind, sharp-witted, and fascinating. People like Aggie were rare. She was like a flawed jewel from that bygone era when everyone's scrawled secrets remained tucked away in journals and not spilled all over social media.

Tears rolled down my cheeks.

Sympathy coated David's eyes. "Aggie was very fond of you, Ava. At first, it *was* a game. Just as you've said. It was Aggie's way of getting back at Justin Lockhart for setting you up, Bronson." He returned his attention to me. "But as she got to know you, Ava, and then discovered that you'd become romantically involved with Bronson, Aggie's spirit lifted. It was no longer revenge that she sought but to see you both together."

"How was she going to get back at Justin through me?" I asked, blowing my nose.

"I'm not sure even she knew. But when Aggie learned of Bronson's false incarceration, she became justifiably furious. She needed a way into that family, and the only way—at least, the only way that satisfied her love of the dramatic—was through you. We discovered you were seeking employment, and the rest is history, as they say." He raised an eyebrow.

"But why the painting?"

"To whet your appetite for adventure."

"How were you to know that I wouldn't run away? I mean, there were times when I did consider that."

"By paying you generously." He paused. "Also, Aggie knew of your creative inclinations. She sensed that you'd be too curious not to return. Aggie also loved theatrics. It kept her going." He chuckled. The way his eyes misted over at recalling Aggie's quirks revealed his devotion to her.

I released a tight breath and gazed at Bronson, who sat back in his armchair with his legs crossed. His face was relaxed, while those sultry chocolate eyes beamed back at me.

David said, "I'll give you some time to think it over." He handed Bronson a large envelope. "Everything's in there."

Bronson took the envelope and shook David's hand. "Thank you. I'll be in touch."

David's stare intensified. "You look exactly like him."

"Monty?" I asked.

He nodded.

"So, you knew him well?" Bronson asked.

"Yes. I've been with Aggie from the days of Ashley. I was his attorney. We're like family."

I rose and shook David's hand. Before leaving, I stared over at the balcony wistfully. My eyes landed on the stemmed glass, complete with pink lipstick stain, and a half-open pack of cigarettes, while on the white peacock chair, in which I'd always sat, a shimmering finger of sunlight pointed down onto *Wuthering Heights*.

That scene held so many memories that tears splashed over my cheeks. It had been an extraordinary few months.

Bronson led me out by the hand.

When we were on the street, Bronson looked up at the building that was now his.

"Are you going to move in?" I asked.

"Depends on you, Ava. Everything depends on you." He stared at me long and hard.

"Aggie was determined to see us together," I said.

He took me by the hand. "Let's go to the park. It will help clear our heads."

When we arrived at our bench, I lowered myself onto the seat and took a deep breath. The smell of earth helped ease my nerves as I pulled Aggie's letter out of my bag.

It read:

Dear Ava,

Initially, my plan was simply to connect to someone who knew Bronson, in the hope of gaining access to him, while seeking revenge on his evil brother. I can't tell you how thrilled I was to discover that you'd fallen into Bronson's arms, and in so doing ruffled the feathers of that cad, Justin. That in itself brought me back from the brink of death.

The shock that came from seeing that cameo was indescribable. I hadn't expected that! You see, I spent a good part of my early years convincing my family that Monty hadn't stolen it. Apart from the flood of memories that came after seeing that family keepsake again, the mystery of its disappearance was also finally solved, even if it did bring me cold comfort, for I knew that Monty had stolen it to escape the pain that I'd brought him after marrying

Ashley. Over and above everything, however, the cameo brought Bronson straight to me in an organic if not extraordinary way.

You are the perfect woman for Bronson. That's why I put in place that stipulation that Bronson marry before attaining my substantial wealth.

A man like Bronson needs the steadying influence of a woman like you, Ava. Not that he would need much convincing, given that I witnessed firsthand how besotted he was with you. Not to mention that twinkle in your eyes whenever you were around him. I recognized that well, for I too gazed that way at Monty.

As you recently observed, I saw myself and Monty through you and Bronson. Preposterous though that might seem, you've got to understand that the supernatural has become more tangible the closer I step toward eternal darkness.

Bronson's resemblance to Monty wasn't just physical, for I recognized Monty's intensity in Bronson. I beseech you, Ava, take that man and hold onto him forever. Monty self-destructed when our paths diverged, which sent me tumbling into a life of regret and sadness.

I apologize if the theatrics spooked you. That being said, I am pleased with the outcome. Even my need for revenge was satisfied, given that men with big egos like Justin's are riddled with insecurity, thus having his girl taken by the brother he envied would have torn him apart.

But nothing gives me greater pleasure than knowing that you'll be with Bronson forever. Just as I will be with Monty forever.

A FEW MONTHS LATER…

Brushing my hair, Cassie stood behind my chair. "Wow. It's so thick and long. I'm surprised you didn't wear it up."

"Bronson loves it down. In any case, I've got diamante combs to pull it back away from my face."

Shaking her head with wonder, Cassie looked at me in the mirror. "You look beautiful."

"Thanks," I murmured with a big smile that seemed permanently planted on my face.

As I stood before the mirror, I felt like a princess. Moving my head from side to side, I studied my pearly silk Yves St. Laurent gown with its flattering, sleek line that pooled into a tulip shape on the ground.

"Those earrings are exquisite," said Cassie.

I had to agree as I jingled the diamond chandelier earrings that had come from Aggie's considerable collection of jewels.

"It's a shame it's not one of those magazine weddings. You're going to be the hottest couple in the whole of America."

I smiled at Cassie's enthusiastic if not slightly exaggerated comment. "I'm glad it's small," I responded.

"It's such a fairy tale. This house. The Hamptons. Thanks for letting us stay."

"You can all stay for as long as you like. It's such a big house. I'm still getting lost in it. I spend half of my time looking for the bathroom." I giggled. "Anyway, it's everyone's house now. Bronson and I want it that way."

"And to think you left him hanging for over a week. Why?"

I sighed as I recollected that week following the reading of the will. A part of me resented being forced into something as life-changing as marriage, whereas Bronson didn't even question it. He didn't even give it a moment's thought. He was just happy. Happier than I'd ever known him to be.

"It was a huge step to take. I just needed to know."

"What did it?" she asked.

A wide smile claimed my face. "I watched Bronson frying eggs for breakfast. Shirtless, of course." I raised a brow. "With his hair all tousled. Those big dark eyes stealing glances at me and smiling shyly, even after we'd made love all night. I knew then and there that I wanted to be with him all my life."

Cassie smirked. "And the fact he'd become a billionaire had nothing to do with it?"

I shook my head. "Bronson could have been totally broke, for all I cared."

"Who could have been totally broke?" my mother asked, entering the bedroom.

"I just said that I didn't marry Bronson because of his money."

"But he has got money. Plenty of it." She embraced me. "Well done. I knew your beauty would deliver."

"You weren't exactly nice to him the first time you met him," I said, pulling away. My mother seemed to have a knack for bringing the mood down.

"No. But he's grown on me. And the new home he bought us has helped me change my views, that's for sure."

"Yeah. I bet it has," I said with a cool note.

"Oh, come on, Ava, this is your wedding day. Don't go all sour on me," she said, lowering her chin.

I looked at Cassie, who, with a subtle shrug, nodded. "Doesn't Ava look beautiful?"

My mother ran her eyes over me. "Ava would look beautiful in a sack. It is a pretty dress, but I would have gone for something modern. It's a bit old-fashioned."

"Yves St. Laurent is never old-fashioned," I said, mimicking her dismissive tone.

When she left, I turned to Cassie. "Nothing I ever do pleases her. Only my marrying wealth has put a smile on her face."

"Oh… come on, Aves, she's your mom. You know parents. They're generally hard to please."

My father entered. When he saw me, he stopped and his face lit up in wonder. What a contrast, I thought. How did this sweet, gorgeous man end up with my tough, hard-nosed mom?

"You look so beautiful. Like one of those classic Hollywood beauties."

"Thanks, Dad. Mom wasn't as impressed."

"You know your mother." He turned to greet Cassie. "You look lovely too, Cassandra."

My best friend did strike an elegant figure in a turquoise chiffon-silk empire-line Dior gown I'd gifted her from the vast collection that Aggie had given me.

My father rubbed his hands together. "Are we ready?"

I nodded. My eyes misted over.

"Come here, sweetheart. You're going to do well. Bronson's a great guy."

"Do you think so?" I asked. I needed one parent to love him.

"I liked him from the first time I met him. I suppose the fact we share a passion for wood helped." He chuckled. "And the new workshop he had built at the back of the palace he bought us stole my breath."

"That was probably so that he could hang out with you whenever we visit." I smiled, picturing Bronson spending his whole day cutting, sanding, and hammering away.

Even though we'd moved into a pretty two-story, blue Colonial-style home in the suburbs, during the weekdays I commuted to Aggie's old apartment, where I'd set up an office. The rest of the apartments, ten in all, were rented out cheaply to struggling writers.

Fearing that the charming gray stone edifice would be bulldozed, Bronson adamantly refused to sell it. That came as a relief, because every time I stepped into what was once Aggie's home, a surge of inspiration overwhelmed me. Stoking my imagination with memories and images, the balcony soon became my favorite place to write.

Taking my arm, my father led me out to my future husband.

Cut by one of New York's finest Italian tailors, the black tux with a red rose in the lapel molded perfectly onto Bronson's strong body. My breath hitched when I saw him.

Bronson turned. A smile grew from the corners of his lips, while his eyes sparkled with desire when he saw me.

Even the day was perfect. The sun was out, and the air was calm.

We stood on the terrace of our new home by the sea. Behind us, the ocean roared out our wedding tune, witnessing a moment that I'd never expected would happen so soon, especially surrounded by such unimaginable opulence.

As our hands entwined, Bronson's heat flushed through me.

"Will you take Ava Rose to be your wife?"

Bronson turned to face me, and an emphatic "Yes," left his lips.

"Ava Rose, will you take Bronson Lockhart to be your husband?"

I took a deep breath, and in that moment, I saw fear in Bronson's eyes. It was as if that one breath had trapped time.

"Yes" floated out of me like a butterfly on a sunny afternoon.

The release in his chest was palpable. I could only assume that Bronson feared that I'd had second thoughts.

He took me into his arms and flying high on his scent, I melted into his strong body.

Lowering his head, Bronson whispered, "Take my heart... it's yours."

My breath hitched again as I tipped my head back to gaze up at him.

Bronson's smoldering gaze softened into a twinkle of promise, making my own heart flutter.

THE END

A NOTE FROM THE AUTHOR

Dear Reader, thank you for arriving at the sweet end. I sincerely hope you enjoyed this story. If you did, would you be so good to leave a review? I will send the romance fairies to grace your lives with gorgeous romance! I'd also be forever grateful. Reviews are everything, and without them I cannot continue publishing my stories.

Thank you! *J. J. Sorel*
https://jjsorel.com/
https://www.facebook.com/JJSorel/